rs

by

Martyn Tott

2009

Six Magic Numbers Ltd

SIX MAGIC NUMBERS

ISBN 9780956380609

Fiction - Romantic Contemporary/Drama

Author's note

Reports surrounding my encounter with a missing lottery ticket are documented in the media. *Six Magic Numbers* is fictional and *inspired* by events in my life, it is not a literal account and similarity to persons either living or deceased or organisations is coincidental.

Thanks

Mum, Dad, Family, and Friends who always support me. Having you all in my life is better than winning any lottery!

Laura Turner for reading the many rewrites, listening to me droning on whilst being patient and cooking amazing food. Lesley Jackson for commentary on the first edit. Test readers who actually read and critiqued early drafts, too many to list and I might leave someone out and never hear the end of it. Katherine King for technical assistance, Sally Garner for website design and Nic Cornwall and the cast and crew for working on the promotional trailer.

Sylvester Stallone for the interview that inspired me to persevere, Anthony Robbins for advice and anyone I have forgotten because I'm going to leave someone out I'm sure.

Finally of course, thank you so much for buying this book. If you enjoy it please spread the word and join the mailing list and cyber groups for updates on the feature film, more books and projects.

Dedicated to the memory of Colin, Fiona, Tony and Wiz.

Websites

www.martyntott.com

www.sixmagicnumbers.info

PART ONE – ENGLAND

*'Someone said to me once, life is just a game. Couldn't find the rule book but
I played it all the same.'*

-Jules Landau,
'Grand Nimbus' by Omega Minus 1988.

CHAPTER ONE

Are our lives governed by luck or belief? Does it matter which path you think you've chosen if it's predestined for you? Do chance encounters with strangers change the entire course of your life in a moment without you realising? Mark often thought that people made their own luck in life but his philosophy was about to be challenged as he stared into the spinning wheel.

A summer bike ride to the pub had started out as a good idea until reaching the meadow with the thistles. It had looked so innocent from the wooden gate, an ocean of tall golden grass in the Warwickshire countryside waving in the gentle breeze but once inside it was like barbed wire in places. He inspected the punctured inner tube as it whistled out a final jet of thin air that felt cooling to his face under the blazing sun.

His friend Will had disappeared into the woods oblivious to Mark's calls for him to wait, with his iPod on he was in a race to get a beer and drown out the summer heat. Mark sat back in the tall grass and unwittingly wiped a line of chain grease across his face.

A noise from the top of the field distracted him. He thought it might be Will coming back to see where he was, instead a woman on horseback appeared cantering towards him. As she drew nearer he couldn't help but notice how pretty she was and somehow familiar. Maybe the puncture wasn't such a bad thing after all, he thought to himself.

The horse slowed down and stopped right next to him.

'Hey, you got a flat?' She said in an American accent.

'I've got it under control.' He lied.

Mark thought that she was beautiful. With her dark hair poking out in wisps from under her riding hat and soft brown eyes she reminded him of his favourite actress, that was why she looked familiar.

'Well if you're sure you don't need help I'll leave you to it.' She said and began to ride on. Mark didn't want her to go, he had to say something quick, anything.

'I love Stallions.' He blurted out, regretting it as soon as the words left his lips.

She stopped again and turned. 'Really? He's actually a Gelding.'

'Oh. I'm sorry.' Mark said, clueless as to what that word even meant. For some reason his brain was blank and his tongue was twice its normal size.

'You really don't know much about the equine world do you?' She said.

'I do. I know loads about fish.'

'Fish huh?' She was obviously unimpressed but he was making her smile. He just needed to keep her there a little longer, build a rapport.

'Has anyone ever told you that you look like that famous actress?'

'Which one?'

'Oh you know, erm.' He rummaged for the name. Mark had suddenly forgotten the actress's name. He had seen her films so many times and even had pictures of her on his wall yet now he just could not put his finger on it.

'You know the one. *Aliens.*'

'Are you suggesting I look like an Alien?' She said, dropping her jaw.

'No. Oh wow no. I mean the actress.'

'Sigourney Weaver?'

'No the other one, the heroine.'

'Sigourney Weaver played the heroine in *Aliens.*'

'Not in the last film.' Mark said.

'Yes she did.'

'Sure?'

She nodded. 'I have the DVD set.'

'Oh.' Mark said, picking at a handful of long grass. His legs trembled when he looked at her. He hadn't had that before either, maybe he was allergic to the thistles or the horse.

'I must be thinking of another film.' He scratched his head wiping a bit more grease across the side of it.

'Did you mean Winona Ryder?' She smiled putting him out of his misery and wondering if she should say something about his messy face.

'Are you winding me up here?' He smiled up at her and she raised her eyebrow. He liked it when she did that.

'Maybe I would have got it if you'd said *Alien Resurrection.*'

Mark patted the horse. 'I see, well I can tell you're not from round here.'

'Very observant, I'm from Sweden.'

'Really? I would have said America.'

She raised her eyebrow again.

'Oh right, you're still winding me up.'

'Sorry, it seems to be easy and yes I'm from the States.'

'Cool!' He stuck his thumbs up like the Fonz from Happy Days and wondered what he was doing. He'd have to think of something better than that to impress her fast.

'Have you ever been?' She asked.

'I've been to McDonalds.'

'Did you really just say that?' She said, indignantly.

Mark twisted the grass in his hand like a naughty schoolboy and grasped for something else to say. He tried his best Homer Simpson impression and the horse made a weird snorting noise and reared up. He could have sworn the animal shook its head at him.

'I'd love to stay and be insulted a bit more,' the young woman said, 'but I have to get going. I think my shake and fries are waiting.'

'You thought it was okay to tease me though?' He said, confused.

'The operative word there being *tease* and not *offend*. Try looking those up in the dictionary.'

She gave a fleeting glance and shook her head. As quickly as she had ridden into his life she was gone and he stood there bewildered by the encounter.

~

Mark puffed and staggered up the field with the bike, through the woods and along the lane to the pub. He could see Will leaning against a wooden bench outside, he was over six feet tall and with his shaggy mop of hair and goatee beard he was always easy to spot. In front of him were two pints of beer, one of them almost empty.

'Blimey, what happened to you?' Will laughed.

Mark took the bike off his shoulder and propped it up on the side of the bench.

'I had a bloody puncture.'

'You should have said, I've got a spare inner tube in my bag.' Will sipped at the last of his beer.

'Yeah nice one except my phones' in your bag too.' Mark slumped down and reached for his pint. Before he could take a swig Will shook his empty glass in front of him. 'And it's your round.'

Mark took the empty glass and made his way to the entrance. Will called out after him.

'You might want to wash your face before you order.'

Mark walked into the pub as Will attended to the puncture. He kept thinking of the American woman on the horse. The dirty face probably didn't help make a good first impression but it was more than that, Mark had never been so tongue tied in his life. He could usually think of lots of funny things to say, so what had come over him?

He rubbed his face with his T-shirt arm, got a beer then began weaving his way through the drinkers outside. He handed the pint to Will who was fiddling with the bike.

'That's the beauty of these quick release wheels you know, you can change a flat in minutes.'

Mark wasn't interested in the wheel though, he was too busy watching the two horses trotting past. Upon one rode the American woman from the meadow and this time she was with a man deep in conversation as they went along the lane. Mark felt an overwhelming compulsion to speak to her again. She was unlikely to cross his path a third time so it was now or never.

He watched them turning the corner.

'Will. I need to do something. That woman who just rode past on the horse, that's her.'

'Who?'

'On the horse, she's the one. I don't know why but that's her.' Mark said.

'But you said that about the last one?' Will called out as Mark sprinted off up the lane.

'Excuse me?' Mark called out as he approached them.

The two riders stopped and looked back, she seemed surprised to see him again.

'Hey Tom,' she said, turning to her friend, 'this is the Fonz. Or was it Homer Simpson?'

'It's actually Mark; nice to meet you.' He stood beside the huge horse and held his hand up. She hesitated then accepted it into hers, it felt soft and he didn't want to let go.

'I'm Jo. It's my pleasure to meet an English eccentric.'

'You two know each other?' Tom asked. He was also American.

Mark thought that perhaps it wasn't such a good idea to hit on her if it was his girlfriend. He seemed much more of a threat up close but as Mark looked back up at Jo there was something that compelled him to be bold. Or stupid.

'We've met briefly.' She said.

'Give me another chance?' He suggested desperately.

Tom looked at Jo.

'Jo, what's going on?'

'Look,' Mark said, his voice was speeding, 'I saw you ride up to me and you looked like Winona Ryder and I really like her and I had to think of something to say and I just made a tit of myself okay.'

'So what do you want then, you tit?' She laughed.

'I just wondered if you'd meet me for a drink later?'

He looked her in the eyes; it was as if the rest of the world had stopped.

'After you've cleaned up?' He added.

Jo did the eyebrow thing again.

'The compliments just roll out of your mouth don't they?'

'I don't mean you're dirty I mean once your finished riding your Goldwing?'

'Gelding.' She corrected him.

'He's a lovely beast whatever he is. The horse I mean.'

'And what is Tom going to do if we go out?' Jo winked over to her companion on the other horse. Mark had a moment of realisation, it *was* her boyfriend after all so he decided to hold his hands up in submission.

'Look I feel a right idiot and I'm going now. I just wanted to try and yeah anyway I'm sorry to bother you, again.'

Mark walked away. At least he knew he'd given it his best shot. As he turned the corner he could see Will and the other drinkers at the pub and needed that pint more than ever now his mouth was bone dry.

As he neared the pub he heard the sound of heavy hooves on the road behind him. Tom, the American who had been with Jo was following him, Mark thought he looked angry and began to speed up his walk.

'Hey wait.' Tom shouted, as the horse began to trot.

As Mark got closer to the pub he decided he didn't want to stop and find out what Tom had to say to him, instead he grabbed his bike from Will who was just finishing pumping up the wheel. He jumped on, pedalling as fast as he could up the lane until he made the mistake of pulling up to get more leverage. The wheel came away from the frame and as it went one-way Mark went the other, crashing through a hedge.

Tom caught up and tried to spot him but Mark was already legging it across the field. Will, who had followed them called out after his mate,

'I hadn't tightened the release nuts up yet you idiot!'

Tom looked down at him and pulled on the reins turning the huge horse around.

'You know that guy?'

Will looked nervous.

'I might do,' he puffed his chest out, 'I do martial arts you know.'

'That's nice,' Tom said, 'I just wanted to tell your friend that Jo's cool to meet up for a drink later. She thinks he's freaking hilarious.'

~

That evening Jo and Tom met up with Will and Mark in Warwick. Jo looked very different with her shoulder length hair worn down touching the top of her Ramones T-shirt. Mark had also spent more time preparing what to wear than usual, spiking up his hair and trying on loads of clothes. Will and Mark might have to work in an office during the week but they were still rebels at heart and often reminisced about escapades in their old rock band.

'I played with them once.' He said, pointing to Jo's T-shirt.

'What, my breasts?'

Mark nearly choked on his beer. Jo laughed. She was quick witted and it made her even more intriguing. Will challenged Tom to a game of pool leaving Mark and Jo alone and soon they were engrossed in conversation. Jo could play the guitar and had written some songs, Mark suggested a jam session but she didn't have enough time, they were heading back via Oxford towards London after the weekend then flying home to the USA.

Neither of them wanted the evening to end and Mark began to realise that the symptoms he was experiencing whenever he looked at Jo were possibly connected to finding *the one*. The myth that he had heard about, seen in movies but never thought really existed at least not in his twenty-eight years.

As they walked back to Jo's hotel Will insisted on introducing Tom to his favourite après beer snack from *Take Bap! VI*. He wasn't sure where the other five restaurants were but this one did the best take out for miles. Mark and Jo walked on alone through a small park that ran alongside the main road.

'Don't you just love that?' She said, looking up at the sky.

'I've never really noticed it before, how did that get there?'

'Ah, you joke but people really don't notice it. This world is full of beauty that everyone misses. My favourite is right where I live, the lakes and the mountains in the fall; so many colours.'

'I've always wanted to go to America. Maybe if I had someone to visit?' Mark said.

Jo smiled at him and looked up again. 'So what do you think when you see all that up there?' Jo said.

'Aliens.'

'Are we back on that now?'

'Sometimes when I look at Will I think they've already landed.'

'I can see where you're coming from.' She said. 'How about God?'

'I think it's more about random chaos and luck. You?'

Jo was hesitant in her response.

'Okay. If you laugh I'll push you through that hedge over there.'

'Two in one day? That's not fair.' Mark said.

She turned around and looked at him intently, deciding to let him into her world just a little for now.

'I think life's like a movie. You know when you watch a film and it's already there. We're just playing a part of it right now.'

Mark began to laugh. Jo punched him on the arm. 'You're going through that hedge.' She grabbed him around the neck and wrestled with him.

'I'm not laughing at you. I promise.' Mark gasped, trying to get free. 'I'm just so glad that we met.'

'You just don't want to be pushed through another hedge you liar.'

'I loved what you said, it was a nervous laugh, honestly.'

Jo let go and put her hands on her hips. 'Hmm.'

'I'm serious Jo I've never met anyone like you ever. This whole day has been like a dream. Like... '

'A movie?' Jo suggested.

Mark stepped closer to her and looked into her eyes, he reached forward and took her hand in his. 'Like a movie, exactly! And if it didn't sound so naff I'd tell you that I wish I had a pause button right now.'

'That would be kind of pushing the cliché,' she laughed, 'Mr B movie!'

'I'm just trying to be romantic.'

'There are other ways.' She winked at him.

He put his hand onto her face and lent in to kiss her, she tilted her mouth up to meet his. At last he would get to kiss her, he'd wanted to all night and it really was about to happen.

Unfortunately Will and Tom shattered the moment bursting through the park entrance.

'Oi! Oi!' Will shouted as he swerved towards them.

'Want some of thissergghhhh.' He tripped, skidding along the grass on his knees without spilling any of his food. He looked up, very proud of himself.

'Are you okay?' Jo asked.

'Don't worry I'm surprisingly bouncy.'

Tom swallowed a mouthful of chilli sauce. 'Oh shit, my mouth is on freaking fire.'

'Weren't interupting anything were we?' Will said.

Mark helped his mate to his feet, smiling over at Jo.

'No, it's fine, just give me a chip you idiot.'

CHAPTER TWO

A year later Jo was strolling along the same Warwick streets that she had done on that memorable summer evening, not as a tourist this time but as the wife of the amusing man whom she had stumbled upon in the field. They had fallen in love and made a great start towards a life together. Despite living five thousand miles from her hometown, friends and family she was happier than she'd ever been. Jo had found a part time job in a trendy florist shop on Warwick High Street and as it was Friday she stopped at the newsagent to pick up their lottery ticket. She pushed her hands through her hair, padding along in her Converse boots and black jeans.

Walking into the shop she began her weekly routine. The lottery operator *Kabelson Industries* ran several games and she always entered *Six Magic Numbers* the main draw everyone wanted to win. She took a form from the stand and grabbed the chewed biro taped to a short piece of string. It was a challenge to get the nib onto the paper so she yanked the pen until it pinged off in her hand and filled in the same six magic numbers they chose every week.

The odds of winning a jackpot were about one in fourteen million but someone had to win it so why not keep dreaming just in case your numbers came up? The shop owner inserted her form into a machine with a bright orange ball on top. This was the smiley-faced lottery logo and it was everywhere you went. She picked up some of Mark's favourite sweets, Jo liked to take him something home no matter how small and it showed that she was thinking of him. Collecting her ticket she began the short walk to their house, unaware that her life was changing with every step.

~

Mark was feeling happier than he had for years since Jo rode into his life. He was probably at his happiest since his old band *Castle Rox* had been in the indie download chart. Formed in bedrooms and garages in his college years with Mark on bass and vocals; Will, his best mate on guitar and Stevie, a huge Scottish guy on drums who could lift the kit up with one arm. They would dress up as Knights for performances in local pubs with their fans slam dancing wildly in front of them. They couldn't afford real armour and chain mail so they went down the local toyshop and purchased plastic armour kits for boys. They were on the small side but at least they didn't weigh as much as the real thing. They had songs like *Marching on (and on and on)*, *Heavy Horse Thunder* and a comedy waltz for festive gigs *The Jester's Balls Are Clanging for Christmas*.

They had achieved a reasonable amount of success, playing alternative clubs and releasing an EP that sold a few thousand copies getting them into the bottom end of the indie charts. He still had the music paper review pinned up on his bedroom wall in a space between Bruce Lee and Rocky Balboa. They had met Marky Ramone from the *Ramones* once in Camden and this meeting had grown into an actual gig *with* the band according to folklore but it never really happened, it was used for kudos purposes when getting gigs. Despite living by the *Ramones* anthem *I don't wanna grow up*, sometimes you had to and when Stevie became a father Castle Rox was put on ice at least until they reformed in their forties like most bands, they joked. Stevie's son Jack was already showing interest in his father's drums however it was usually climbing inside the bass drum to hide with a packet of biscuits until he was sick.

Mark and Jo were expecting a new arrival too, it wasn't planned but it was about to surprise them; from their wedding night the clock had been ticking. As Jo walked home from the florist that evening Mark sat watching the news, his attention drawn to an urgent appeal.

> *'The mystery winner of a three million pound jackpot is still yet to come forward and claim. They have just one hour left!'*

Mark strummed his guitar thinking how awful it would be for that person to miss out on a fortune and not know about it. The poor sod would probably be stuck in traffic struggling back through the rush hour after a day of stress and toil. He was so glad that they knew their own numbers and checked them regularly.

> *'We would appeal to everyone who might have purchased a ticket in the Warwickshire area to go and hunt for their tickets and double check for those six magic numbers. Fast!'*

Mark wondered if he knew the unfortunate person who was about to miss out on that fortune, it was after all somebody in his county. He put his guitar down by the side of the sofa exchanging it for a TV magazine and a bag of crisps. He made a mental note of a few shows that he wanted to watch and put a huge handful of crisps in his mouth. The news reader began to wrap up the item announcing that the *six magic numbers* people should be checking for were on the screen.

He lowered the magazine curious to see the numbers that had beaten amazing odds. His life slowed down, the world stopped except for him and the six numbers now on the TV. The unlucky person who was unaware of the millions of pounds at stake was closer than he thought, much closer because they were Mark and Jo's numbers. Once the information had sank into his brain Mark spat the crisps out of his mouth in a jet across the room, slinging the magazine into the air. He stood up and bounded over to the TV checking the numbers again for a second and third time growing more ecstatic, he jumped up and down clapping his hands and whooping.

'This is it! No more work, no more suits, no more rush hours, I'm free.' He took his tie off and threw it on the floor. 'I won't need you mister tie.' He stamped on it and looked at the TV again charging over to kiss it, recoiling from the static shock. He laughed then spun round jumping onto the sofa yelling with excitement. Then, he stopped. There was one vital thing he would need to claim the fortune that they had won. The ticket.

He started to look through the draws beside the TV, turning out pieces of paper, tablemats and pens. As he did this, his mind was turning to a house, a big house with lots of land, a music studio and rehearsal room where he could invite Will and Stevie over for a jam. He hurried to the next drawer that was full of note pads and guitar magazines, yanking it out completely and tipping the contents onto the floor. A pile was forming quickly on the carpet but there was no time to tidy.

He ran upstairs into the bedroom throwing open wardrobes and plunging his hand into the first of many coat pockets, some of them fell to the floor but he didn't care there was only one mission, to find the three million pound ticket. He was so involved in the hunt that he never heard the key in the lock downstairs and the door opening.

Jo walked in and immediately saw the mess in the front room. The sound of banging came from above. Looking up the staircase she guessed that it was a burglar and decided to call for help. She slowly backed towards the door pulling her mobile phone from her bag, dialling the police, but before she pressed the last digit Mark appeared at the top of the stairs. She yelped and dropped the phone.

'Oh my God Mark. I thought it was a burglar.'

'Where do we keep the lottery tickets babe?' Mark puffed as he descended the stairs jumping the last few steps. He put his shaking hands on her shoulders.

'You scared the hell out of me you idiot.'

'The lottery, they've been waiting for a winner to come forward. I just saw it on the news it's us we're the mystery winners!'

'Are you sure?'

'It's the same numbers we always use. Where do we keep the tickets?'

'In the drawer by the TV or in my bag.' She said.

Mark snatched the bag off her shoulder tipping it upside down and emptying the contents. A ticket fell out and Mark studied it.

'That's the ticket for tomorrows draw.' Jo said.

He started pulling the bag inside out.

'Mark! It's my new bag be careful.'

'How many bags could you buy for three million pounds?'

Jo pulled the hair away from her face and stared at him.

'How much?'

Mark grinned. 'Three Million.'

Jo's eyes widened. After a moments thought she dived onto the floor and began rummaging through the contents with him, screaming with a mixture of adrenaline and panic.

~

Across town on the other side of Warwick the phones at Kabelson Industries were ringing much more than usual. The main receptionist was so overwhelmed that she had diverted all incoming calls to the claims hotline. The television appeal had ignited the nation's interest, it seemed that even without the ticket many wanted to have a go at pretending they were the winners. The stories ranged from the mundane like putting it into the washing machine, to the bizarre *It's in my Aunt's coffin.*

Two operators working for Kabelson Industries, Lisa and Emma felt as if it had been the longest shift ever. Lisa finished another call, removed her headset and puffed her cheeks out.

'That must be the fiftieth one saying their dog ate it. Unbelievable.'

She glanced down at her copy of *Glossipz* magazine and stroked Brad Pitt's face on the cover.

'I bet Brad and Angelina wouldn't even notice three million.' She sighed.

Her phone line buzzed and she put her headset back on.

'Here we go again,' she said, pushing Brad aside, 'Kabelson claim line...the three million jackpot, it's you is it?'

Lisa rolled her eyes at Emma, it wasn't the first time she'd heard this statement and it most likely wouldn't be the last before the night was over.

'Oh, you don't have the ticket?'

Emma shook her head. 'What a surprise.' She mumbled, picking up a post-it note and placing it between her teeth holding her hands up like dogs paws.

Lisa struggled to keep a straight face.

'Well you won't be able to claim without it.' She said to the caller.

At the other end of the phone line an anxious Mark was desperate to make his claim before the deadline. There was only ten minutes left, with or without the ticket he knew they were in with a chance and told Lisa it was just a matter of time until they found it and he wanted his call logged officially.

Mark and Jo continued searching for the ticket as if their lives depended on it tearing the place apart looking in pockets, bags, cupboards, and shoeboxes, behind the sofa, under the sofa, inside the sofa, in the washing machine, nowhere seemed too crazy to look when it was that amount of money. Three million pounds was within their reach, if only they could hunt down that tiny slip of paper that had once been in their hands. Without it they were just one of many hundred callers that night making a claim for the fortune.

Jo pulled a box full of scrunched up carrier bags from inside a kitchen unit, they liked to re-use them where possible after all it would be their children inheriting the planet. What a wonderful start if they could claim their winnings she thought, they would be able to get a bigger house with a long garden for the kids. Her thoughts turned to her family and friends in the US, she missed her homeland and they couldn't afford to visit just yet, not unless they found that ticket, it could change their lives in so many ways. She rummaged near the bottom of the box and spotted a white bag with a small square shadow inside. Rushing back to the front room she waved it at Mark.

'It was in with all the carrier bags, I can't look.'

Mark pulled the top of the bag open and hesitated.

'Go on then.' Jo said.

'Okay. Give me a moment I need to catch my breath. This could be three million pounds.' Mark put his hand in and picked out the piece of paper. It was a lottery ticket. He turned it over and they both examined it.

'Same numbers.' He said positively.

'How about the date?' Jo said.

'June.'

They looked at each other, unsure whether or not to celebrate. 'Is that it then, when was the winning draw?' She waited desperately for Mark to answer.

'I don't know I wasn't paying attention to the news item at first I just caught the numbers. Show me that ticket you got today, it must tell you the claim time on it somewhere.'

Jo located the ticket she had purchased on the way home from work and studied it.

'It says you have ninety days to claim.'

They looked at each other realising that it wasn't the ticket. Mark cursed and kicked a DVD across the floor.

'Mark, that's our wedding DVD, you idiot!'

She picked it up off the floor. Mark looked at her apologetically and walked over holding her tightly and kissing her neck. He breathed in her familiar scent that anchored him and always felt like home.

'Sorry babes. Look it's a sign we kept some old tickets right? I mean we just need to remember what we were doing on a Saturday three months ago.'

Their gazes simultaneously came to rest on the wedding DVD in Jo's hand. It wasn't a surprise they'd forgotten to check the numbers, they were busy taking their vows and celebrating rather than seeing their magical jackpot win. Mark had got the ticket on the way to the Church as Jo had been off work that week, he had picked up the buttonholes for the wedding from Jo's shop then purchased it next door. He remembered it clearly because the other customers were wishing him well for his big day.

Jo sat back on the sofa as Mark opened the DVD case and put it into the player. They soon came to an early scene with him and Will, the best man waiting at the Church.

'I still don't know how he seduced her.' Will joked.

'Well actually you make your own luck in life Will.'

On screen Mark pushed his hand into his pocket and produced a lottery ticket momentarily waving it around. They paused the DVD. There it was, the ticket they were searching for. It was strange how they had never paid much attention to that tiny piece of footage before despite seeing the wedding DVD several times. 'It's got to be in my wedding suit.'

Mark had left the suit with his parents at the hotel wedding reception. They were supposed to take it home whilst he and Jo headed for the airport to go on honeymoon.

Full of excitement and renewed hope Mark called the Kabelson hotline again. He asked for Lisa's extension. 'Have you found the ticket yet?' She said.

'Well yes and no,' Mark said, his voice trembling with adrenaline, 'it's in my wedding suit but I need to get it from my parent's house.'

'There's nothing more we can do tonight anyway, the office is closing for the evening I'm sorry.'

'Lisa, we also know something nobody else does, the winning machine was the newsagent beside the Florist on the High Street. You must have had loads of calls tonight but they won't be able to tell you the things we know.'

'Well I can take the details but without the actual ticket it's not going to change anything.'

'It was the day of the draw, eleven in the morning, I was on the way to the Church on our wedding day. Jo usually gets it on a Friday around quarter past five so you'll see a pattern of the same ticket being purchased as well.'

Lisa looked up and noticed Philippa walking past her desk on her way out. Philippa was Chief of the Anti-Fraud Department, a sharply dressed woman in her early forties, she had joined Kabelson Industries with a solid background in loss prevention and investigating credit fraud for a retail chain. She loved her job and the buzz of unearthing people's attempts at false claims, some of them went to extraordinary lengths to convince her but it made it even sweeter to uncover.

Lisa motioned for her to wait so she paused at her desk, putting her briefcase down and listening. Since the appeal had been broadcast her job had been incredibly hectic. Mark and Jo's details were handed to Philippa; she put her glasses on and studied them.

'Well, well, well.' She said, a broad smile spreading across her face.

CHAPTER THREE

Mark couldn't get hold of his parents by phone. They sometimes went out to see a concert with their friends on a Friday night, not the kind that he would go to, usually some old middle of the road crooner from the seventies still doing the circuit. He left a garbled message about the suit on their answer service and resigned himself to the fact that it would have to wait until morning. He sat down on the sofa beside Jo and they watched more of the wedding DVD, on screen Mark was still talking to the camera.

> *'I love you Jo. Remember, as long as we have each other the rest will fall into place.'*

It had been so perfect on their wedding day, nothing else mattered. That's why the lottery draw had seemed so irrelevant they had more important business, as most newlyweds did.

'So what now?' Jo said, hugging him.

'We keep looking I guess, but I'm sure it's in the suit.'

'So, let's assume it's still there; we drive over tomorrow and collect it from your folks, go to Kabelson and give it to them then...' She trailed off.

'Then we become multi-millionaires.' Mark said. He took her hand and slipped her slender fingers between his lifting it up to his cheek. Looking into her eyes he could see that this was going to be a tough ride for them, their first major test.

'Or we don't find it and we never speak of this again.'

~

Eventually Mark and Jo fell asleep on their bed in the early hours of the morning still clothed, their minds a mixture of hope and anxiety. Even in sleep Mark dreamt about the ticket, he was opening the front door expecting an entourage with champagne and a big cardboard cheque something he had seen lottery winners in the papers getting over the years. Then just as he reached the door he was sucked backwards like he was in a wind tunnel, the more he tried to move forwards the stronger it became.

Mark shuddered in the bed and realised the house phone was ringing. He opened his eyes and shut them again trying to adjust to the morning light.

He slid onto the floor taking the duvet with him, Jo moaned out and slapped the bed desperate to get some covers back. Mark rummaged for the handset picking up one of Jo's shoes at first, trying to find a button on it. He lobbed it across the room and located the proper handset. The voice on the end of the line was his mother's.

'Mum. Did you find the suit?'

'What's going on Mark?'

'The ticket for the six magic numbers jackpot.'

'You were hoping it was you I suppose?'

'We *know* it was us, it was on our wedding day.' He insisted.

'Oh Mark.' She laughed.

'I'm serious Mum.'

Jan was in her kitchen, serving his dad Roger breakfast. She cradled the phone with her neck and poured some tea whilst relaying the conversation to him over his newspaper. He shook his head and folded the paper onto to the sports page, the back sheet scraping across his fried egg.

'I don't think we have that suit anyway Mark.' Jan said.

'I left it with you at the hotel I know the ticket's in there Mum, we saw it on the DVD.'

'He says it was on their wedding day.' Jan repeated to Roger, now inspecting his leaking fried egg.

'This is still runny.'

'Well stick it back on the grill yourself Roger, I'm not an octopus.'

Roger shrugged and attacked the soggy yellow middle with a folded piece of bread. Mark was becoming frustrated on the other end of the phone.

'Mum, please just tell me where my wedding suit is?'

'Of course I remember now, *Will* took it,' she said, 'he offered to as we had a load of stuff in our car. Nan was moaning about her lumbago she wanted to stick her leg up in the back seat where Dad had that old canvas bag, remember we got it in Cornwall in the little shop on the beach where you got your ducky hat? You loved that ducky hat, anyway we couldn't...'

'Are you sure he took it?' Mark interrupted.

'Yes. He said he was going to get it dry-cleaned, anyway Nan wanted to put her foot up and we tried to move everything around we had my bag behind the seat, hang on, no it was on the floor and the canvas bag was on the seat wasn't it Roger?'

The line went dead.

'Hello?' Jan said. 'Oh charming, *how are you mum? I'm fine son.*'

Roger looked at his cup of tea, took a sip and winced.

'What's that face for?' Jan said, putting the phone back in its cradle.

'Have you put Soya milk in this?'

Mark tried Will several times but his mobile number was ringing endlessly. Sometimes he worked Saturday mornings. Jo was pacing around wondering about what Mark's mum had said because if Will had taken the suit to be dry cleaned then it was going to be a ball of dried mush by now and not their passport to a three million pound jackpot. There was a tiny chance it survived maybe, just legible enough to prove their claim, she hoped.

Mark was about to hit redial when the phone rang.

'Will?'

'Mark?' A woman's voice. 'This is Philippa from Kabelson Industries. I think it would be a good idea if I came over and had a chat.'

~

The doorbell rang. Mark opened the door to a tall blonde woman in a sparkly red dress holding a huge cardboard cheque, behind her was an entourage of cheerleaders with champagne, photographers and neighbours cheering. Mark drank in the moment he'd seen so often on television and in the newspapers, now it was his turn. He called out to Jo who ran into the glorious sunshine and they embraced then held the huge cheque up, posing for the photographers as the flashlights popped in the sunshine that seemed so bright that morning, it was unreal. Jo suddenly stopped smiling and shouted at him, he didn't know why. Then she slapped his face and began to repeat his name.

Mark snapped out of his daydream as Jo shook him.

'Mark, wake up, they're here.'

He sat up on the sofa where he'd dozed off, the severe lack of sleep from the night before was catching up with him. Jo went to the door and opened it to find a woman and a man in suits looking more like CID than public relations from a lottery company.

The woman with the tightly scraped back hair held out her hand.

'You must be Jo? I'm Philippa and this is Nigel.' Jo forced a smile. Unlike Mark's dreams of a large cardboard cheque the woman simply held a black case that knocked Jo's knee as she ushered them inside. Mark sat perched on the sofa waiting anxiously.

'That was quick.'

'Well our offices are here in Warwick.' Philippa said.

'I never knew that, what a Coincidence.'

'That's what we thought.' She said, looking over at Nigel and pulling out a clipboard from her case.

'You didn't bring the cardboard cheque then?'

'No,' Philippa spotted the ticket on top of the TV, 'unless you've found the ticket of course?' She stared at Mark looking for signs of nerves. She could spot a fraudster easily.

'Sadly that's not it, that's for this week. Not that those numbers are likely to win twice, I mean it's fourteen million to one odds right? That must have gone up even more for us now.'

Philippa gave a fleeting smile as Nigel began scouring the room like a detective. Bags, clothes and most of the contents from the front room drawers were still scattered across the floor.

'Excuse the mess. We've been searching for that ticket like mad as you can imagine.' Jo said.

'Don't worry, it's hard being a housewife I expect?'

Jo went to correct her but she continued too quickly.

'Sorry to come mob handed but Nigel is with me for back up. Some people can get very cross you know, especially when you tell them they can't have lots of money,' she laughed to herself, 'who'd have my job, I ask you?'

She adjusted her pad. 'So lets go through the basics again shall we?'

Mark tried to calmly explain how they had worked out how it was their win, where the ticket was and that Will would be bringing it over as soon as he got hold of him. Nigel seemed to be more interested in the room and its contents than the conversation while Philippa began busily scratching notes onto her pad. She looked over at the wedding DVD. 'Married long?' She said.

'Three months, the draw was on our wedding day.'

'Congratulations.' Nigel said under his breath.

'That's why we never saw it.' Mark handed the DVD to Philippa.

'You have your marriage certificate?'

'Yes. Why?' He said.

'Just thinking ahead.'

Philippa inspected the DVD and looked at the cover a collage made from stills of the day. 'Aw, how sweet.'

'Coffee?' Mark asked.

'No thank you.' She went to recline onto the sofa next to a pile of clothes stopping as a sharp coat hanger began digging into her backside. She stood up again holding it out.

'Oh my goodness I am sorry.' Jo said, trying not to laugh. Philippa handed the offending object to Nigel who inspected it.

'You can move the washing if you want to sit down as well Nigel?'

'He'll be fine standing thank you. So, have you lived in Warwick long?' She said tapping at her pad with polished nails.

'I came here in my teens for college. Grew up about half an hour away,' Mark said, 'I liked it so much I got a job here.'

'I take it y'all not from around here?' Philippa asked Jo, breaking into a mock American accent.

'I've been here since we married.' Jo said, not amused.

Philippa spotted Mark's guitar. 'Musical are we?'

'A bit yes,' Mark said, 'it relaxes me. We used to have a band going a few of us round here have you heard of Castle Rox?'

'I don't seem to recall the name.' She said.

'We played with the Ramones at the Marquee.'

Jo rolled her eyes as Philippa continued scribbling. Jo knew that it was all hype but she'd gone along with it because she loved him.

'R.A.M.?' Philippa stopped and looked up at Mark. 'The Ramones, how are you spelling that?'

'Oh no I wasn't in the Ramones.' Mark laughed. 'Blimey, I wish, well they're not around now but we supported them at a secret gig. We were in our first band at college and they were on their last tour, it was *Castle Rox* that I was in.'

Philippa scratched out what she was writing, looking slightly annoyed.

'Are you music fans then?' Mark said, hoping to establish some common ground.

'No, not really.' Philippa said, her eyes drilling into him, searching for signs that might give him away if he was trying to fool her.

'I'm partial to a bit of freestyle jazz funk myself.' Nigel said.

Philippa frowned, 'Let's keep to the business at hand shall we?' She placed her palms down on her clipboard like a makeshift lectern. 'Let me explain the reason why we're here. My role is with the Anti-Fraud Department at Kabelson Industries and I'm not here for any other reason than to investigate the claim you made last night. A formality so let's not get excited without the ticket, we had quite a few calls about the three million jackpot as you can imagine.'

'But it was us. The others don't have any proof and we do.' Mark said earnestly.

'Your information on the machine and time may have set you apart I agree however we're a long way from *fourth base* as you say in the States.' She looked at Jo with a tight-lipped grin. 'You wouldn't believe the things people say to claim, *'My dog ate it'*, *'it's in the washing machine'*, I'm used to those but then there are the other ones, the more serious attempts to claim. Some actually try to fake tickets.' Philippa looked across the room.

'You see that join in your wallpaper over there?'

'What join?' Mark said.

'Exactly,' she proclaimed, 'you can't see that from here but it stands out like a sore thumb to the trained eye.'

Mark and Jo both craned their necks trying to see the join.

'The two halves trick,' Philippa said in a secretive voice as if letting them in on a conspiracy, 'sometimes more than two spliced together. One chancer is doing eighteen months in prison as we speak.'

The couple looked at her. Did she think they were fraudsters, was that what she was insinuating?

'Why that machine and those numbers?' Philippa said, tapping her pad sharply.

'It's right next to where I work and we always use those numbers, you'll see tickets before and after that lucky draw. Mark's birthday is the twenty seventh of June and mine is the fifteenth of February, he's never got an excuse to forget unless he misses Valentines as well so his life just wouldn't be worth living,' she joked, 'then it's door numbers, ours is thirty-two as you can see and Mark's Nan's is forty-four. We noticed that forty-four also came up a lot in draws.'

'Will, my mate, says it's because it has greater ink coverage and weighs the ball down more than others.' Mark interjected.

Philippa gave a tight lipped smile and asked for proof of identification to clear up the first four numbers and the full postal code of Mark's Nan's house. She told them that the press had been very keen to discover who the mystery-claim was from and warned them not to mention it to a soul, because if their identity leaked out the media would hound them and make their lives a misery.

Philippa stood up and paced to the hallway, turning to face them. Nigel, who had been looking through their CD collection turned and followed.

'We'll call you as soon as Will gets here with the suit.' Mark said.

'Here's my direct dial,' she handed Mark a card and winked at him, 'don't lose it.'

Jo couldn't believe what she was seeing, was this woman actually trying to hit on her husband whilst investigating them or just referring to their lack of ability with retaining small pieces of paper? Either way she was out of order.

'You don't have long to come up with the ticket and remember what I said, nobody wants to be known as the couple who let a three million pound jackpot slip through their hands.'

'We haven't lost it.' Jo said.

Philippa looked her up and down.

'You have until the end of the day.'

She opened the door and they walked down the path leaving Mark and Jo more anxious than ever.

CHAPTER FOUR

Mark and Jo heard the sound of a car pulling up outside. Will, jovial as ever had no idea what was going on as he entered the house.

'There is a slight confession about that suit,' he said, 'I know I said I'd get it dry cleaned but I forgot.'

Their reaction was quite different to the one he had expected. Jo put her hands on his face and kissed him.

'Will, I love you.'

'Really? Blimey, maybe I should forget more often.' He said.

Mark was busy unzipping the suit bag before it had hit the ground searching for the ticket.

'Why the rush for this suit then, are you going for an interview or something?' Will said.

Mark checked the main pockets but the ticket wasn't there, he turned this attention to the inside ones.

'Remember the wedding day?' Mark said. 'We got lucky.'

'You did and if you weren't with this woman I would marry her in a second.' Will put his arm around Jo.

'Like one in fourteen million odds lucky.' She said.

'I know Mark told me that meeting you was better than winning the ... Oh my God it's you isn't it?' Will took his arm away from Jo. 'You're the mystery winners, the thing they've had on the telly I can't believe it!'

Jo nodded as Mark continued his unsuccessful search, checking the trousers and the suit bag.

'So the suit's for the presentation right, to get the cheque, can I come?' Will said.

Mark cursed and threw the suit down.

'I needed the suit because we thought the bloody ticket was still in the pocket. They won't pay without it.'

Will scratched his head.

'I guess that's quite fundamental in the construction of a claim.'

Jo and Mark looked at him. Will held his hands up.

'Sorry, just thinking out loud.'

'I don't understand,' Mark said, 'we changed after the reception and you got this from my parents right?'

'Yeah, it was when they were loading the car they had so much stuff to take back and your Nan had something wrong with her. You'd gone off on your honeymoon'

'Lumbago.' Jo Said.

'I thought you went to Miami? Anyway I offered to have it cleaned and pop it back when you returned and sort of left it in my wardrobe instead.'

If the ticket wasn't inside then Mark knew it had gone astray between the start of the wedding service when they were filming and Will's house. It was definitely there when they were outside the church, the DVD confirmed it.

'Will, we need to check your car, your wardrobe, it could have fallen out anywhere.'

The phone next to the television rang making them jump. It was Philippa.

'I got bored waiting to hear from you Mark. Have you found the ticket?'

'Not exactly, we're close though.'

He covered the mouthpiece and told Jo who it was. She whispered not to tell her they hadn't found it in the suit, they needed more time to think.

'Mark, you and Jo seem like a nice couple but rules are there to be followed and the board need to close this one down. The deadline is past now.'

'So, does that mean we have more time or not?'

'I'll contact you in the morning. Goodnight Mark.'

He pressed the red rubber button and stared at the handset.

'So?' Jo said.

'It's not over yet.'

Shuffling forwards towards Jo he leant on her shoulder. She kissed him.

'We need to find that ticket.' Mark said.

'We're going to be okay aren't we? Promise me this won't send us crazy.'

'I promise.' He hugged her tightly.

'I promise too.' Said Will, patting them on their heads.

They looked at him curiously.

'I was feeling left out.'

~

Philippa pushed the newspaper over to Nigel and reclined in her high backed office chair. The headline read *The Six Million Dollar Man - Just who is the mystery claimant?* The media had been pestering Kabelson Industries they wanted to know more about the jackpot winner, was the prize going to be paid out or would it still be the largest unclaimed amount since the lottery began?

Philippa didn't have much sympathy for people who would let that sort of money slip away although she thought Mark was cute. She had to face lots of situations every day with folk trying to con her but among these were genuine winners and she hoped that her work would mean those would at least get their money. The fact that Mark and Jo lived in the same town aroused suspicion initially but after looking at their claimed patterns of purchase, Jo working next to the newsagent, reasons for picking the numbers she knew there were too many confirmations for it to be coincidence or fraudsters. Kabelson Industries relied on computer technology to track everything that was how they could announce winners straight away and instantly know which machine had sold a winning ticket because they were all hooked up to the mainframe system. This made it more perplexing to Philippa why it was taking the board so long to reach a decision. The government watchdog that kept tabs on the lottery had been asked to comment too, layers of decision makers operating behind closed doors.

Her phone rang; it was the Marketing Director speaking in abrupt staccato bursts through the receiver.

'Philippa this has opened a huge can of worms.'

'I know, I was hoping we could give them an answer soon.

'This isn't a decision that we are going to make quickly, how are they coping?'

'Well they're on tenterhooks as you can imagine.' She looked at her nails one of them had chipped.

'I mean from a security angle, are they likely to go blabbing to the press? We've been inundated with calls, they want to know what's going on.'

'I told them not to talk to anyone. I'm pretty sure that they'll be fine as long as I keep them updated.'

'Try to tell them without telling them if you get my drift. Don't indicate the delay means anything positive.'

'Do you really think we might pay them?' She leaned forwards.

Nigel stopped reading and watched her face as she listened, it was cold and calculating and rarely gave anything away. He wouldn't want to play her at poker and yet he found her strangely attractive at times.

~

It had been another long and stressful night for the couple, snatching bits of sleep when they could. Mark moaned as he scrambled around for the ringing phone. He slid to the edge of the bed taking the duvet with him but

Jo pinched enough to stop him stealing all of it this time. She reached for the handset that was by her dresser and pressed the little green rubber button.

'Hello Jo, it's Philippa. Did you sleep well?'

'Not exactly.' Jo said, sitting up.

'There's still no news.'

'What's the hold up?'

'Well, I can't tell you that either. I'm at the end of a long chain and I have no idea who the person is at the other end but they are far more important than yours truly as you can imagine.' She gave a loud fake laugh down the phone. Jo pulled it away from her ear and handed it to Mark.

'Mark? Oh I thought it was Jo having a moment there with that manly voice.'

'No, it's me. What's the latest?'

'Well as I said to Jo we're no further to making a decision at the moment.'

'They haven't said *no* yet?'

'More importantly they haven't said *yes* and it's highly unlikely without the ticket they ever will. What happened with this suit?'

'No luck, it must have fallen out somewhere but we can show the ticket to you on the wedding DVD. Isn't that proof, I mean I hold it right up to the camera at one point?'

Philippa smiled and twisted a strip of her hair that had fallen down from her tight ponytail. Nigel had now finished reading the newspaper article and was drawing a cartoon moustache and glasses onto a famous celebrity on the opposite page.

'As much as I'd love to get some popcorn in and watch your happy day Mark it's not the same as having it in your sticky little hands is it?'

She advised them to keep hunting for the ticket and that she would be in touch unless she heard from them first.

Mark fought back the tiny ray of hope rising, he didn't want to start believing that they might really get the money. Surely if it was definitely a negative decision they would have made it immediately, he thought. It was such a dangerous thing to hope for because let loose in his brain it could ferment and spread then he would have to come back down to earth with a hefty bump.

'How was your girlfriend then?' Jo said.

'What does that mean?'

'She fancied you, I saw the way she looked at you yesterday.'

'Nah.'

'And I caught you looking at her too.'

'She's not my type, you are.'

'Nothing wrong with an older woman Mark, must be all that power she has over people.' She broke into laughter.

Mark tickled her playfully.

'You realise that we are possibly multi-millionaires? He shouted, excitedly.

'And what if we aren't?' She said, pulling his hands away.

'We were happy before, it'll be okay.'

'We need to prepare for the worst though,' she said, putting her finger on his lips, 'money can do weird things to people.'

Mark smiled and pulled the duvet across her back cocooning them inside as he held her tightly. He wouldn't let anything come between him and Jo he loved her too much to let that happen.

CHAPTER FIVE

One year earlier...

Jo was wearing her army surplus jacket, tight black jeans and Doctor Marten boots. She checked her hair in the hallway mirror and looked outside the hotel door to see Mark waiting by his car. She had been looking forward to their second date in as many days.

'How's your head today?'

'Better than Wills. I left him on the sofa with the remains of his takeaway glued to his cheek.'

'I haven't heard anything from Tom's room either.'

He opened the car door for her and she climbed inside picking up a CD by the band *The Cure* from the seat.

'You like indie music too. I keep meaning to get this album but I can only find it on download back home.' She said.

'Mostly I'm a rocker, indie, heavy. Don't like dance music but I do make exceptions for Shakira.' He grinned.

'Yeah, I wonder why.' Jo said, as he switched the car stereo on and the opening bars to *Just Like Heaven* filled the air. They pulled away into the traffic and headed towards Stratford upon Avon.

'I hated reading all that Shakespeare stuff at school but I'm going to show you this place for historic reasons.'

'I hear it pre-dates our first McDonalds restaurant?' Jo quipped sarcastically. It wasn't something she'd expected on a vacation, to meet someone who she could have such fun with so easily. Her last serious boyfriend had been jealous and controlling. She thought that men behaved exceptionally well until they felt that they had you then they would reveal their true colours. Even so, deep down she knew that she would have to step out from behind her walls eventually because without risk there was no chance to really find unconditional love and it was out there somewhere. There was a long way to go before she'd be convinced Mark was anything more than a holiday romance but he was proving a welcome diversion to her planned itinerary.

They walked along the River Avon, Mark pointed out the Clifton Suspension Bridge towering over it in the distance. Jo wanted to come back and see more of the historic old country someday as the trip was only scratching the surface.

After lunch they stopped at a record store, flicking through second hand albums and her knowledge of rock music and passion for vinyl surprised him, Mark always made a note of a woman's musical preferences as it saved arguments over the stereo if they were to date full time.

He walked up to the counter and asked if they had a copy of the *Castle Rox EP*. The spotty youth stared blankly at him then typed something into his computer.

'It's not listed.'

'Well I'll speak to my record company. Next time I come in I want to see it on the racks or I'll not do anymore signings here.'

The youth made some grunting noises and shrugged. 'I'll ask my Dad if he remembers them, he's about your age.' He turned and disappeared back into the storeroom.

'I'm only twenty eight!' Mark called out.

'We all look old to teenagers.' Jo laughed as *Just Like Heaven* came on the music shop speakers.

'Oh I don't believe it. This song again.' She said.

'Does that make it our tune? I mean this was released years ago, it must be a sign.' Mark gave her a hug.

'Hey, easy tiger it's just a song.' Jo pushed him away and began to spin and dance. 'I thought you didn't believe in all that anyway.'

Mark tried to be sexy and do some cool moves but he looked more like *Mr Bean*.

~

As they walked out into the street Mark pretended that he had left something in the shop and ran back inside returning with a bag and handing it to her. It was *The Cure* CD on a rare picture disc. She thanked him, taking his hand in hers and squeezing it tightly.

'As it's your last night here there's something I want to show you later.' Mark said.

'Excuse me?'

'No, I'm not being a pervert. Trust me.' He smiled.

It was almost nightfall as they finally arrived back in Warwick. Mark stopped outside Warwick Castle.

'Want to go in?' He asked as they peered through into the entrance courtyard, lit by torches.

'Aw would love to but it's closed.'

'Not if you know security.' Mark winked and whistled loudly in three sharp bursts. The huge gates opened in front of them and they walked in. Jo was speechless as he began to tell her all about its history, how it started out as a wooden fort in the early sixteen hundreds and then later became a stone castle. There was history there beyond her comprehension, he reeled off stories about William the Conqueror, Lady Jane Grey and Knights of old in battle. Jo was amazed by his knowledge and Mark was thankful to his friend Richard on Security who had given him a quick potted history when he'd phoned him to arrange the *surprise* trip.

He took her by the hand and led her across a courtyard and through a stone floored narrow street lined with timber framed houses. All they could hear were their own footsteps echoing around the fortress.

They entered a tower and ascended up to the battlements overlooking the River Avon. The sun was now disappearing on the horizon.

'Mark, this is just beautiful, I don't know what to say.'

'You could always just kiss me instead.' He mumbled.

She laughed and they embraced, before he knew what was happening their lips met and his heart was thumping through his shirt; everything made perfect sense for the first time in his life. They had to be together, they would be and it was no longer *how* it was *how soon*.

~

Within a month Mark flew out to California to visit Jo. He had seen America on the television and in films but never been there. As he looked out of the plane window he felt a rush of excitement and checked his wallet inspecting the dollar bills that all looked the same, they weren't a different size or as strongly coloured as English currency, it felt like pretend money. He noticed that during the trip people were frequently asking him how he was and thanking him for his custom when he got a drink or a paper. It was like he had stepped into an episode of one of the shows he and Will watched on a Friday night and he liked it.

Jo lived in a beautiful picturesque town called Rocklin, a few hours North East of San Francisco, California. She was waiting outside the airport in a car waving at him.

'You made it.' She said, running over to him.

'I know. I can't believe I'm here.'

Mark put his red backpack in the trunk and then went to get into the drivers seat.

'You sure you want to drive?' Jo laughed.

'What's this steering wheel doing in the passenger seat?'

Mark felt disorientated at first, speeding along on the right hand side of the road, it reminded him of a camping holiday in France when he was little, they'd driven on the right back then. He looked out of the window as Jo took the Interstate. He could have taken another internal flight but she wanted to show him her country and Jo was a road trip fan, she would often go for ten hour drives with friends on a weekend and just camp out or find a motel somewhere new.

It didn't take long until they were out of the city limits and into country.

'It's so green out here.' He said.

'What did you expect?'

'Skyscrapers like they had back in San Francisco or desert.'

'And you guys say Americans stereotype the world?' Jo laughed.

They stopped in a diner for a break and Jo ordered Mark a double espresso shot.

'Gonna need that if you want to stay awake the rest of the ride.'

'How far is it to your house?' He said.

'Oh it's got to be twenty five to thirty.'

'Hours? Oh my god.' Mark sat back.

'Twenty five miles.' Jo laughed, flicking a sugar packet at him.

They drove up to Rocklin catching up with news on the way and feeling happy to finally be together again. Mark met Jo's parents and once inside their large white wood panel house he presented them with some English tea in a caddy shaped like a London bus. Jo's father was a big man and although quiet he was friendly enough towards Mark. Her mother however seemed distant and cold, she thought that this man might take her daughter away if things got serious and she was quite happy for Jo to stay there in Rocklin and marry a local man like Nicholas, her ex-boyfriend. She had approved of him.

Jo showed him up to the guest room, a huge open space with en-suite bathroom and bay window overlooking the garden. The room alone was the size of the place that Will and Mark shared in England and he found out later that he could have purchased a whole house out there for an equivalent price. He put his case down on the bed and looked at Jo in the doorway and he knew that it had been worth the trip across the ocean just to see her face again.

They spent their time mountain biking around Lake Tahoe, rafting and camping with her cousins, it was a world away from packed rush hours and congested towns back home. Most of all he liked being with Jo in fact he was *in love* with her and working up to telling her during the three week stay. The day before he returned home they were sat in a beautiful rocky cove overlooking Lake Tahoe. As they watched the sunset he turned to her.

'Okay. You have until the sun disappears to answer a question.'

'I do?' Jo said.

'I was hoping that's what you'd say.'

Jo's eyes widened.

'Mark what are you saying?'

'I'm not saying anything, I'm asking.'

'Are you asking me to marry you?'

'It's too far for me to go home and then wish I'd asked you. I knew the moment we met you were different and whether I come back again one more time or a thousand times it's so obvious we're right for each other.'

'You waited three weeks and then do this on our last evening together?'

'Yes, why?'

'Because if you'd done it sooner my folks would have let you stay in my room you idiot.' She leaned over and pushed him back onto the ground kissing him hard.

'You can take this as a yes.' She whispered, unbuttoning his shirt and sliding her hand onto his chest.

CHAPTER SIX

The couple decided to start their married life in the UK and after months of planning they took their vows in a small English Church near Warwick and moved into a modest terrace home. Jo's family and friends made it over for the special occasion and despite the longer plan to relocate to the USA her mother was very upset. Her mood wasn't improved by one of Will's jokes during the best man's speech even though everyone else found it very funny.

Moving to a new country had its pressures though and Jo missed her closest friends back home despite new friendships with Gillian, her boss and Lauren who was married to Big Stevie. Occasionally Mark would forget that Jo had made a huge leap of faith in him by moving and she would have to remind him to support her emotionally. It wasn't that Mark was thoughtless it was just that he was used to thinking about himself. Mark and Will had spent so many years in Warwick they would inevitably bump into ex-girlfriends at the pub and Mark would go over old times with them in front of Jo, expecting her to join in and laugh with them but she felt threatened and vulnerable, it was his history and something that she had never been a part of. These occasions would sometimes spark a row and end up with Mark usually going off to sulk for a few hours, then reappear with his guitar and a song for her, some were sweet, some were funny and some were just bloody crap but they usually did the job and got her smiling again.

Jo hoped that the pressure of the lottery ticket saga wouldn't come between them and planned to work hard to retain a sense of normality. She was realistic, all marriages would go through trials they just hadn't expected one so soon after the ceremony. Matters were being made worse as it was dragging into yet another week and phone calls from Kabelson were vague.

She returned home one evening to find Mark and Will with a tape machine. Jo put her bag down and looked curiously at the pair of them.

'Insurance.' Will said.

'You're going to record a song about it?'

Mark told Jo to call the landline and test the device. She reached over to her bag and took out her mobile walking into the kitchen and dialling. Mark pressed the green button and answered.

'This is the lady from the Church.' Jo said.

'Erm, what are you wearing?'

'I'm wearing a big potato sack, support tights and Wellington boots.'

'You sound really sexy why don't you come over.'

Mark put the phone down and started to rewind the tape. It worked, the recording was clear. 'Let's see if we can get some juicy conversations on this thing next time Kabelson call.'

'If only that ticket would turn up somewhere.' She said, sitting down next to him.

'We've searched everywhere it could have possibly been babe. Will's house, his car, the church, I even went up to the hotel where we had the reception.'

'Nobody else could have found it, could they?'

'They would have handed it in by now for the money.'

Will picked up a guitar magazine and started flicking through it. 'I've looked loads of times in all the places where that suit might have been from the wedding to the day you called me. It must have fallen out of Mark's pocket somehow, I know it doesn't help but...'

Jo reached into her bag retrieving a neat parcel. She handed it to Mark. Inside he found a silver guitar pick holder, on the side was engraved *Castle Rox Reunion*.

'What's this for?' Mark said.

'You need something else to think about. I was talking to Lauren the other day and we both think that it's time you lot did a reunion gig as I never got to see you perform.'

'Yeah, I'm up for that,' Will said, 'mind you Stevie was moaning about his back again so he won't be keen to hump that gear around like we used to.'

'He'll just have to avoid picking the kit up over his head like Keith Moon then.' Mark said.

They began reminiscing about gigs and the fun they had, the wild nights often being paid in beer, sleeping on fans couches and waking up in a different town with a hangover and the time they nearly got a session on the radio for the Legendary John Peel Show after bumping into him at a festival.

Will decided that he would go home and dust off his old gear.

'Can you drop me at the take away en-route?' Jo said. 'I'm going to treat Mark to dinner on one condition...'

'What?' Mark said.

'We try to forget about the lottery saga for at least one night?'

~

Mark was stepping out of the shower when the doorbell rang; he wrapped a towel around his torso and padded down the stairs singing an old Castle Rox song.

'Did you forget your keys?' He said, opening the door to a surprised Philippa.

'Have I caught you at an awkward time?'

'Sorry, I thought it was Jo.' Mark tried to cover his nipples suddenly feeling exposed. The towel began to drop and he grabbed it with one hand.

'Can I come in it's a bit awkward in the street?'

'Now?' He said.

'I've seen a naked chest before and you're not going to attack me are you Mark?' She laughed, stepping inside the hallway before he could answer, her case knocking against his knees.

Mark excused himself and got changed into shorts and a T-shirt. As he returned downstairs he noticed the tape recorder on the side. He adjusted the microphone setting to turn it onto ambient recording and placed it on the floor as closely to the front room as possible.

He found Philippa sat on the sofa looking through a photo album.

'I hope you don't mind, it was on the side and...'

'No, it's okay,' Mark said, wondering how long Jo would be, 'so why are you here?'

Philippa was distracted by a photograph that tickled her and she laughed.

'Sorry, I don't mean to laugh, you still look cute.' She stood up and replaced the album onto the shelf unit. 'They've asked me if I'd do some more checks on you that's all.'

'Checks?'

'Yes. Just to confirm you are who you say you are.'

'But I thought you took all that last time?'

'Different sort of evidence at this stage and I'm sorry to do this because I'm convinced it was your ticket.'

'You believe us?' Mark's jaw fell open.

'As far as the ticket purchase goes. The machine, the time, the combination of numbers is in sync with your details and reasoning.'

'So, it is good news then?' Mark said.

'Don't get too excited please, it doesn't mean you'll get the money. They want to know where you have been working and living for the last ten years. Utility bills, payslips, mortgage details.'

'Bit severe isn't it?'

'Are you going to refuse my request Mark?' She said, stepping close to him and getting too close for comfort.

'No, not at all I just thought it was a bit extreme to want all that info but I'm happy to oblige if it helps.'

'I hope I'm not keeping you from anything by the way?'

'Just three million pounds.' He muttered, looking out the window for signs of Jo.

Every now and then Philippa thought she could hear a faint whirring sound but couldn't work out where it was coming from. Apart from her involvement there had been no attempt at offering support to the couple and the big decision on their win was supposedly on the agenda at the Kabelson board meeting each Friday. There had been several of those now and it had dragged on without conclusion.

There was also a new thorn in the side of the decision makers, the issue of other people who had already been paid out. Philippa and her team had been tasked to look back and check if anyone else had ever been paid outside the rules, and they had, over one hundred times. A huge error in the enforcement of the rules would be very embarrassing if it leaked out. Secrets were kept behind closed doors and agreements made without record at high levels in corporations that only a very select few are privy to share it often seemed.

Philippa finished making notes from the paperwork that Mark had dug out. Once she was satisfied that there was enough information she looked at her watch and put her folder back into her case. She flopped back onto the sofa and patted the seat next to her.

'Sit down, you're making me nervous.' She laughed.

Mark stopped pacing around and sat down as instructed.

'Thank goodness it's the weekend.' Philippa loosened her suit jacket as Mark shifted on the sofa.

'Jo should be back soon. She's gone to get some food.'

'Mark do I make you nervous?' Philippa sat forwards and looked at him with widening eyes and a large smile.

'No, It's just that this whole situation is weird.'

'Do you have any idea what three million looks like in notes?'

'Not really.'

'It's about three wooden pallets, that's roughly the size of a car.'

'Any sort?'

Philippa looked away quizzically.

'Something sporty with perfectly curved bodywork I expect.' She studied him, he looked like an innocent puppy and she wanted to pet him and teach him tricks. Men always did as she told them or she dumped them. She tipped her head forwards and let her fringe fall down a bit, peering up at him.

'I'm just a woman doing her job Mark. You wouldn't believe how hard it is to do effectively. I'm treated either like royalty or dirt depending on the outcome of investigations and all I'm doing is looking for the truth. You respect the truth don't you?'

He nodded.

'Well the truth is this Mark,' She lent forwards to within inches of his face causing him to back into the armrest.

'The truth is...'

'Not interrupting anything?' Jo's voice cut through the room so fast that Mark and Philippa both jumped up. Suddenly the hard-nosed inspector looked like a schoolgirl caught smoking behind the bike sheds.

'Why is the front door locked, I had to come round the side door?'

'I must have done it by mistake. Philippa was just inspecting my things I mean papers, your papers. They need more information on us.'

Jo looked between them and marched into the kitchen with the take away bags. Mark raced after her and found her busily opening the silver take out trays onto plates.

'You haven't even warmed the plates up, shall we set the table for three or do you want me to just serve?'

'Babe, she wanted to see more information.'

'I think she wanted more than that Mark.'

Philippa's voice came filtering through from the front room.

'Well I think I have all I need, I'll be in touch.'

Jo looked at Mark.

'Are you going to show your girlfriend out?'

CHAPTER SEVEN

The whirring tape machine had recorded clearly. Not only did it prove Philippa believed that they were genuine, it also helped Mark prove what had happened during the visit. More phone calls followed and with no final decision on their claim the couple began to let themselves dream of how they could spend the money. At work Mark would sit at his office desk gazing out of the window imagining the three million pounds. He would surf the Internet, looking at the latest Porsche or huge house, some of them had outrageous mod cons like a private cinema or music studio. They could invite friends over to see movies and enjoy parties without the worry of disturbing any neighbours. None of this helped his day-to-day work in the office which began to suffer as a consequence of his distractions.

Will worked opposite him and had tried his best to keep him grounded.

'Hey you up for rehearsal tonight?' Will said, summoning Mark from his daydream. 'We're supposed to be organising this reunion gig and Stevie keeps asking questions. Can't I tell him what's going on?'

'No. If it gets out then we're stuffed.'

'But he's our mate, he won't tell anyone.'

'He'd tell Lauren and then if she lets it slip to her mum and then she tells a neighbour... you know how things get out of hand.'

'I suppose. Talking of things getting out of hand I need to speak to you about this months report mate.'

Will motioned for them to adjourn to the staff kitchen and once there he explained that he had been covering for him, correcting slip ups. Mark wasn't surprised, since the ticket saga began he had been glued to the phone waiting for a call to say his six magic numbers were paying out. Every call deflated him, why wasn't it Philippa calling to congratulate him and ask them to hurry down to get that big cardboard cheque? The mental stress combined with the potential of getting the money was beginning to get to him so no wonder he wasn't inputting the correct data, all he could see were pound signs. When company execs mentioned millions for the profit and loss accounts he would twinge and be reminded again. The lottery was everywhere, on the news, in the papers, adverts in shops. He had never noticed it before until now but people were always talking about the lottery in offices and he couldn't escape it. *'If I win I won't be in Monday'*, they would joke. Mark had to simply sit there and hold his tongue while inside he wanted to stand on the desk and scream out;

'It's me, it's my bloody money I have proof and they just won't let me touch it yet but it's mine, it's mine I tell you.'

Mark thanked Will for watching out for him and they returned to their dull brown desks. They had always just been *desks* before but since he had come so close to living a millionaire's lifestyle they had become dull, crap desks. He didn't care to be there and by rights he shouldn't have to be because he'd beaten one in fourteen million odds and won millions and could prove it, if it wasn't for the stupid ticket that they'd mislaid then he would be in that big house right now looking out of the music studio window at his Porsche and not at his dull, crap, shitty shit desk. He had even prepared a packed carrier bag full of his personal belongings for when the call came through. He would simply tell Bob, his boss, he was leaving and go to collect that huge cardboard cheque from Kabelson Industries.

He closed the drawer again and took a mouthful of tea from his mug, the one that Jo had sent him during their engagement. It read on the side *As long as we have each other, the rest will fall into place.* That had become their manifesto. On his computer screen was a bright orange ball, the lucky mascot or *gonk* as Will called it, resembling a lottery ball with a smiley face. He had bought it before he met Jo, when he was in the office syndicate. Each week they would shake the gonk and six small balls would drop into the base section, from this they would pick the six magic numbers to play that week.

'I'm taking you with me whatever happens mister.' He flicked it with his finger. It rattled and six balls appeared but Mark wasn't interested in the numbers, he already knew *his* winning combination.

~

That evening Mark and Jo were driving through an exclusive neighbourhood, windows down pointing at houses which had become their indulgence since the wait had gone past the one month mark. They would venture out to a leafy village on the outskirts of Warwickshire and look at the beautiful houses. It was one thing to look at a seventy thousand pound car, another to live in millionaires' row. They knew from looking on the Internet that these houses would set them back up to two thirds of the winnings, but it still left a million pounds in the bank and the interest alone would provide a comfortable income, enough to start a family without worrying about where the next meal was coming from.

'Mark, stop the car.'

They pulled up outside a beautiful huge detached house with iron gates suspended between columns opening up onto immaculate rolling lawns. The house was timber framed with painted white brickwork and complemented by the Aston Martin on the driveway.

'Now this is what I'm talking about.' Jo said as they got out of the car and approached it.

'I thought we'd never agree.' Mark squeezed her hand tightly and kissed her cheek.

'I can't believe we're doing this it's crazy. What if we don't get the money?'

'Philippa said that the longer it goes on the more hope we have, if they were going to say *no* then they would have said so by now. It's nearly two months babe, they're just sorting out the red tape.'

'I'm scared. I don't want anything to change what we have.' Jo looked at him, her eyebrow cocked in that way he loved. Mark put his hand to his chest, knelt down and took her hand kissing it.

'As long as we have each other the rest will fall into place, isn't that what we live by?'

She nodded slowly.

'I would never abandon you. In fact we'll come back and buy this house,' he paused looking into the grounds, 'but probably get rid of the mock Georgian pot plants.'

'You shouldn't make promises you can't keep.' Jo said.

'Rubbish, those pots need to go.'

'Idiot.' She folded her arms and laughed at him, he could still give her the biggest boost out of anyone she knew.

He stood up and put his arm around her, feeling her smooth warm skin and pulled her close.

'This is our time babe it's going to be you, me, kids and a huge house to fool around in.'

She looked up and kissed him and they lost themselves in their own little world as they often did. Life was about moments like that for Jo, not about money and expensive things. Sure they could help you but when the door closed at the place you called home it was whom you shared it with that really mattered.

The owner of the large house interrupted this particular moment of peace by knocking on a window. They looked across to see a woman waving them away in the manner you would shoo away a stray dog. The couple waved back so she opened the window.

'This is private property.'

'We want to buy it.' Mark shouted back in a very posh voice.

'I beg your pardon?'

'We want to buy the house, we like it.'

'I'll call the Police.'

'Come on, let's go home.' Jo tugged at Mark's hand and they turned to walk back to the car.

They had approximately thirty minutes of carefree uncertainty left in their lives.

CHAPTER EIGHT

Mark and Jo turned the corner of the road and their hopeful mood swiftly turned to anxiety as they recognised the people outside their door. Philippa and Nigel.

'I'm glad we caught you, can we come in?' Philippa said. She didn't have a case, a pad or more importantly an entourage with a big cheque. They went inside and the couple sat down preparing for the news on the final decision, they knew that there couldn't be any other reason for the third visit. Philippa got straight to the point.

'Kabelson Industries have decided that although they believe you purchased the winning ticket, they just can't pay out. I'm sorry.'

Mark and Jo tried to absorb the information. It had seemed so long since the first time they had sat there with Philippa discussing the ticket. Months of waiting, dreaming and having hopes raised and dashed, of waiting by the phone, of not knowing if they would ever touch the money they knew was theirs. Now it was over. Time to swallow the bitter pill. They weren't going to get their hands on their three million pounds. End of dream.

The room was silent for a while, it was like the information would not lodge anywhere in their minds. Finally, Mark began to come round to reality.

'You said we were the genuine owners of that winning ticket?'

'I did and you are, they just can't pay out and make a precedent because you lost the ticket and the watchdog agree with them.'

'Everyone knew that all along, what were you doing all this time?' Jo said.

'We were trying to see if there was a way to pay you, bend the rules.'

'Trying? Either the rules are black and white or they aren't?'

'I've brought Nigel with me to help you.' They looked at Nigel who had been standing there observing them quietly. His face changed into a concerned smile. 'You're probably feeling very shocked right now. This is a natural part of the process.'

'What process?' Jo said.

'Healing.'

'What are you on about?'

'Nigel here isn't just anti-fraud, he's a counsellor.' Philippa said.

'As many session's as it takes,' Nigel said, 'I'm here for you.'

'You're offering us counselling?' Jo said.

'Free of charge, Kabelson Industries have offered to foot the bill for as long as you need me.'

'We don't want counselling we want the bloody money.'

'Mark can you calm down, we know this is a shock.'

'I've got it on tape,' Mark said, 'proof that it's us so what are you going to do about that?'

'You recorded me?'

'The night you came round, the calls, it's all on there and going straight to the media as soon as you leave here, in fact you can piss off now.' Mark's head was spinning, he shook with anger as thoughts whirled and jostled for pole position. He needed space and time to really let it sink in. Jo was trying to calm him but even her attempts to hold him were shrugged off.

'If you could just let Nigel help you.' Philippa pleaded.

'I understand what you must be feeling.' Nigel said, trying to put his hand on Mark's shoulder.

'Get off me you tosser. Have you had three million pounds dangled in front of you, knowing it was yours?'

Nigel shook his head.

'Have you had to give over your personal details to a total stranger, I mean what the hell was that about Philippa?'

'We could sue for that.' Jo said.

'Not in England you can't.' Philippa smirked.

'I've heard enough, just get out.' Jo said, marching to the door and throwing it open.

'You can't use those tapes,' Philippa said on the way out as she wobbled on her heels, 'the press will hound you they'll make your life a misery.'

'I think you've done a pretty good job already, don't you?' Jo said.

Nigel turned and held out a card with his details. 'Just in case you change your mind, my number is on there and...' They slammed the door before he could finish and walked back into the front room.

Philippa's car headed up the road as the sky turned from blue to slate grey, a storm was coming. Jo put her arms around his waist.

'As long as we have each other, we'll be fine. remember?' She said stroking his neck.

Mark stared at the car taillights as it turned the corner. They may have denied them the payout but the next move was his.

CHAPTER NINE

Mark sat under a wall of framed newspaper pages as his tape recorder on the desk beside him played back the Kabelson phone calls. A hand pressed the stop button. Fraser was a PR Guru, Mark had seen the news enough to know that there was only one person to go to with the story if they wanted advice.

'So they put you through all that and then said *no*?' Fraser said, leaning back in his chair and nesting his fingers into a steeple under his chin.

'Apart from offering us counselling.'

'Counselling?'

'To cope with the news.'

Fraser laughed out loud and put his head in his hands. It was the familiar tune of large corporations dealing less than tactfully with everyday people. He could see the key facts of the story beneath the web that Kabelson Industries had spun for two months. Walking to the window he peered outside, below the city rumbled on in the familiar relentless way that they did across the globe, it wasn't an ideal environment for everyone but he loved the energy of it all. Fraser lived in the media world and knew how it worked, he'd been at the top of his game since before Mark was born and seen it all in his time.

'Never stops, does it?' He said, sitting down again and playing with some cuttings on the desk. Mark looked at them and recognised a pop star caught in a precarious situation under a headline pun.

'Let's get you another coffee and I'll make a few calls.'

'You'll help us?'

'I'll help you tell your side of the story. That's what you want right?'

'I want the truth to be known.' Mark said, earnestly.

Fraser shouted in a Jack Nicholson voice, slamming his hand down onto the desk. 'Can you handle the truth?'

Mark smiled, he had been hesitant to approach such a media heavyweight with a reputation but he'd made him feel relaxed and welcome.

'Fraser, there was one thing we were concerned about.'

'What's that?'

'If this story goes to the national press there's going to be some publicity obviously.'

'That's the general idea.'

'What's it like?'

~

The doorbell rang. 'It's so early. Who's up this early on a Sunday?' Jo said.

'I'll get it.' Mark groaned, sliding out of bed. He pulled on a pair of jeans and scratched at his unkempt hair. On the way downstairs he picked up a T-shirt that was hanging over the banister, put it on backwards and stomped down the stairs as the doorbell rang again. 'Alright, alright.' He shouted padding down the hallway. A shadow peered through the fogged glass in the front door. He opened it and squinted in the morning sunshine as a dozen cameras and journalists swarmed towards him.

'What's it like to be Britain's unluckiest couple?' One of them shouted.

'Who lost the ticket?' Demanded another.

'Can we hear the tapes?' A woman shoved a microphone in his face.

Disorientated, Mark panned the scene. In the street behind the journalists he could see more film crews setting up, vans with satellites on the top. He noticed a neighbour watching from his front gate and waved at him.

Fraser had certainly got them exposure. After playing him the tapes Mark had spent Saturday afternoon with a journalist at his offices going through the story. It felt so good to finally speak about it to people but he hadn't expected this much fuss. A newspaper was thrust into his hands.

'Can you just hold that up for us Mark?'

He looked at it. The front page was a picture of him and Jo on their wedding day with the headline *It's the Six Million Dollar(less) Man!* Oh come on, he thought, was that the best headline they could come up with? He tried to bat away the sea of cameras and microphones.

'Guys could you speak to my agent about anything to do with this, I'm sure you all know where to find Fraser and I need a cup of tea.'

He shut the door. Jo appeared at the top of the stairs.

'How many people are out there? It's ridiculous.' She said.

He held the newspaper up. 'Welcome to your fifteen minutes of fame.'

Jo put her head in her hands.

'What did you say to them?'

'I told them to speak to my agent.' He laughed.

They went into the kitchen and read the article together. The couple had somehow made the national headlines.

The phone rang.

'Mark, we've got a situation here.' His mum's voice came down the phone line in speedy bursts. 'There are men at the door wanting to know about you. What have you done?'

'Mum, it's us, we're the lottery winners I kept trying to tell you but you wouldn't believe me.'

The phone went silent for a moment.

'Hello? Mark, it's your dad Roger.'

'I know your name Dad.'

'They are offering money for pictures of you. How much is a good price?'

'Dad! Don't sell my pictures.' Mark suddenly had images of old pictures leaking into the tabloids, his hair bouffant and quaffed up, eyeliner exaggerated up to his temples during his brief Goth phase at college.

'Well we've got double prints of some of them you know what your mothers like there's hundreds to choose from. I mean we're quids in lad never mind the lottery money.'

Mark's mother looked outside to find a cameraman on her flowerbed and opened the window.

'Oi! Yes you, David Bailey. Get off my bloody plants.'

The next phone call that Mark and Jo received was from Fraser telling them he was on the way to collect them and they were about to go on national television. He assured them that he would guide them through the media frenzy. 'This is the biggest morning show on TV but don't be phased. Tomorrow it will be old news so just enjoy yourselves.' He laughed. They had expected a small *bad luck* article, a column or two, tomorrow's chip papers as Fraser rightly pointed out. It wasn't the end of the world and the couple knew that much more serious events were happening everywhere but for some reason the theme touched people, it was something everyone identified with, the dream of winning millions on the lottery and the nightmare of losing your ticket. Whether they thought the couple deserved their winnings or not, they had an opinion. It was travelling around the world fast and becoming a talking point in most countries that had a lottery.

On arrival at the studio, they were taken to make up. At first Mark protested at having *his shine* taken away or wearing make up but then he saw a poster on the wall highlighting the difference.

'I feel stupid.' He said, sitting in a chair under the mirrors as they powdered his face.

'You get used to it.' Came a voice from the chair next to him. It was a famous impressionist that he'd seen many times on the TV.

'Oh wow, I love your show.'

'Thanks.'

'I do impressions...'

Before Jo could stop him, Mark was doing his Homer Simpson impression and the TV personality was doing his best to remain polite.

'Very good.'

'Hey I couldn't come on your show could I?' Mark asked.

'Well, it's not that simple...'

'I'll come down and do it for free, I know you do a Christmas special so let me know when and I'll be there.' Mark jumped off the chair and bounced out of the room looking very pleased with himself as Jo mouthed an apology.

'Behave yourself on camera.' Jo said to him as they waited in the green room looking through the newspapers. Mark held one up with their faces on the cover.

'Very weird, one for the kid's scrapbook eh.'

'Or Grandkids.' Jo added, kissing him on the cheek.

Fraser had been on his mobile phone since they arrived. He finished his call, sat down next to them and grinned.

'That was one of my contacts. Been digging around for info on Kabelson Industries and oh boy, have we got news for you.'

~

The inside of the TV studio looked really tiny. When they had watched shows at home they had imagined sprawling great rooms. Every few feet there were huge cameras on wheels, cables snaking everywhere, people with clipboards and headphones almost tripping over each other. Mark and Jo navigated nervously through the chaos as quietly as they could. A man walked up and clipped a microphone onto their clothes then ushered them to the sofa next to the presenter. They immediately felt the heat from the bright lights pointed towards the set. It seemed surreal to actually be there looking at the opposite end of the camera for once.

The presenter talked them through the basics of the story and assured them that it would be a relaxed interview. Jo squeezed Mark's hand and kissed him on the cheek, smearing his foundation a bit. The make up lady whispered something and went to step forwards but the floor manager was counting the studio back in from the commercials. The autocue began rolling and Mark mouthed it along with the presenter as he began his link.

'Welcome back, now unless you've been on the moon you'll have heard of our next guests, they're being called the unluckiest couple in Britain after losing a whacking three million pounds on Six Magic Numbers, the game run by Kabelson Industries.'

Mark and Jo watched the red light illuminate on the top of the camera facing them, they were being broadcast to the nation.

'Talk us through what happened Mark.' The Presenter said.

'Can I just say hello to my Mum and Dad?'

'Erm, yes but let's get back to this amazing story ...' the presenter chuckled.

'Hello.' Mark interrupted looking right into the camera, 'Oh and Will and Stevie and anyone who knows me. Jo, say hi to your folks, does this go out in the states?'

'No it doesn't. So back to this story, Mark, I'm over here.' The Presenter was trying to get Mark's attention but he was still staring into the camera.

'Sorry, I've never been on TV before.'

The production manager bellowed into the presenter's earpiece.

'Go to the woman quick, quick.'

'Jo, if I could turn to you sweetheart, how did you manage to lose the ticket?'

'The draw was on our wedding day and we were so busy with other things.'

'Nudge, nudge. Know what I mean, say no more.' Mark did a Monty Python impression and smiled at the camera again. Jo elbowed him in the ribs.

'Kabelson Industries say that without the ticket they can't pay out.'

'Yes, we understand that, we just wanted to play the recordings to people and show the ridiculous way they went about it when they could have told us on day one.'

The presenter sat back and the camera switched to a wide shot.

'Well, we can perhaps pose that question to them now, joining us by satellite is the head of Kabelson Industries Anti-Fraud Department.'

A screen to the side of the room came to life and there was Philippa, complete with earpiece and clip-on microphone.

'Philippa, good morning to you.'

'Good morning.' She said, confidently.

'We've got Mark and Jo here and obviously they're in shock still regarding your decision not to pay out.'

Philippa pursed her lips, 'Can I just say that it wasn't my decision to deny them the money,' she glanced sideways into the monitor at her end of the link. The corner of her top lip seemed to flick at the sight of Jo, a fleeting sneer, 'it was a company decision, that's Kabelson Industries along with advice from the Government watchdog.'

The presenter looked down at his notes, 'Surely if you went to all that trouble proving they had won you could pay up, what's stopping you?'

'We cannot make a precedent case of anybody I'm afraid.'

'So why the two month wait?' Mark said.

'We had to be sure that your claim was genuine.'

'And like it says on the tapes, you proved we were then you took every bit of personal info you could get your hands on, where we lived and worked for years?'

Philippa shifted in her seat at the mention of the tapes. She had really got it in the neck from her bosses over that one.

'Why not give them something if you know it was genuine, soften the blow, come on we all saw how much profit your company made last year?'

'Absolutely not, we cannot set a precedent.'

'So Kabelson are saying that nobody has ever been paid without a ticket in this situation Philippa?' The Presenter said.

'Correct.'

'Well we have someone here who begs to differ, if we could ask Fraser to join us.'

Fraser, who had been waiting in the wings, joined the couple on the sofa. Philippa watched him on the monitor from her end and her face twitched again, she knew who he was and he wasn't there to join her in backing Kabelson Industries.

'Morning Fraser, I believe you have some interesting information on this situation don't you?' The Presenter looked gleeful, as he knew what was coming next would be good television.

'I do. It seems that Kabelson do have a precedent already, in fact if you'll pardon the pun, they've had more *precedents* than Jo's country has in several hundred years.'

'Is this true Philippa?' The presenter asked.

'Well, I can't... I mean I... refute what Fraser is saying.'

'You said that you haven't paid out to anyone in similar cases?'

'I... look I came on here this morning to answer questions on this case only. I am not on trial here.'

'Why can't you answer the question?' Fraser said, 'Either you have paid out before or you haven't.'

Philippa was now red and looking around the studio as Fraser dealt another blow. 'I have also spoken this morning with the Downing Street Press Office and the Prime Minister has backed Mark and Jo. Let's get real here, they have recordings, you know it's them, we know it's them and now it seems you've paid others already. What's the real issue here?'

They sat and waited as the link went back again to Philippa who was just staring at the camera. She cursed inside at her bosses for sending her into the firing line like this. Why hadn't one of the senior decision makers offered to do the interview, after all it was their decision and not hers? If it was her decision then she would have let them have the money but she couldn't say that on national television or she would be sacked.

'You can't deny it can you Philippa? You have paid other people and this pretence about setting a precedent doesn't hold water.' Fraser said.

Philippa looked down at the monitor and saw the faces from the studio peering back at her, waiting for an answer that she could not give and retain any credibility.

'This interview is over.' She tore off her lapel microphone and stood up. Unfortunately as she walked off screen she had forgotten that the earpiece was also still attached and her head pinged back into shot, hair wildly splaying around. Mark and Jo giggled as the link screen went blank.

'We appear to have lost Philippa.' Said the presenter.

'Blimey, it's bad enough us losing a ticket but a person?' Mark said.

~

The interview had actually been fun after all the stress of the previous two months it was good to get the story out and discuss it with other people. The couple were immediately whisked off to a radio interview and then another television station, Fraser knew there was a short window of time before news focus moved onto something else.

After a day of media interviews they arrived back exhausted at his office. A curly haired man in a pinstripe suit was waiting for them. Fraser was pleased to see him and introduced them to the couple.

'This is Terence, he's been following your story.'

'Are you a reporter?'

'I work for a litigation firm, I'd be interested to look at your story closer.'

'Thanks for the interest but we could never afford to take on a huge corporate like Kabelson Industries.' Mark said.

'You might not have to. Are you familiar with no-win no-fee?'

'We just want to get back to our lives.' Jo said.

'Not yet,' snapped Mark, 'we won that money Jo and I don't care how long it takes to get it.'

He looked back at Terence. 'Tell me what you can do for us.'

CHAPTER TEN

The long pool was shaped like a gigantic dollar sign with a bar at one end, a waterfall at the other and a Jacuzzi on the side. It had been two months since the meeting with Terence and accepting his offer of a no risk legal battle, now Mark and Jo were on a paradise island near Fiji. It was a world away from the lottery struggles that had dominated them for so long as they splashed around in the sculpted swimming pool. Whatever they wanted they just had to ask. They were living the millionaire lifestyle that they had been held from at arm's length and there was no danger of it being a daydream.

Beyond the pool was a crystal blue sea where Mark would go sailing, maybe across to one of the neighbouring islands or scuba dive to see fish in the shallow reefs. Jo would play tennis with a coach who was boated in especially for her lessons then sunbathe and watch for Mark to return. He didn't exactly look like James Bond when he came up out of the water with his stringy legs but he was the man she loved. In the evenings they would decide what the Michelin Star Chef would cook for them and to walk it off they would take a moonlit stroll along their private beach before retiring to bed in the master bedroom overlooking the bay.

They swam towards the bar, propping themselves up on the edge. A tanned man in a crisp white shirt appeared and asked them what they would like to drink.

'Can we have two of those cocktails you made us last night please?'

The barman smiled warmly and went to locate a silver shaker.

Mark put his arm around Jo.

'Not a bad life for a couple of losers.' He said.

'Shall we have a barbeque here tonight?'

'Whatever you want babe.'

'And I'm not dreaming this am I?'

Mark called over to the barman.

'Can you tell her this is real?'

'You aren't dreaming.' He smiled, putting some ice into the shaker.

They took their cocktails down to the beach finding a small cove overlooking the bay. Mark put his towel down and they huddled together feeling the warm sunshine on their bodies. 'As long as we have each other.' Jo whispered.

They laid there for a while and fell asleep in each other's arms.

~

The sound of a boat landing on the beach woke them and they watched as a man unloaded fishing equipment. He saw them and waved, they stood up and walked over to him.

'You must be Mark and Jo?' He bypassed their outstretched hands and hugged them both warmly. 'How are you enjoying the island?'

Sir David had invited the couple to his own private island as guests after learning of their story. He was a self made billionaire and maverick inventor who'd been turned down by lots of corporations before forming his own company to produce inventions that spread around the world.

They walked back towards the main house with him asking about how he had made his fortune, most of his drive and motivation stemmed from not wanting to work for other people and the freedom to be creative.

'You know, some people see me and they say *'He's got millions and all I would need is for him to give me one of them and I'd be happy for life'*, he looked at them intently, 'but they're missing the point completely. You can be rich and unhappy too, it's not about all this.' He pointed to the beautiful main house they were approaching. 'This is a by-product but on its own its nothing. You need to find out what you love, what you really feel passionate about doing in life and do it. True success is what you feel on the inside. The physical can all be taken away but what's created from inside of us and how we use it is the real treasure, it's unshakeable.'

Jo put her arm around Mark. 'Listen to the man.'

'You guys might still get that money if your court case comes out but it doesn't mean it's going to be the end of stress and struggle. You won't have to worry about the bills but it brings different problems, believe me.'

~

The time on Sir David's island meant different things to the couple. Jo thought it was a good return for a pound on the lottery; she was always trying to put things into perspective. When she was travelling around Europe living out of backpacks Tom used to paraphrase something from a Monty Python song, *We come into this world with nothing and leave with nothing. What have we lost in between? Nothing.*

Unfortunately Mark wasn't quite in the same place. He was pinning their future on Terence winning the legal case and a continuation of the delights they had sampled on the island. He had now tasted the lifestyle and wanted it all the time. Litigation was notoriously long winded and it might take years but he wanted to fight it all the way, or he would grow old and bitter wishing that he had exhausted all options. For Mark it was also about standing up to the corporations, the faceless people who had remained in the shadows otherwise it would feel like the family in Dickens's Bleak House, an unresolved hangover for generations. It was real gold at the end of this rainbow and he was going to chase it.

At the barbeque by the pool that evening, Jo wore a new dress she had found whilst shopping on a nearby island. It was a sleek blue strapless fit with a daring plunging back. Mark used to pay her so much attention but he didn't even comment on it. She put it out of her mind as they enjoyed the wonderful food that the Chef had prepared on a grill in front of them.

After they had eaten they sat drinking and talking to him about the island. The conversation turned to money and then Mark began relaying the whole lottery drama, something they had agreed to avoid as much as possible during their break.

'Great. Here we go again.' Jo said.

'It's interesting.' Mark snapped, taking a swig of his drink and jabbing a cocktail umbrella up his nose.

'Maybe to you but not everyone wants to be bored with it.'

'No it's fine Miss, I heard Sir David talking about it,' The Chef said, 'so where are you now with the court case?'

Jo drifted off and gazed at the beautiful sunset on the horizon. She put her hand on Mark's shoulder.

'Look at that sunset. Mark, come down the beach with me, you'll miss it.'

'Okay, in a minute.'

Jo walked from the bar to the private beach leaving Mark talking. She walked to the sea, feeling the cool water run between her toes. She took in a deep breath and looked out at the sunset.

'Come on, you'll miss it.' She turned to see Mark deep in conversation under the light of the poolside bar. Mark wasn't going to let go of the lottery money and she knew it. The plan had been to get away for a while, away from all the stresses that had been eating away at them for so long. Time out to re-charge and focus on their relationship. Jo had hoped for at least seven days so they could have truly left it behind and searched for the love they used to share. Instead she watched the sunset alone and wondered if things would ever begin to get back to how they used to be, before their numbers came up.

CHAPTER ELEVEN

The dream holiday had been a double-sided coin, it was something they never would have experienced before, a week on the island was worth tens of thousands of pounds per person plus the first class flights on top. On the flip side it was a taste of the life that Mark felt had been snatched away from them. Kabelson Industries had sentenced him to another forty years or so in an office rather than pay out his win. It was becoming a mental stumbling block for him to get on with the rest of his life.

Even if he could work out how to do that there were reminders of the lottery in newspapers, TV adverts, billboards, signs outside shops. Slow progress on the litigation case made things harder. Terence had written to the couple once he had examined all the details of their case to inform them that it was not as clear cut as he had initially thought. There were tight curves to navigate with litigation and contract law. He reminded Mark that it wasn't always a court of *justice*; it was a court of *law* and to be patient.

Like the legal curves Terence faced, it was proving to be a time in Mark's personal life that he was struggling to manoeuvre round. Jo was behaving differently towards him, not engaging in conversations like she used to especially if it was about the lottery. She buried herself in books or went out with Lauren and Gillian.

Mark was showing pictures of Sir David's Island to Will and the rest of his colleagues. They looked in awe at the views and the beautiful surroundings. Bob, his boss had noticed the small throng and called over.

'Mark. Can I have a word.'

'Sure,' he replied holding up another picture for the others, 'that was the view from our window.'

They all took a good look at it, passing it round. Bob tried to get his attention again.

'Now please Mark.'

'Ok, just a second.'

Mark pointed to a picture of himself on a hammock overlooking a crystal clear water bay.

'That's where Sir David does all his thinking, for his inventions and stuff.'

'Listen to that, all chummy with Sir David.'

'My mate Dave you mean.' Mark grinned.

Bob was getting impatient. 'Mark. I haven't got all day.'

Mark stood up and joined Bob over at the water cooler outside his office.

Bob poured himself a cup and gulped it down.

'Look. I'm glad you had a good break Mark.'

'Aw it was amazing thanks we got to fly first class and then a boat picked us up with champagne and...'

'...And I hope that we can get to see some hard work from you now.'

Mark was taken aback by the sharpness of the comment.

'It's time to come back down to earth now,' Bob said, 'I know it was a shock this lottery business but you have to face reality, it's over. This is nine to five and you have a job to do just like everyone else.'

'I'm trying hard to keep it together Bob.'

'Well show me you're the guy I hired, I can't have you uncommitted to your job here Mark while you're rattling on about losing the lottery.'

'Bob, I'm good at what I do here, I've been through a lot of crap lately but this holiday was a tonic.'

'And I'm glad. Now let's get back to work please.'

Mark began to walk back to his desk.

'And leave the happy snaps to lunchtime.' Bob called out.

'Cock.'

'What did you say?'

Mark turned around.

'I said Okay.'

'You never did. I heard it and that's a verbal warning.' Bob said.

'Well if you knew I called you a *cock* why ask me?'

The office fell silent.

'That's a written warning.'

'Hey everyone, Bob's being a cock.'

'Mark. Pack this in now.'

'No. Everyone needs to hear this, Bob says I need to come down to earth is that what you all think?'

Nobody answered him. He looked at Will.

'Will, what are my reports like this month?'

'They're pretty good actually.'

'Don't encourage him Will or you'll be on a warning too.'

'But he is performing.' Will said, quietly.

'See I'm performing Bob, here on earth, I'm back on terra firma are you happy?' He jumped up and down a few times to make his point.

'Okay, that's enough Mark. Go outside and cool off or I'll call security.'

'Mark let me buy you a drink,' Will said, standing up, 'come on don't lose your job over this.'

It was too late. Mark was already way over the line.

'I'll calm down if you admit you're a cock, Bob.'

'Mark. Why are you doing this, you know I'm going to have to fire you?'

'Just admit it here in front of everyone and we'll forget all about it, just say *'I'm Bob the cock and I have an attitude problem'*.'

Bob stormed over to him. 'You're fired.'

'Who do you think you are now, Alan Sugar?' Mark laughed.

'I mean it, you're out of here.'

'Bob's search for his apprentice continues but nobody wants to work for a cock?' Mark mimicked. 'I quit anyway you puffed up windbag. It's people like you across town who made the decision not to give me my money, hiding behind your job titles and corporate brown nosing and treating people like shit.'

Mark walked to the photocopier, tipping out the last ream from a box of paper which hit the floor and fanned out. He stomped back over to his desk, putting his mug, photo frames and other belongings into the empty box. He yanked open the drawer and grabbed the plastic carrier bag that held his remaining possessions. At last he was getting to tell Bob he was leaving and walk out with it, even if it wasn't to collect the cardboard cheque he was buzzing just to be escaping those miserable drab offices.

'Don't worry; I'm not taking office property. This pen is mine though,' He held up a bright felt tip pen, 'and the gonk, I'm taking the lucky gonk Bob, don't even attempt to stop me.' He tried to peel the bright coloured lottery mascot off the top of his screen. The balls inside rattled then the cartoon face ripped off in his hand. 'Argh his bloody face has come off! See what you made me do Bob? You killed him, not me!' Mark yanked the gonk harder knocking the pen pot from his desk. He kicked at it and it shot across the room, pens, pencils and paper clips spraying around Bob's head.

'Eat my goal.' He cackled manically as he strode towards the emergency door. Will ran after him down the stairwell and watched Mark boot the fire exit door open, setting off the alarm. He caught up with him as he reached the street.

'What was that about? This isn't bloody *Jerry Maguire* it's your income you've just thrown away.'

'After losing a three million pound ticket I hardly think it warrants any fuss do you?' Mark said.

'Look, just calm down a second.'

'I can't stay there Will.'

'Come on let's get a nice mug of tea over at the cafe. You can calm down and I'll go back and smooth things with Bob, it'll be okay.'

'It's not okay Will, I mean look at that.'

Mark pointed to a newsagent across the road, on the pavement stood a *Six Magic Numbers* sign with the bright orange logo.

Will tried desperately to pacify him. 'Forget about it. Come on mate I'll get you a tea I'll even throw in a toasty and a copy of *The Beano*, just take a deep breath.'

'It's everywhere though, I mean on adverts, in shops, I'm never going to escape reminders it's always going to be around me.'

'It'll get easier. What about this guy Terence and the court case?'

'It could be years.'

'So that's good, you have that in the pipeline and we're getting the band back together, we were always at our happiest with a rehearsal and a few beers and a take away right?' Will smiled.

'But I'm losing it I can feel it. I was fine for so long and now it's just taken me over like a broken record in my head.' Mark paced around.

'It'll be fine seriously don't let this cost you your job. They've won then haven't they, Kabelson Industries?'

'They have already; sentencing me back to forty years of hard labour in shit-holes like that.'

'We all have to work for a living.'

'But I shouldn't anymore Will, don't you get it? I had the ticket, I had Charlie's golden ticket to the flipping chocolate factory. That is my money they are keeping from me so why should I just walk away?'

Mark lifted the orange gonk out of the box and tried to stick the face back on.

'What are you so happy about, you weren't lucky at all were you?'

He threw it into the road. They watched as a car ran over it then a lorry, squashing it into an orange pancake. Mark shrugged and looked up the road at the lottery sign, a 2D cousin of the orange gonk smiled back from the artwork. Will patted his friend on the shoulder and started walking to the cafe.

'Come on mate. My treat yeah?'

Instead of following Will, Mark turned the other way, breaking into a run with the copier box full of odds and sods. He charged at the lottery sign with a flying kick but it was heavier than it looked, his foot sliding outwards and his shin scraping across the top bar as it clanged to the ground. Mark lay on top in a crumpled heap. He rolled over holding his leg, cursing. Passers-by stopped. The newsagent rushed out of the shop.

'What the hell are you doing?'

Will ran over trying think of an excuse for his friend. 'Mate that's dangerous leaving that sign there, he could sue.' He said to the newsagent.

'What are you talking about? He just kicked it I bloody saw him. I mean I expect it from the hoody brigade but you should be ashamed of yourself at your age.'

Mark was scrabbling around for the box.

'The mug! I haven't broken the mug have I?'

Will picked up the box and looked inside.

'It's fine, it got wedged in.'

He helped his friend to his feet. The newsagent began to pick up the sign and took a good look at Mark.

'Hey aren't you the guy who lost that ticket? What a state, gee.'

He shook his head and walked back into his store.

Mark tried to stand on his foot and winced.

'How am I going to explain this to Jo?'

~

Jo stood with her arms folded looking at Mark who was sat on the sofa with his leg up, a bag of frozen peas draped over his bruised shin.

'You did what?' She said.

'I kicked a lottery sign.'

'I mean your job. You quit?'

'I can't do it anymore.'

'How long do you expect us to live on my salary? We didn't win the money, remember.'

Mark adjusted the peas. 'I just lost it, Bob was on my case.'

'We need some normality back in our lives. Not more drama.'

'How can we just switch back to normal now we've seen what we should be doing with our lives Jo? That island is stuck in my head. I want to be there, not here.'

'It was just a holiday Mark, we were fine before.'

'I know and I don't want an island but we could be in that big house we looked at or going on a cruise somewhere. Not stuck here.'

'Well *stuck here* is real Mark and that money isn't, the island isn't nor the big house. You need to wake up to that and move on.'

Mark wondered why she was acting like this she seemed argumentative and always looking for a fight with him lately, why couldn't she understand that he was simply determined to get the money and secure their future?

'If we don't win the court case I'll get another job, it's no big deal.'

'You'd better get down the job centre then.'

'What do you mean?'

'This came today.' Jo reached for a letter on the side unit and threw it at him. He noticed the familiar franking mark at the top of the page.

'Terence is pulling out, they think it's too high risk to carry on.'

Mark opened the letter and read the legal jargon, the type of fabled prose that solicitors use even though the majority of people wish they wouldn't. In Mark's case they could have reduced it to two words, *Game Over*.

He read the last paragraph and for a moment his sense of despair lifted. According to Terence, they could proceed if they moved from a *no-win, no-fee* legal case to a *subsidised fee* but Mark and Jo would need to find the solicitor's fees plus a guarantee of over two hundred thousand pounds should they lose.

'Did you read the last bit? It's not over completely.'

'Mark, where are we going to find two hundred thousand pounds?'

'We could re-mortgage this place and borrow the rest?'

'Are you out of your mind? We'd never be able to borrow or repay that much.' Jo said.

'Maybe we could offer a deferred fee by asking some wealthy businessmen or something?'

'You're losing sight of reality, don't be ridiculous.'

'Come on let's finish this.'

'Finish what? This will finish *us* Mark, this is our home.'

'If we'd kept the ticket it would be a bigger home.'

'Oh great! Here we go again round in endless freaking circles.'

Mark threw the letter across the room.

'I'm trying to fight for us Jo, why can't you bloody see that?'

'You are going crazy and I don't want to be with a crazy person Mark, where's the happy funny guy who told me he just wanted me and then things would be fine?'

'He's still right here.'

'Well show me.'

'I'm trying to but you keep picking fights.'

'Me?' Jo said.

'I never thought you'd be like this.' He said, shaking his head.

'Like what?'

'Like the women you hear through the neighbouring wall with shrill nagging voices and you thank God they aren't married to you.'

'You see me like that?' Jo's jaw dropped.

'I don't plan to end up like one of those poor blokes who could have walked away when they had the chance and found someone who appreciated them.'

'You stupid bastard.' She screamed, arms flailing in the air.

Mark recoiled and put his arm up in defence, he'd never seen Jo explode like that, she grabbed her bag and stormed out slamming the front door. Mark sat there for a minute then climbed off the sofa and hopped after her, holding the peas in one hand. As he stepped outside he caught his foot on the doorframe and tripped, the bag of peas split open and exploded across the driveway. He lay there staring up at the sky with his leg really throbbing. A neighbour walking past with his dog stopped to see if he was okay. The animal began licking madly at the peas.

'You alright there Mark?'

'I've had better days to be honest with you.'

CHAPTER TWELVE

Jo arrived at Stevie and Lauren's house in floods of tears. She was furious with Mark on so many levels. It had been tough for both of them but she thought they could get through it if they both looked after one another. She used to feel so protected and close to Mark but he had started to turn into someone different and that evenings outburst had shaken her to the core. With no job and no court case on the horizon it was going to be an impossible struggle for her to keep up the mortgage payments. He knew that so why put her in such a situation? She had always been so supportive for him and they had always discussed major decisions together.

Lauren opened a bottle of wine, they continued talking and gradually Jo began to compose herself. The phone rang in the hallway and Stevie who had been reading their son Jack a bedtime story, came downstairs.

'That was Mark; he wanted to know where you were lass. Told him you were fine but best you stay over 'til things calm down eh?'

'Are you sure?' Jo said.

'Its cool,' Lauren said, topping up their glasses, 'we can have Jack in with us, that's if you don't mind sleeping in a five foot plastic racing car?'

'You want me to go and have a word with him?' Stevie said.

'No, just leave the great tit to stew,' Jo said, downing half a glass of wine, 'let him stew on it for tonight.'

'Its not like him to be like this, I've known him for years.' Stevie said, sitting down with them.

'Well he won't be speaking to me that way again or it will be the last thing he does.' Jo said, holding out her glass for a top up.

~

Jo held her head as she walked slowly along the high street to work the next morning. She'd taken a few tablets before leaving Lauren's house and a half-hearted attempt to eat some of the fried breakfast Stevie had rustled up. The drink had helped numb the anger and emotions after her argument with Mark but it came back worse in the cold light of day. She suddenly had a very strong desire to see her family, she hadn't seen them since the wedding and for the first time in England, she felt really lost.

Gillian, the manager at the florist had been noticing Jo's mood changing as well. 'Not like you to have such a hangover.' She said, as she watched Jo arranging a display near the window.

'Gillian, would it be okay if I went home for a while?'

'Go on then, you look terrible.'

'No, I don't mean now I mean like a vacation.'

'You mean *America* home?'

Jo nodded and pulled herself onto the counter staring at the floor.

'Can you afford it with Mark quitting his job like that?'

'I'd need a month's salary, in advance. I haven't seen my folks since the wedding and I need time to think.'

'You're going alone? I thought you couldn't bear to be away from Mark.'

'I've never seen this side of him before. Its just me paying the bills and for what, so he can sit at home waiting for a court case that's never going to happen?'

'Jo its not the best time, I don't know if I could pay you that much in advance and I'd need to get someone in, besides you need every penny right now. I mean how long are you thinking?'

'One way open ticket?' Jo frowned, her shoulders dropping. She began to get tearful then shook herself out of it. 'Sorry, I just need my folks right now. I feel pretty lost and Mark's behaving stranger by the day.'

Gillian put her arm around her and gave Jo a squeeze.

'He'll come round, you'll see. I bet he's home right now preparing a fancy dinner or writing a romantic song to apologise.'

~

Mark was watching the wedding DVD in his pyjamas with the sound down whilst Kelly Clarkson belted out *My Life Would Suck Without You* on the stereo. He was unshaven with a half empty bottle of wine on the unit beside him. He idly strummed along with his acoustic guitar, longing for the time before things got complicated. The front door opened and Jo walked in, she put her bag down. He wondered what mood she would be in.

'I remember those people, the happy couple at the Church.' She shouted over the music, nodding towards the television.

'Babe I'm so sorry about last night. I'll get a new job.'

Mark did his best puppy impression and turned the music down but Jo wasn't so easily swayed this time.

'Bit early for boozing and singing the blues?'

'They say you can't sing it until you feel it.'

'How is the leg?'

'Much better, got a big bruise on it though.'

Jo sat down at the other end of the sofa and watched herself on screen in her wedding dress.

'I remember when you used to write songs for me.'

'I have an idea for a new one.'

'Come on, you know what I mean, what's happening to us?'

'Nothing's changed.' Mark said.

'I don't remember this,' she replied, leaning over and stroking his unshaven chin, 'or these smelly pyjamas and drinking in the daytime.'

'I'm the same person inside.'

Jo moved over closer to him and leant on his shoulder.

'Just unshaven, stinky and unemployed on the outside?'

'Hey I resent stinky.' Mark said, sniffing his armpits. 'Okay, stinky can stay in there but I'll find a job I promise.'

They watched the wedding footage. The camera was panning around the Church as Jo walked down the aisle with her father and she could see her old friends looking on.

'I haven't seen Tom and the others since the wedding.'

'We could go visit them sometime,' Mark said, 'maybe next summer once I get myself together and earn some money.'

They say that *anger dies quickly in a good person* and Jo wanted to give him a chance, after all he hadn't known about the lottery case and Terence's letter when he walked out of his job. They finished watching the DVD and began talking for the first time in ages about things other than the lottery, about life, music and their dreams of a family, just like they had done when they met. The photo albums came out and they put on records that reminded them of people and places. They messed around just as they had done when they met, laughing together and for a while forgetting about the troubles outside of the moment they were sharing.

Jo prepared a meal as Mark joked with her and attempted to help. As they ate and drank the mood was light and relaxed again. She wondered if they could put it behind them after all. There had to be some small period of adjustment after any major event or upset in life but it would pass.

Mark finished a mouthful of wine and lent over to kiss her.

'Ooh, too stubbly, you need to shave mister.' Jo rubbed his face.

'I'm tired.'

'Shame. I picked up a rather sexy little outfit last weekend and I was planning on surprising you one evening. She arched an eyebrow, tilted her head and peered up at him through her fringe, a look she knew always worked on Mark. As if throwing a switch inside he stood up full of energy and clapped his hands together.

'Okay. Here's the plan. You get changed while I clear plates away then I go and shave. We rendezvous in the bedroom in,' he looked at his watch, 'fifteen minutes?'

Jo laughed. 'Well I hope you start mustering up this sort of enthusiasm for a new job search soon.'

'Absolutely. I swear.'

She stood up and put her hand to his face, looking deep into his eyes.

'We're going to be okay aren't we Mark?'

He kissed her forehead and reassured her. Jo went upstairs to get ready while Mark drained the last of the wine.

As he went to stack the plates his phone beeped.

~

After half an hour later Jo gave up waiting in the bedroom and walked back downstairs into the front room in a risqué black bra and suspender set. It wasn't hard to please him in that department especially compared to one of her ex-boyfriends who had asked her to dress up as the university baseball team mascot and spank him.

Mark was on the sofa with his laptop open, still unshaven in his pyjama bottoms and T-shirt. The dirty plates remained stacked on the table.

'What are you doing?'

'Sorry, I just wanted to check something online.'

'Can't it wait; I thought you were coming to bed? You haven't even shaved.'

'Just got to read this then I'll be right there.'

Jo stared down at him playing with the sexy outfit. 'Aw babe. You can hunt for a job in the morning, look what I got for ya right here and now.'

Mark didn't even look up.

'Its a case, Will sent me a text about it, some lottery claim under scrutiny.'

'You are joking me.'

'No. You should read it,' he said enthusiastically, 'I think this may help us.'

Jo couldn't believe what she was hearing.

'Mark for once I thought we were having an evening like we used to. I thought

I finally saw the man I fell in love with tonight.'

'Yeah. I am babe. Look at this though this bloke said he'd lost the ticket then went into a store. They told him to...' Jo pressed the round power button on the corner of the laptop switching it off.

Mark looked up at her in disbelief.

'What the hell are you doing?'

Jo turned and walked away. He put the laptop down and followed grabbing her arm.

'You stupid cow that was important.'

She span round and slapped him hard across the face.

'Don't you dare touch me!' Jo yelled and ran upstairs leaving Mark dazed, nursing his stinging cheek.

She sat against the door in the candlelit bedroom. It had all been prepared for him but she knew that he didn't care anymore. The haunting piano intro to *Nature's Law* by *Embrace* came on the stereo, it was a mix CD that Mark had put together for her when they were missing each other across the atlantic. Jo burst into tears, her fresh make up running. He had never touched her before in any way but with affection, even just grabbing her arm like that had been so unlike him. Despite her attempts to keep their marriage together she knew Mark was changing from the man she had fallen in love with, slipping away more each day. Jo felt alone and without Mark beside her she was increasingly homesick for America.

CHAPTER THIRTEEN

Mark begged Jo to let him have another chance, blaming it on the drink and stress; he even went to the Doctors to seek help and agreed to some counselling sessions. Despite her desire to return to the States she relented and gave in. It really was just one more chance for him and she gave it everything on the condition that they drew up a plan together. She tried to help him, setting up interviews and encouraged him to go out more rather than watch the television and mope about.

He put on a show for her initially but after a while he stopped attending the interviews, instead he would take his iPod with him and sit in the park or a café for an hour. Months passed and while Jo hung onto any shred of hope for their relationship, Mark continued to put on a front whilst descending into his own world, obsessed with somehow finding a way to get the money that had long since been forgotten by everyone else.

As Christmas approached Jo realised that Mark wasn't being honest about the job search, confronted him and they had another row. She went to Lauren and Stevie who informed her that he hadn't been showing up for band rehearsal either, something else in the bigger joint plan that they thought would help him in his recovery.

A week before Christmas Will took a card over to Mark's house in his lunchtime. He could see him in the front room through the window playing on an old Scalextric set, staring at the cars going round and round. Will banged on the window and eventually Mark opened the door.

'Nice pyjamas.' Will said, handing him the Christmas card. *She Loves Me Not by* the band *Papa Roach* throbbed out of the speakers.

Decorations sat in half opened boxes on the dining table next to a bottle of mulled wine. It was nearly empty. 'Help yourself to wine,' Mark said, turning the stereo down, 'then you can be the green car.'

'Just tea for me mate.'

'I know what you're thinking,' Mark said, 'it's too early.'

Will looked at his friends unshaven face, the dark rings under his eyes ageing him beyond his years. He watched Mark top up his own glass with the last drops of the bottle and then he walked towards the kitchen, unsteady as he trod on a piece of track. Will followed him and was surprised by the food wrappers and unwashed pans everywhere.

'Excuse the mess dear boy, I think Jo's on strike.'

'Well, you know Christmas is a busy time eh, I thought you'd have those decorations finished by now.' Will said.

'I know. Jo was so excited when we got those last year, she insisted on being in charge when we put it all up. Besides I've been busy looking for jobs online, not that she notices.'

'Any luck?'

'There's nothing out there.'

'What sites are you looking at? I know a few agencies in town.' Will said, getting his pen out of his top pocket.

'All of them.'

'Have you tried the one at the end of the high street?'

'Yep. All of them.'

'List them for me and I'll tell you if you've missed any.'

'What is this, a bloody interrogation?' Mark snapped.

'I'm trying to help out you miserable sod. I knew when I heard that song blasting out you were going to be in one of your moods.'

'Alright, alright I'm sorry.' Mark said, rubbing at his unkempt hair.

'I might have some good news actually.'

'Don't tell me, you've found a girlfriend at last?'

Will tried to keep him focussed but Mark's eyes were *like piss holes in the snow* as Stevie would say.

'I spoke to Bob about you coming back.'

Mark began to laugh, it wasn't the natural easy laugh he usually did, it was slow and juddered his whole body. 'Bob?'

'Mark, you need to pay the bills its been months now.'

'I can't go back there I'd rather starve than work for that cocking cock.' Mark belched.

'He's alright really.'

'Arsepack!' He shouted, falling onto the side unit and steadying himself.

'So what are you going to pay the bills with? You can't expect Jo to keep both of you.'

'Nag, nag, nag. You sound just like her. Who's side are you on?'

'What bloody side? You're a couple and we're mates, there are no sides in this.'

'Well she's been weird lately, clearing out clothes, not speaking to me and we haven't played horses for ages.' Mark tapped his nose and winked but he was so inebriated that both his eyes shut and opened at the same time.

'Maybe a shave and a shower would help?' Will said.

'Yeah, go ahead mate. My home is your home'

'I mean *you*, you're starting to smell a bit ripe.'

'Nah. She's trying to make me suffer when all I want to do is get this money for her. She doesn't think like that though, she thinks I'm just after an easy life slobbing around.'

'She loves you Mark. She's worried, we all are.'

'And how would you know that, talking behind my back together?'

'Shut up and stop acting like a dickhead will you. Lauren mentioned how concerned Jo was and its understandable, you know they're going to cut your electric off soon?'

'They don't do that these days.' Mark giggled as he poured cold water into a mug of coffee and handed it to him. 'There ya go. Black, like my wife's heart.'

'You don't mean that.'

'Will.'

'What?'

'Go back to work, I've got important race this afternoon, I think the blue car is going to take the title in the living room Grand Prix, unless you fancy your chances with the green one?'

He looked around for his wine glass and drained it.

Will watched as Mark started to open another bottle, kicking some empties across the floor that clattered around like bowling pins.

~

Mark woke up with his head banging and his throat dry and sore. It was still light outside so he wasn't sure how long he had been asleep or unconscious. He thought he should clear up a little before Jo came back from work. He knelt up, the thumping head seemed to get much worse and he moaned loudly. Looking up he saw a pair of feet at the doorway beside one of the small racing cars.

Jo was looking at the Christmas tree, half finished.

'Hey babe,' he said, 'I'll do the tree now. Will came over earlier and interrupted me.'

'You mean yesterday.' Said Jo flatly.

'What?'

'That was yesterday. I came home around six to find you playing *The Clash* at full blast, I asked you to turn it down and you told me to *'Go and boil my tits'*, before collapsing on the spot where you are currently kneeling, oh and be careful of the sick by your left hand.'

Mark looked down at the stained carpet and retched. He couldn't remember much after Will left.

'My cab will be here in a few minutes.' Jo said.

'Where are we going?' Mark fought the rising nausea.

'I tried Mark, God did I try to make this work but you just pushed and pulled at it until it all broke and now I have nothing left to give.'

Mark stood up slowly and felt another jab of pain through his head.

'I'll change. You can't go anywhere now, its Christmas.'

Jo shook her head, she looked different to him, something about her maybe it was her hair or her outfit, he thought. Then it hit him like another headache jab, it was her eyes that were different. Where once there had been a soft glow now there was just an empty stare.

'You're supposed to be helping me with the tree,' he laughed, turning to grab a can of spray snow from the side unit, 'come on I left the spray for you, I know you like that bit,' Mark continued messing around with the tree branches, straightening sections, 'I'll clean this mess up, I'll clean myself up, get a job. Hey, Will said Bob wanted me back. At least I think he said that, I was a bit pissed but that will stop too, honest, no more boozing.'

'And when were you planning this Mark, when they cut off the gas as well as the electric or were you going to wait for the bailiffs?'

Mark went over to a box and got some plastic mistletoe. He held it over her head and closed his eyes. She turned and stepped back towards the hallway.

'You stink of stale wine,' she said, 'and sick.' She looked at his T-shirt, one of their favourite bands *Mega City Four*, the front was a lyric from a song, it read *Don't sit on your arse while your world just falls to pieces*. Instead of taking heed of that he'd used up his three strikes and there was nothing she could do now but say goodbye.

Mark saw the suitcase behind her. He needed to claw something back before it was too late, maybe he had a chance, he thought. She'd given him plenty before. 'I started writing a song for you, a new one,' he walked over to his guitar, sat on the sofa and strummed a few chords, 'there's no lyrics yet, do you like the tune though?'

Jo took a deep breath. She began to feel the tears rising inside her but before she could say another thing to him a car horn sounded outside.

'That's my cab. Please don't make this harder than it already is.'

Mark put the guitar down and went back to the tree.

'You think we should put more tinsel on it?' His voice was shaking.

'There was never going to be a good time to leave, I know that.' Jo said, her eyes filling up.

'Maybe a few more baubles?' Mark scratched his beard and ran his hands through his unkempt hair.

'I'm sorry Mark.'

Jo wanted to go to him, to hold him, he looked like a lost boy but she knew that she couldn't stay. There wasn't enough strength in her to fight for two anymore and she deserved better besides he had to help himself because everyone else was out of ideas.

'I haven't told your parents any of this, maybe you need to go and talk to them.' She said, a tear running down her face.

'I've been trying to fight for what's ours can't you get that into your head? I don't think you can because you'd understand the end game if you tried. It's us against them.'

'You might not understand this right now Mark, but sometimes there isn't someone else to blame when things go wrong, maybe you need to look in the mirror.' Jo wiped her face and picked up her case.

'Is there someone else?'

'I'm not even going to answer that. I'll arrange to have my things collected and get them shipped home.'

'*America*? I thought you were going to a friend's for a few nights?'

'Just try to enjoy Christmas okay. I'm sorry.'

She turned and walked out. He circled the room a few times unsure of what to do then he dashed outside and called after her. The cab driver had put her case in the back and opened the door for her.

'Let's finish the tree first,' Mark shouted, 'I was going to hide small presents in there for you like we did last year.'

'I have to go Mark.'

'Jo, come back this is stupid.'

'I can't.'

'But we can still win this, together.'

Jo went to turn and look at him one last time but something stopped her. She knew that she had to get in that car and go for her own sake no matter how much she loved him.

'I'm sorry.' She got into the cab, Mark walked over to it oblivious that he was in pyjama bottoms and flip-flops in the middle of the street and the neighbours were starting to curtain twitch.

'What do you mean '*you're sorry*'? We can work this out.'

The cab pulled away and he began shouting, running alongside it, trying to make it stop. Jo kept her eyes ahead as the car turned the corner and sped away.

Mark walked back to the house. He picked up the can of fake snow and sprayed a bit onto the tree.

'I hope you haven't spent too much on me,' he said glancing at their wedding picture, 'when you get back we can finish the spray then Will can pick us up and we can go over to see Stevie and Lauren. It should be fun like last year.'

He sprayed the tree with more and more snow. It began dripping onto the carpet. Mark looked down and saw that he was standing in a mixture of snow spray and his own stale vomit. He grabbed the top of the tree and yanked it out of its stand kicking it and stamping on some of the decorations. He took a huge swig of mulled wine from an open bottle on the side. Wiping drops from his chin he pelted the bottle across the room smashing it into the wedding picture. He staggered over and slumped onto the side unit, sliding down to the floor. Picking up the broken frame glass pieces cut into his fingers as Mark stared at the picture, tears dropping from his face mixing with the blood.

PART TWO - GO WEST

'There's a big hole where your dreams should be, just waiting to be filled.'

-Darren 'Wiz' Brown,
'Start' by Mega City Four.

CHAPTER FOURTEEN

Mark looked through his window, across the freshly cut lawns and out to sea for the last time. On the horizon tiny boats went to and fro, they looked like moving specs in one of those seventies computer games his uncle had. It was a view that he had become accustomed to and one that helped him remain calm during the tougher days. Spring was his favourite season and the sun was starting to come out earlier each day. The birds that had settled in the box on the tree to the right of the main gardens were helping their young venture out into the world again, it was fascinating to watch and he could spend hours happily sat there observing them. Now it was time for him to leave the nest as well.

The chime on the clock meant that it was breakfast hour so he shaved and dressed, packing his belongings neatly into the case on his bed. He walked out into the long corridor that led to the dining room. The tables were neatly laid out and as usual he sat down next to the serving trolley. He would help distribute the main meals at lunchtime as one of his duties, he didn't have to but it had made him feel useful and a routine was something that helped to build up a sense of purpose again for the first time in months.

It had been a very different lifestyle to the one previously in Warwick. After Jo had left Mark descended further into a black hole. The drinking had got worse and then the isolation became too much for him to cope with, wandering around the house with the curtains drawn, no electricity and just a single gas fire for warmth. Over Christmas Will had taken him to visit Stevie and Lauren and Mark's parents saw him once on Boxing Day but they had no idea how bad he was. On New Years Eve he decided to stay in with a bottle of whisky and by midnight was running round the garden dressed in just his pyjamas, an overcoat and Wellington boots with *Slade's* rocked up version of *High Ho Silver Lining* blaring from a battery operated guitar amp. He looked around at the garden and decided that it needed tidying up, filling the wheelie bin so high that it overflowed. As a solution to this he stood on an upturned plant pot and hopped onto the bin stomping it down and promptly flipping it over and knocking himself unconscious. It was only after a neighbour complained about the noise in the early hours that the police found him and called for an ambulance.

Mark was diagnosed with depression and it was either pills or a retreat in the country. His parents and friends agreed on the latter and drove him down to Cornwall. They took his guitar and a box of music books and magazines to keep him occupied; it was a relaxing sanctuary with few distractions. He managed a few jokes about being institutionalised and ending up like Randle McMurphy in *One Flew Over the Cuckoo's Nest* but he was glad not to be going back to the house, too much of Jo still remained there.

He spent his days walking along the beach or sitting in his room watching the waves, reading or playing his guitar. The people who ran the retreat told him that it was usually a slow and steady return to form that was best. They had seen many different visitors passing their way, each with varying reasons for being there. They advised his parents that people didn't usually snap out of depression; they crawled out inch by inch. For the second time in his life Mark started learning to crawl again.

Part of his therapy was to stay away from technology and get outdoors, to forget the quest for the lottery money and messing around on the internet in order to remember the simple pleasures in life. He learnt to appreciate his basic health, family, friends, a simple meal and conversations with the other residents at the retreat, these things were increasingly being overlooked in the credit rich society and communities seemed to thrive online in cyberspace instead of within the vicinity of bricks and mortar of a real home.

He would sit at his desk and write down his thoughts with a pen and pad, something he hadn't done for years. It was so easy to e-mail people that the art of writing a physical letter was almost nostalgic and noble to him. Quite a few of these sessions ended up with letters to Jo, he sent them via her parents address in Rocklin USA. He felt the need to apologise to her for what he had done, for what he had allowed himself to become. Deep reflection and time in recovery made him realise how badly he had treated someone he was supposed to care for.

If he spotted an airmail stamp in the post room his heart would jump but it was never a reply from Jo. He wondered if her parents even forwarded his letters to her. They hadn't really approved of Mark marrying her in the first place, especially her mother. He had after all taken their daughter to the other side of the world and broken her heart.

He wrote to his parents and friends recounting memories of things they had done, explaining why they were so special to him. Sometimes he sat doodling cartoons for hours, something he used to do at college. His life was a blank page again and it was up to Mark what he wanted to put down on it.

The pace of life on the west coast suited Mark and he eventually found a job in a music shop, something he wished he'd done years ago instead of ending up in a career completely unsuited to his natural skills, interests and passion. He had been offered a small room in a shared house near to town, out of season the rent was quite cheap. In late spring, a longhaired man in his twenties came into the shop. Mark got talking to him about bands and sold him a flight case for his guitar. He then asked if he could put something up on the notice board, usually this was where the local musicians placed wanted adverts for band members. When he had gone, Mark noticed that it was about a Church meeting. He wondered if he should take it down before Darren the Manager saw it. Instead he began reading.

Are you struggling to cope? Do you think you have everything and still feel you have nothing? Come and talk to us at Holy Fire Coastal Church.

There was a meeting there that weekend and it was on the way to a seafront restaurant where Mark would go for Sunday lunch. He'd seen the Church hall before so he thought he would take a late meal and drop in on the way back. Since his meltdown he had decided to be open to new ideas and experiences. He used to think that as you grew older you became more certain but it was quite the opposite, the older you got the more questions you had.

Mark had begun to take an interest in spiritual things since the breakdown, he didn't believe in things like horoscopes but there were mysteries out there to investigate, perhaps it wasn't just about luck, like the phone ringing when you thought of someone for the first time in ages, deja vu, healing of illnesses. So many people experienced these miraculous moments then dismissed them.

He hesitated outside the church hall willing himself to take the first step on the wooden staircase leading up to the open doors. He was about to walk away when a man popped his head out. 'You like donuts?' Mark shrugged and nodded. His genuine smile put Mark at ease. 'There's three left and my wife is approaching the tea table at a speedy rate of knots so best be quick. I'm John by the way.' He disappeared back inside and Mark followed. There were people of all ages milling about, some in groups, some pottering around looking at posters on the walls. He spotted the longhaired man from the music shop. A lady poured Mark a cup of tea and he managed to secure the last jam donut, finding a seat near to the back of the hall where he people watched, something him and Jo used to like doing in café's.

The meeting began with John welcoming everyone and asking then to stand and sing a few songs. 'Or just open and close your mouth if you don't know it very well.' It wasn't the sort of music that Mark liked or was used to but it was more up-tempo than the drudge he expected at a church. He busied himself watching the guitarist, trying to work out the chords he was playing. After the music finished John walked over to a wooden lectern, fiddled with some notes and then took out a lottery ticket from his shirt pocket. Mark winced.

'Have you got yours?' John said, waving it around. A few people laughed, some said they had and others said they never did the lottery. Mark sank down in his seat wondering if it was a bad dream.

'We all want the winning ticket don't we?' John continued, 'because it's got the answer to all of life's problems on it.' There was a silence in the room. 'Folks, if this is the answer to life's problems and what everyone is after then my God we really are in serious trouble.' People around the room nodded and agreed. 'It's not wrong to dream, we all need to dream but be careful you don't get confused by the true meaning of wealth. Some dictionaries say it's an abundance of possessions but I disagree. I want you to think about this...'

Mark listened intently as John continued his sermon about the pursuit of happiness and how different people and cultures viewed *wealth*. It reminded him of something Sir David had told them on the island but he hadn't really understood it at the time. The God of the present day was consumerism and instant reward. People who wanted to look out for each other and their community were on the decline and being replaced with a more insular culture despite the advances in technology.

It wasn't quite what Mark had expected after some of the services he saw on songs of praise at his Nan's house, it actually seemed relevant and made him think about life. He was expecting to be bored rigid but John was a good speaker and an hour and a half passed without him noticing. Mark felt involved enough to speak up a few times and hoped nobody would recognise him in relation to the lottery saga.

John wanted to end the meeting by asking people to close their eyes as he said a prayer that they would get home safe and that their families would be healthy and well. He then asked if everyone could remain with eyes shut and if anyone would like personal prayer they should raise their hands. Mark felt an urge to leave and peeped to see if he could slip away but there was a woman at the end of his row obstructing his exit. He had not come here to be a sunbeam for Jesus he just wanted to have a nose around. Mark heard the sound of scraping chairs as some people stood up. Once more he felt an urge but this time it was to raise his arm. He fought back, closed his eyes tighter and sat on his hands to keep them still.

'I feel that there are one or two of you here that would like to raise your hands tonight but it's causing a battle inside,' John said, 'I want to speak to those people and ask you to forget about everyone else. This is between you and God and if you feel something tugging at your heart then try to let go. We aren't here to embarrass people. I will ask one more time, if you wish to come forward for prayer it's up to you.'

Without thinking, Mark gave in and raised his hand. He opened his eyes and could see that a few people had gone to the front of the hall where John and two other men were standing. He saw a lady head in his direction. She smiled at him and motioned for him to join the others at the front. He made his way forwards and stood near John who was praying for a woman. She began to shake then fall back, was caught by another member of the church and rested on the floor. They began praying for her, some spoke in a foreign language. John turned to Mark who was already halfway back up the aisle heading for the door. 'It's nothing to worry about Mark, speaking in tongues just sounds odd at first'.

'I don't even know why I put my hand up, I best be off.' Mark said. John walked up to him, 'I promise not to put a spell on you, it won't take long.' Mark felt self-conscious at first then started to listen to John praying for him. He began to feel a sensation in his foot, a small tingle rising up; he resisted at first and then went with it, it came up through his torso and out the top of his head. It was comforting but he didn't want to fall down like the lady and to his relief he didn't. John's voice spoke clearly and softly and after a few minutes he stopped. 'Are you going overseas?' John said.

'Not planning to.'

'I get a vision of you heading overseas and being by water. It could be a huge harbour or lake.' He smiled. 'Some say that water is a sign of burial.'

'You think I'm going to die?' Mark said, horrified.

'Burial *and* rebirth, don't worry.' John laughed.

Mark shrugged and sat at the back of the hall. He watched the guitarist play while the prayer session continued. He wasn't sure what had happened to him and there had certainly been no thunderbolts, but it had been very calming.

The people eventually drifted off into the evening until it was just John, his wife and the guitar player packing up. Mark walked over. 'Nice sound.' He said pointing to his guitar.

'Thanks, I really like this case you sold me by the way.'

'You been playing here long?' asked Mark.

'A few years, I moved down from London, got fed up with the pace. It's a lot more chilled around here. I'm Ben by the way.'

John, the pastor began turning the lights off. His wife appeared at the door with a set of keys. 'You guys coming up the pub with us then?'

Ben looked at Mark, surprised.

'You okay with that?'

'Yeah. I just thought you lot didn't drink.' Mark said.

'Nonsense, if Jesus didn't want us to drink then why turn all that water into wine?' John said, holding the door open.

'Mind you, I'm not sure what he would have made of *Flaming Sambucas*.'

CHAPTER FIFTEEN

Jo stepped out into the warm summer day, arranging the flowerpots along the front of the store. It was good to be back on familiar territory, getting her old job back a first positive step. After a week of working there at the florist she had seen a familiar face too, he had walked past the window and her heart had raced. Since then she had been looking out for him each day, bumping into him now after so long would be exciting.

A woman approached her and asked if the shop did wedding bouquets. Jo pulled out a card from her jeans and handed it to her, returning inside. She took a mouthful of coffee and then the door opened. There, holding a bunch of purple carnations stood the man she had been waiting to see.

'I thought it was you,' he smiled, 'what are you doing here?'

'Working.' She laughed, pushing her hair back around her ear nervously.

'You look amazing.' He beamed.

'I'm a mess,' she looked at her work clothes, 'you look good though, haven't changed a bit.'

'I thought you moved to England.' He said.

'I did.'

'So what happened?'

'Long story.'

It had been many years since Nicholas and Jo had dated but you never forgot your first love. They had attended the same high school and college before going their separate ways.

'What time do you finish working? I'd love to catch up properly.'

'I should be done here around five then I need to change.'

'Where are you living?'

'Back at the folks.'

'Really, that bad eh?' He laughed.

'Like I said, long story.'

'Can I buy you these flowers then? I remembered you like purple and when I saw you from across the street I just instinctively grabbed them on the way in.'

She took them in her hands. He had remembered correctly and that was a few bonus points in his favour.

~

Jo's parents were pleased that their daughter was smiling again. It had taken a long time to get her back to the bubbly lady who had set off to England years before. They had always liked Nicholas; so had Jo for a while until he had got insanely jealous of her friendship with Tom, a lifelong friend of the family; they were like brother and sister. Nicholas couldn't deal with their closeness and was always suspicious of Tom especially when she went off to university and got placed in the same halls of residence.

The jealousy was amplified whenever Nicholas visited and came to a head the summer of their second year together. Nicholas had to go and work on his father's farm and Jo wanted to go travelling with Tom and other friends from the university. Nicholas gave Jo an ultimatum, the trip or him and she answered that ultimatum by booking a trip to Italy with three friends, including Tom. It was the first of several trips to Europe and gave her a taste for travelling. She hadn't seen Nicholas since then and perhaps on reflection she'd forgotten all the good times too. Everyone was entitled to make mistakes and get another chance, heck, look at the chances she'd given Mark before he became unbearable to live with.

A car pulled up outside the house. Her mum called up the stairs.

'Jo. You have a visitor.'

She walked down and saw Nicholas there in tight jeans and a leather jacket. He really did look the same as he had in his teens and even in the nineties he'd looked slightly dated.

'You look beautiful.' He said.

'Oh it's so nice you two are back together.'

'Mom!' Jo shot her a glare and Nicholas laughed.

They drove across town to a restaurant where they used to go on dates. Jo felt relaxed and happy, talking about old times, people they'd bumped into and relationships they had had since their time together. She even covered the difficult time in England with some philosophical poignancy. Nicholas had never married he had a few girlfriends after Jo but remained a bachelor. When he told Jo that she'd been an impossible act to follow, she blushed and stared into her wine glass. After the meal they drove out to a hill overlooking Rocklin, a spot they used to go to.

'Look in the glove compartment Jo.'

'I'm not that sort of girl.'

Nicholas went red and started to try and explain but Jo started laughing.

'Relax; I know you wouldn't be dragging me up here for that. At least not yet I hope.' She found their school yearbook, a huge volume that covered all the ages during a school year, a headshot and a few lines underneath about each student. She was eager to flick to their year where she picked out Tom and roared with laughter.

'Oh my god, Tom! He looks so young.'

'Do you still see him?' Nicholas asked.

'Yes I saw him last month it was so much fun. He's engaged now.' Jo said.

'Look. I'm sorry about that business.'

'Forget it Nick, it's a long time ago now.' Jo ran her finger across the page and turned it over. There, looking just as he did in the flesh beside her was Nicholas.

'I was a jerk back then. I was young and jealous and, oh this is embarrassing.' He looked out the window at the town. The lights were coming on and the sun was fading. Jo asked if she could change the radio station, Nicholas had it on a dance channel and it was ruining her mood. She found a college radio DJ playing indie music. 'That's better.'

'You never did like my taste in music.' He said.

She grinned and patted his cheek.

'Ditto I seem to remember.'

'I'm sorry it didn't work out for you in England.'

'Sometimes it feels alien being back, not looking out at those streets or seeing the castle. I miss my friend's son Jack too, they change so fast, even in three months.'

'Do you wish you were back there?'

'I don't know, is it possible to leave part of you somewhere if you experience deep emotions there?'

'Now that I do know, from dating you, I never got that part of my heart back.'

'Oh you're smooth.' She laughed.

'Seriously, I should have supported you more Jo, I know you liked Europe and I wish I'd come with you sometimes.' He said.

'No you don't you hated the idea of Europe.'

'You're right,' he laughed 'I would have hated it. Not as much as I hated the years missing you though.'

She looked embarrassed and flattered as he moved closer and put his hand on hers. 'I thought I'd lost you from my life forever. Do you think this could be our movie story ending, meeting up again?'

He pulled her closer. She hadn't been held like that for so long and embraced him, his mouth was close to hers. They moved together and began to kiss. It felt strange for a few seconds, to be kissing someone different to Mark but then she remembered Nicholas's kisses from the old days. The only weird thing was he wiggled his tongue and it tickled. It took her by surprise and she pulled away as *Just Like Heaven* by *The Cure* came on the radio, the track that Mark and Jo had danced to in the shop in Stratford, the one she would sometimes play when she read his letters.

Jo started punching the radio buttons to find any station that wasn't playing songs that reminded her of Mark or that period in her life.

'Jo, what's wrong?'

'I think we should call it a night.'

'I'm sorry, it was too soon.'

She forced a smile and kissed him on the cheek. 'No it's just me, I'll be fine. Memories, that's all but they can't hurt me anymore.'

They drove back to her parent's house and agreed to meet up soon. It was time that she learnt to go out and have fun again, for too long she had sat in at night going over her failed marriage and trying not to get upset by the letters from Cornwall that Mark kept sending. Maybe he would give up soon because she never replied to them, there was nothing you could say when someone had hurt you that much, they were consigned to the past. She just wished that you could stop loving them too.

CHAPTER SIXTEEN

'It's cancer Mark, don't be afraid it's just a word.'

Mark didn't know how to respond. His friend looked so small laying there on the sofa with a blanket over him.

'Can they do anything?'

'They've started him on some tablets to try and shrink the growth, it's too big to operate on the liver.' Lauren said.

'These tablet's make me really dizzy. It's almost like being pissed sometimes.' Stevie forced out a laugh.

It had been five months since Mark had first gone to the West Country. He was still living in Cornwall and working in the music shop but he would go back to see Will and the others as much as he could. Sometimes they would come down to visit him but for Stevie and Lauren it was more difficult with a family and they had an addition, Jack now had a baby sister.

The pain in Stevie's back that had been bugging him for ages had slowly got worse and it wasn't simply muscle strain; the Doctor had sent him for a scan and found a growth in his liver. It was so large that it had been pushing another organ into his back. He had been for further tests and there were traces in his thighbone. Secondary cancer meant that it had spread and was now at an advanced level.

Mark knew from losing his Aunt how cancer could hit someone, he had watched how it had spread despite many courses of treatment. There were cases where people survived though and he knew that Will's uncle had beaten prostate cancer. It had been Will who called him up and told him to get back to Warwick as soon as he could.

Mark needed to keep his faith strong and prayed fervently that Stevie would be a survivor. He seemed to have the fighting spirit that Doctors said helped.

'I know I'm not quite the strapping jock you saw last time you came up but am I still as good looking?' Stevie asked.

'Yeah. Course.'

'Hey don't you give me that bullshit. It's still me sitting here you know.'

'Okay. You look like shit mate.' Mark said.

'That's more like it,' he laughed and began to cough and hold his side, 'it's okay, give me a second.'

Jack went skipping into the kitchen. 'Daddy looks like shit, mummy.'

Lauren walked in shaking her head.

'Sorry that was my fault.' Mark said as Stevie began to cough again. Lauren helped him sit up and put a cushion behind him.

'Is he okay?' Mark asked.

Stevie grabbed him by the arm. Even at his thinner size Mark felt the power in his grip as he pulled him closer. 'Don't talk about me like I can't hear you. I'm sick of being treated like that.' His eyes burned into Mark and he could see the fear. He wanted to run back out the door and away from there away from the closeness of death. He tried to shut out that word, *Death* didn't belong there with Stevie. He was only in his late twenties, never smoked; he used to drink a bit but no more than the rest of them and was a regular on the football and cricket pitches.

'They say I'll lose this mop of hair.

'How's Jack taking it?'

'He thinks dad is on some sort of diet; keeps feeding me his toy plastic fruit and trying to fatten me up.'

The sound of a baby crying crackled out of a small monitor in the wall. Lauren went upstairs returning with the family's new addition.

'Katie, meet mad Mark.'

The baby looked up and yawned. Lauren handed her to Mark. 'Go on, she won't hurt you.'

He took her in his arms, she was tiny and fragile and it overwhelmed him. Stevie smiled, watching his daughter.

'We want you to be her Godfather.' He said.

'But I'm an irresponsible idiot.'

'You're a *nice* irresponsible idiot.'

He looked down at the baby. She waved her hand, he placed his little finger in her grip and she made some noises and squeezed it.

'Am I a nice idiot Katie?'

She looked at him and cooed. Mark nodded at her.

'You're an idiot.' Jack said.

'Jack!' Lauren waved her finger at him.

'*You* said it.' He shrugged and walked off, befuddled by the adult's irrational ways.

'Of course I'll be your Godfather Katie. Who could say no to such a smile?'

Will was flicking through Stevie's records.

'Stevie have you got our old EP in here?'

'Yep. You can have it if it's there. In fact take anything except my Ramones signed LP, that signed yellow vinyl is coming with me.'

'Stevie, stop it.' Lauren said.

Will turned round to apologise.

'I didn't mean it like that I was just looking for something to play.'

'Och. Sure you were.' Stevie laughed. He lay back on the sofa and winced.

'You have to stop saying things like that.' Lauren said.

'I'm not going anywhere, I'm just trying to wind the lass up.'

'It's nice you've still got your sense of humour mate.' Mark said.

'Aye. I have, it's others who seem to have lost theirs.' He summoned up some energy and threw a cushion at Lauren.

Mark looked at his friend and wondered how he could help. He was supposed to have a newfound faith and here it was being tested to the max. Maybe there was treatment, a special Doctor or therapy? Lauren took him aside to make some tea and warned him that nothing could change what was happening. Stevie knew it too and there was a deep fear behind the bravado of this young man in his prime. Everyone knew the picture was wrong but nobody could fix it.

They walked back into the front room.

'Did you hear this Lauren? Will has got a woman at last.'

'Really, what's her name?'

'Steph, you know the hippy chick from the music shop in town. She's alright for now, three month trial.' Will said.

'Aye listen to the gigolo.' Stevie cackled.

'She's passed cooking and driving so far now I need her to do her laundry exam and then I will consider issuing her with a full license to my heart.'

'I'd be careful with Steph if I were you,' Lauren said, 'Jen saw her in that new rock bar and I think she's already got her advanced license.'

'What?' Will looked concerned.

'She was under the DJ booth until the early hours, Jen was telling me about it this morning.'

Will looked forlorn.

'I just got tickets to bloody *Cats* though. She kept banging on about it.'

'*Bloody cats*, is that the horror musical?' Stevie laughed.

'What about you Mark, met anyone down in Cornwall?'

'No, not me I haven't felt anything for anyone since Jo.'

'You need to move on.' Lauren said.

'Want to hear something sad? I stop by the Church where we got married when I come up here to visit, without fail.'

'I'm not sure if that's healthy.' Lauren said, putting Katie into a little rocker seat.

'I sit there and play that song, you know the one she liked, Avril Lavigne *When you're gone.*' It used to be on a mix CD she put together for me after the first trip over there.

'That's sad,' Will said, 'not the Church bit, I mean it's sad that she's got you listening to Avril Lavigne.'

Mark pushed him into Jack's toybox which flipped and sprayed tractors and lego blocks across the floor.

'You can tidy that lot up.' Lauren said.

Mark turned to her, 'Stevie said that you two still keep in touch. Does she ever ask after me?'

Lauren was unsure if she should go into details about what Jo had told her.

'You want the truth?'

'I know it hurts much less to hear a lie sometimes but give it to me straight, if you know how she feels I want to know.'

'You broke her heart Mark, she gave everything up to come here and you let her down when she needed you. She won't let anyone do that again so you need to move on.'

Mark felt it like a punch in his gut as they stood quietly watching Katie in her chair, making noises and smiling. A new life, a blank sheet, everything ahead of her.

'Mark. You're into all this faith stuff right?' Stevie said.

'I believe in God. Will moans that I preach at him so I don't mention it much.'

'Amen brother.' said Will, still looking through the piles of records.

'Pray for me?' Stevie said.

He was such a proud man; Mark knew it took a lot for him to ask. Lauren walked over to Stevie and held his hand with tears in her eyes. Mark had never prayed for anyone like that. He had received prayer but to lay hands on the sick for healing? That was another thing. He couldn't say no though and either he had faith or he didn't. He certainly believed that some people were cured miraculously. Mark knelt down beside them, Jack nuzzled in.

'Are you talking to Jesus?'

'Yes we are.' Lauren stroked his head.

Jack called over to Will. 'We're talking to Jesus. Close your eyes or the wish won't come true.'

Mark kept it simple and spoke from his heart. He thanked God for Stevie and all the happiness he brought into peoples lives and he asked for healing over the illness. He held his hand to the areas where his friend had the cancer. When he finished, Stevie reached his arm around Mark and held him close in a powerful grip.

'Look out for Lauren and the kids when you can eh?'

'You're not going anywhere mate.' Mark said.

Stevie just slapped him on the back.

'Here it is,' Will said, holding up a record, 'I always preferred the vinyl copies to the CD version.' He placed it on Stevie's old deck. The crackles gave way to a throbbing guitar noise, the familiar sound of Castle Rox filled the room. He stood up and began to windmill with his right arm. Stevie began to tap away on the side of the sofa and Jack screamed with delight, dancing in a circle, even Katie squealed along. Mark grinned at Lauren, shrugged and joined in with his air guitar. They sang along to it with heart and soul:

For two and a half minutes they were young upstarts again, taking the stage by storm, happy go lucky lads with nothing to worry about except a guitar string snapping mid-set. They were on a mission, brothers in arms riding a wave of cheap booze, teenage kicks and excitement. Life was simple and it was spread out in front of them.

Four weeks later, Stevie died.

CHAPTER SEVENTEEN

Mark and Will walked past the parked cars and up the path. The door was half open and they found Stevie's mum in the kitchen arranging sausage rolls and sandwiches. Lauren's parents sat with his dad in the garden. They were joined by two of his brothers; he was from a large family. One of his sisters and her daughter sat playing with Katie, rocking in her chair. She cooed and flapped her arms around bringing a welcome distraction to the adults. Lauren was in the front room trying to coax a biscuit away from Jack, he had chocolate all over his face. She saw Mark and Will and let him go. Jack ran away waving the remains of the biscuit in his hand victoriously.

'He can do what he wants to today.' She said.

Mark hugged her tightly, 'How are you?'

'I don't know I haven't slept properly all week. Kids keep you busy though. Don't have time to think much.'

'Is there anything we can do?'

'Indeed, I have your orders.' said Lauren.

She walked to the stereo and took two envelopes from the top of it and handed them to Mark and Will. Stevie had left instructions for them about things they could do to help out. There was also a list of what he wanted them to have in the way of records and films. He'd already left Lauren a list and a huge brown envelope full of letters when he went into hospital two weeks before. Inside were his wishes for the service and letters to her and each of the children that were to be given to them when she felt they were old enough. She wondered if any child was ever old enough to understand why their daddy wasn't able to stay and see them grow up. It had happened so quickly that she appreciated having that list, the last thing she wanted to do was to sit in a quiet room and actually think hard about the reality of the situation, to let it sink in and absorb the finality of it all.

The doorbell rang and Mark opened the door to the funeral director. No need for many words, somehow everyone knew how to walk through a funeral day. Nobody ever needed a rehearsal, not like a wedding, it just happened. Mark looked out into the street where the hearse was, in the place where Stevie's people carrier usually parked. Inside the glass panelled estate was a wooden box, with his friend's body in. Propped along the side was a large yellow wreath 'DADDY'. It still didn't sink in that he was gone.

Mark had been there at the end. Stevie had deteriorated very fast, the cancer was so advanced that they had to give him the maximum possible dose of chemotherapy followed by radiotherapy, but it was too late and too much for him. If it had been discovered earlier then maybe he would have stood a chance but his body had thrown in the towel long before his spirit. He went from hospital to hospice whilst they stood helplessly by, watching him slip away. The Stevie they knew drowned in a haze of morphine, he wasn't really there. The nurses at the hospice made him as comfortable as possible in the last hour as his body shut down little by little.

Right up to the last breath Mark had felt God could save him; people were supposedly still miraculously healed at the eleventh hour. He had held onto Stevie's arm and looked into his eyes willing for God to heal him, to take away the darkness waiting to consume them in that room. His eyes were cloudy. Mark thought he heard him try to say something, Lauren leant over and kissed Stevie on the forehead and then it was like someone hit a pause button.

The nurse pronounced the time of death and Mark looked at the shell that was once his friend. Stevie didn't look like he was sleeping as some people had described people passing, whatever *made* this man *Stevie* had vanished with his last breath. There was some comfort in wondering where that energy went to.

Lauren appeared beside Mark at the doorway. She looked at the hearse and took in a big breath of air. 'Come on, let's get through this bit then I can have a bloody drink.'

~

The Church was packed. People had travelled from all over the country, many from Scotland. Lots of faces from the band scene appeared; some of them with young families and a few more lines around the eyes. Most of the children who were too young to go stayed behind at the house with Stevie's niece. They played games and ate sweets and wondered why the grownups were letting them get away with things that they were usually told off for.

Mark and Will stood at the Church entrance, handing out the order of service. There was some muttering and pointing at it. Why would Stevie ask for *My heart will go on*, the theme from *Titanic*? Only Mark And Will knew why and they had plugged the CD player into Will's JCM800 Marshall amp. Will had put the number eleven on the volume dial in marker pen as instructed in his letter. When the pallbearers reached the entrance with the coffin there was a loud guitar chord and then a breakneck power punk version by Castle Rox pumped out. The Vicar grimaced and the people either laughed or cried or did both.

The service passed in a fog, it was hot inside the Church with standing room only, Stevie had been very popular. When it was the funeral of someone so young it never seemed real, it was like a childhood game and at the end everyone would be fine. It didn't seem right that the sound of that larger than life Scottish lad hitting those drums would not be heard live again.

The coffin disappeared behind the curtains and Mark played *Where The Rose is Sown* by *Big Country*, just like Stevie had requested. The last thing on the order of service read '*No slouching shoulders, I want you to have a dance for me on the way out*'. Will turned the music up and Stevie's brothers were the first to begin clapping. Others followed; hesitant at first, self-conscious and wondering if they should really do something like that at a funeral.

A few started cheering Stevie's name like a football chant. With every passing second the atmosphere became more charged, the reservations vanished and for a moment it became tribal, people started jumping around as the Vicar stood slack jawed. Stevie's sister laced her arm through his gown and began dancing round him. He shrugged and joined in with Will and Mark doing a jig in the pulpit. Mark thought it was the most wonderful thing he'd ever seen at a send off even though he cried through the whole song.

Outside the air was fresh and the sun had appeared for the first time that day. Mark looked at the flower arrangements at the back of the crematorium; there was a huge one in the shape of a drum kit from Lauren. If Jack had been there no doubt he would have been trying to play it as it sat amongst the ocean of colour along the grey stone floor. At Lauren's request people had made donations to the local hospice and the Macmillan Nurses who had been so good. There were still lots of floral tributes, Mark read some of the condolence cards and just as he was about to head to the cars he noticed a wreath in purple at the end, the writing on it small and neat.

> *Stevie, I still can't believe it. The world has lost a gentle giant.*
> *Thank you for being such a good friend. It meant so much to be*
> *part of your clan when I moved there. Say hi to Keith Moon for me*
> *when you get to Heaven! I will never forget you.*
> *Love Jo x*

At that moment Mark missed her more than ever.

Back at the house the mood was jovial and people were loosening their ties and having a drink. High-spirited Celtic rock music played. Stevie had told Lauren that any sad faces were to be reprimanded and given ten press-ups. Mark found Lauren and Will outside watching Jack playing on the swings with some of the other children.

'He's left you that signed album you know.' Will said.

'The yellow vinyl?'

Lauren nodded. 'Stevie loved that album but he knew how much you loved the Ramones.'

'I don't feel like I deserve it.'

'You were a good friend Mark, you both were.' Lauren put her arms around them.

'He left me *Shit Hot Speed Metal Volume Eight.* Will said, staring into his cup of tea.

It was a weird day for all of them, one they couldn't prepare for.

'Well I didn't ever think we'd be stood here without the big man.' Lauren said.

'It's the most lively funeral I've ever been to. He's looking down on us and loving it,' Will said, 'I don't believe in all that God stuff but I think we carry on in nature if anything. It's all around us isn't it?'

'You've changed a bit haven't you?' Mark said.

'I'm entitled to shift beliefs and if you will excuse me I am going to speak to Stevie over there by that tree because he's there too, omnipresent energy.'

They watched as their peculiar but very funny friend walked off towards the back of the garden. People dealt with grief in different ways and for Will it was humour. He turned and pointed to a tall tree smiling and patting it.

'He's right though, he's still with us.' Lauren said.

'You think he's in the tree too?'

'No you idiot, I saw him in the hallway last night and I know what you're thinking but I swear it happened. I thought it was Jack sleepwalking at first, so I got up and went out to the landing. I could hear music downstairs, thought I'd left the stereo on as it's been a bit of a blur this week so I started to walk downstairs,' she paused, closing her eyes, 'and there he was.' Mark offered her his handkerchief. She opened her eyes again. 'Sorry, you don't want to hear this.'

'Yes I do, go on.' He said.

'He looked up at me,' she continued, 'sort of did this thing with his hands. Some daft rock sign you lot used to do on stage.' Mark put his forefinger and little finger in the air and she nodded, wiping at her face. 'That's the one. And he blew me a kiss and walked back into the front room. I was frozen to the spot, I wasn't scared, I mean it was Stevie so why would I be scared?' She composed herself and played with the handkerchief, rolling it over her fingers. 'Then the music faded and it was just me on the stairs. I must have sat there for half an hour, looking down. I wanted to go and push that door and find him asleep on the sofa, to hold him in my arms.' She burst into tears. Mark embraced her; there wasn't anything you could say in a moment like that. Jack ran up the garden.

'Is mummy crying again?' He said.

'Oh she's just tired.'

'Can I have another biscuit?'

'I think you'll explode if you have anymore,' Lauren said, composing herself, 'here let me wipe that chocolate off your mush.' She took the handkerchief and dabbed it on her tongue in that way mums did. Jack grimaced as she removed the smear of chocolate from his face.

'Yuk.'

'I'm afraid your handkerchief is going to need a wash.' She laughed waving it at Mark as Jack ran off again.

And so the day rolled on, children carried on playing, people laughed, cried, talked of old times and remembered Stevie. When most of the guests had gone Lauren started to tidy up and then bathed the children. She put them to bed and sat halfway down the stairs where she had the night before.

Cars drove past outside, a few miles away in town the bars began to fill up and people carried on with their lives. Some of them thought tomorrow would be just another day while others knew that each one was different. Before Stevie went into hospital he told Lauren that it was wise to be mindful of that and to see each day as something amazing. She had taken his hand and stroked it against her cheek and promised to teach that to their children as they grew up.

CHAPTER EIGHTEEN

The frothy goo spattered and gurgled into the cardboard cup. Mark looked around the service station lounge and felt glad he was only passing through on his way back to Cornwall. They used to stop in these places a lot when they travelled with the band; Will said it was like purgatory, an in-between world of commuters, travellers and breakdown recovery service men. In all the years they had passed through them he had never seen one person sign up, in fact people suddenly took an interest in the photo service envelopes or their shoes as they went by. It didn't stop them camping out at the entrance, he admired their tenacity.

Mark picked up his *gourmet* coffee that looked disgusting; Stevie used to say it was made of *Gollum's armpit paste.* He laughed to himself as the memories came back; he'd been very nostalgic since the funeral.

A woman by the magazine racks was smiling at him. He checked to see if her boyfriend was behind him but there wasn't anyone else near. She kept looking over and so Mark waved back at her. She grinned as her friend joined her. They looked at a magazine, giggled and walked away. Mark shrugged, too tired to care and headed over to the cash till.

It was when he passed the spot where the women had been standing he saw why they had been staring. A magazine had his face on the cover. He picked it up flicking through the pages of boobs and absurdities to the related article. He had managed to get to the top of the charts. It wasn't the indie music charts with Castle Rox but it was a number one at least. *Top Loser of The Year.* He put the magazine down, paid for the coffee and wondered if Pastor John would advise that is was better to forgive and forget or sue the pants off someone. The old Mark would have probably done the latter and written a letter of complaint to the editor, instead he just laughed, threw the idea in the bin with the rotten coffee and strolled back to his car. There were more important things in life these days than worrying about trashy magazine articles.

As he got nearer to the coast he pulled over and took a small A-road towards the sea. He put his iPod on and walked across to the edge of a cliff, looking across the water. *Everybody's Changing* by *Keane* was on repeat since the funeral, Mark found so much comfort in music, it was an amazing gift that anyone could have their own unique soundtrack to their lives, he thought.

Staring out at the ocean he began to wonder what his next move would be, he was at another crossroads and questioning this faith business, mad at God. Jo was thousands of miles away and wanted nothing to do with him, she was always full of good advice and comfort. It was their friendship he missed most, the intimacy and rapport you rarely found in a lifetime. What about Lauren, Jack and Katie? They were left without a husband and father so young. Why would God let that happen and why hadn't their prayers been answered? When Mark and the Church prayed for him they believed in a miracle, if God could create the universe then he could cure a small cancer growth surely? Mark had so many questions to ask Pastor John when he got back to Cornwall. John preached about not holding onto possessions which was one thing, Mark could grasp that concept but what about loving people? They could be stolen from your life without warning too.

He grabbed a stone and hurled it off the clifftop into the sea.

'You still throw like an old woman.' Came a Scottish voice.

'Stevie?' Mark backed up and tripped over.

'No wonder we always lost at cricket.' Stevie looked at him and grinned.

'You're not real. Are you?'

'I don't remember looking like this since we were in the band. Why am I wearing my old tartan trousers?'

Mark looked at him, incredulous. He'd heard of other people seeing apparitions but could not believe whom he was seeing now. If it was a trick of the mind maybe he could change the trousers to jeans. He concentrated for a second but it didn't work. 'I can't change the trousers.'

'Och. At least I've got my thick hair again he said patting his head and pulling at it.'

Mark stood up slowly and moved closer. 'I must be dreaming.'

'I would have dreamt of someone like Angelina Jolie over you Mark. I bet your disappointed pal.'

Mark shook his head and stared at him, he didn't look like a ghost he seemed very real.

'So, how's Lauren?' Stevie said.

'Gone to Scotland with your ashes.'

'Lay me where the rose is sown, just as I asked.'

'I became Katie's Godfather. We had the Christening Saturday.'

'You keep a lookout for them.'

'Of course I will. Can't you just sort of float over and see them if you can appear here?' Mark said.

'I'm not sure, I think this is your apparition so it's kind of personal you know? Subconscious. Come on Mark I'm no more real than we ever played with the Ramones.'

Mark knew that if he thought too hard about what was happening maybe Stevie would disappear. 'I don't know what to do Stevie,' he said, 'I keep losing things, ticket's, people, faith, now reality.'

'I don't think it's over with Jo.' Stevie said.

'Now I really do think I'm imagining you,' Mark said, 'that's never going to happen, Jo's gone and she won't come back, you were there when Lauren made that perfectly clear to me.'

'What was that song you used to play in the car over and over when we were in the band?' asked Stevie.

'*Don't stop believing*? You hated that song.'

'I know, it was shite but you need to remember it. You can't give up.'

'It's so hard to believe though I mean what is it worth? I prayed for you, the whole church did.' Mark bent down and picked up another stone and tossed it out to sea. When he turned around Stevie had gone.

~

Back in Cornwall Pastor John and Ben were able to help Mark work through some of the issues he was facing with his faith but even after several months he found that life without one of his best mates weighed heavily on his heart.

He was closing up the music shop one evening when a woman approached.

'I'm just closing sorry.' He said, pulling the shutter down.

'Mark?'

She was vaguely familiar to him and she certainly seemed to know who he was.

'Who are you?'

'My name's Carly and I want to discuss this.' She reached into her bag and got out a copy of the magazine with the *Top Losers* article.

Mark's face dropped.

'Can't you just leave me alone?'

'Just wondered if you could spend a minute discussing it?'

'Not really.' He said.

'I freelance for some of the national papers, I was hoping you'd be up for telling your side of the story?'

'I don't talk about it anymore.' Mark checked the door lock and then walked off. The woman followed him up the street.

'Mark, please listen to me. I know that article was derogatory but don't lump me in with those trashy magazines. I'm a real journalist and I want to tell your side of the story.'

'There's nothing left to say.' He said.

'It's been nearly a year since you spoke to the press face to face. I remember covering it when the news broke and obviously a lot has happened since then. Don't you want the chance to tell your side?'

'I've told my side of the story. It's over.'

'What happened with you and Jo and the breakdown?'

'What about it?'

'You don't want people to think you just rolled over and that's it do you?'

'I didn't just *roll over,* I learnt from it.' He snapped.

'So tell them, show them that you've moved on or just be remembered like you are in these magazines.'

She seemed sincere to Mark but it was her job to come over that way, people had warned him about journalists but in fairness the ones who broke the story had done a good job on the piece.

'Let me buy you a coffee. Just hear what I've got to say about my idea for a feature. What have you got to lose?'

Mark looked up and down the street wondering if it was a good idea. He certainly didn't want people to think he was stuck in the rut he had been in at Christmas. Maybe Jo would read a copy somehow, Lauren or Gillian at the shop might send her one and he could use it as a chance to publicly apologise to her.

'Okay Carly, a double espresso and you get ten minutes.'

'Half an hour and I'll buy you a cake too?'

Mark led the way to a nearby cafe, still unsure whether it was a good idea to start digging up the past.

PART THREE – CALIFORNIA

'If life gives you lemons...squeeze them in your enemy's face.'

- Will.

CHAPTER NINETEEN

Jo and Mark were in bed relaxing. She was so pleased that they had managed to work things out. He had begged for her forgiveness and she had given him one more chance to prove he had changed. After turning up on her door with the intention to get her back, she could see he was different and fighting for her. This time they would be together forever. She felt his face next to hers and heard the birds singing outside the bedroom window. There was a noise in the next bedroom; their baby son was awake. He would start babbling and rattling his cot around six in the morning.

'It's your turn.' She whispered.

He began to stir. She squeezed him tight, pressing her lips against the nape of his neck. Mark turned around and smiled, the same smile he had given her when they first met in the meadow of golden grass.

'Wake up.' He said.

'No. It's your turn.' She said stroking his face and then drifting back into sleep.

He told her to wake up again, she was now dreaming about the meadow but Mark was in the distance. Hundreds of bicycles were moving in front of her. She was on the horse and tried to get it to go forwards but there was no way through, it reared up on its hind legs and she began to feel herself falling backwards.

'Wake up.' Jo opened her eyes. Nicholas was staring at her and he looked angry. She tried to adjust to the room, worried about her son next door. But there was no son. She propped herself up on one elbow and rubbed her eyes.

'Dreaming about Mark again?' He said, getting out of the bed.

'I can't help what I dream about.'

Nicholas shook his head and walked into the bathroom.

Jo was having the dreams again. It had been eight months since she had left England. Nicholas had been understanding about it at first but since she had moved into his place permanently he had become more irate and prone to sulks. He was a good man but he could still be jealous and snappy at times. Nicholas did make her happy although there was a lack of butter-flies and spontaneity. At least he was unlikely to go off the rails. Her parents always approved of him, solid, dependable; her mother had always been resistant in her acceptance of Mark.

Jo had kept in touch with Lauren and discussed going to England for the funeral but Nicholas wouldn't let her go alone and in the end she decided that it would be too awkward to bump into Mark anyway. He would of course be there and it was an emotional occasion for Lauren as it was without any added tension. Instead she organised a wreath through Gillian at the shop in Warwick and on the day of the funeral had gone out to a quiet spot and remembered times she had spent with the couple. They had been so kind to her when she'd moved to England.

It was around the time of the funeral that the dreams started. Mark had reappeared in them and won her trust, they settled in Rocklin and had a baby. She felt a sort of sadness when she woke to find herself in the real world, sometimes she would try and get back to sleep desperately trying to find the dream but it was gone.

Nicholas walked back into the room knotting his tie.

'So are you going to make a decision about the divorce?'

'Soon.'

'I'm going to be late for work, look why don't we go out tonight and talk about it?'

Jo rolled over and faced the window.

'I'm sorry about snapping sweetheart,' Nicholas said, 'of course you can't help dreaming, I just want us moving in together to be a perfect new start. Just us and the future I mean once you get this divorce....'

'Nick, please don't rush me.'

'I may not be your first husband Jo but someday I certainly intend to be the last.' He leaned forwards and kissed her on the nose then the mouth. She responded and he did the funny wiggle thing with his tongue, something that she kept meaning to speak to him about.

Jo showered and dressed, put her jeans on and a silk top that Nicholas had picked out for her. She looked in the mirror and felt awkward, she hated the damn thing and only wore it to please him, it made her look so frumpy. Rummaging about in the bottom of her wardrobe Jo pulled out an old band T-shirt, there were a few things she had kept from her past. She slipped on her converse boots and began to feel more comfortable, more like the

Jo who had set off to explore the world. A song came on the radio, *Katy Perry* singing about being with someone and imagining it was your ex. Jo switched it off and felt a wave of nostalgia for her time in England.

It wasn't all horrible memories from the past once she'd had time to move on and look back from a different view. Most of them before the lottery saga with Mark were amazing; you were lucky to experience that sort of love once in a lifetime no matter how brief. When the anger faded and life moved on she had felt in control and treated any good memories like salvaged photographs; you could simply get them out to look at now and then. It wasn't like actually wanting to go back, she thought as she reached inside the wardrobe for a shoebox. Inside it had a dozen CD's, some cards and letters. It was all she'd kept for sentimental value.

She looked at one of the letters and ran her hand over the Queen's profile on the stamp, the familiar handwriting underneath was irregular and wiry. Mark was so messy at times, hair, clothes, writing. Jo had found it cute when they met but by the end he had overstepped the line and his charm had disappeared completely.

Jo put the letters into date order, and re-read them, from early love notes through to the ones from Cornwall which had remained unanswered.

Nicholas had memories too; she'd seen pictures of his ex-girlfriends in albums and even a framed collage of one of them under the bed. A letter wasn't any different from a photo. No harm in it, she thought as she laughed at a cartoon doodle Mark had done on the next envelope she came to.

~

Mark was much closer to Jo than just memories. He was only a few hours away, stepping into the airport arrivals lounge in San Francisco. He was half expecting Jo to be there but this time there was no pretty face to greet him or a chauffeur up to Rocklin. Instead he pulled his backpack on and headed for the bus depot. It was bustling with people and engine noise and he felt a rush to be back there. When they pulled out towards highway I80 Mark looked out of the window and remembered it all so clearly. It had been nearly two years since he had flown out and proposed to Jo by the side of Lake Tahoe.

He liked the space and the open roads in America and wondered if they had stayed in Rocklin how things might have been different. They could have put a deposit down on a far bigger house and they certainly wouldn't have played that *Six Magic Numbers* game. The saga never seemed to end with that lost ticket no matter how hard he tried to move on but for once it had given him a reason to track Jo down and maybe, just maybe get her back.

A week after Carly's interview was published in the newspaper Mark had received a call, he thought it was another newspaper but it was from a law firm. The senior partner, Gordon was a litigation specialist, some cases he had won were high profile. Gordon explained that he would be prepared to finance a new case against Kabelson Industries, as he believed Terence hadn't explored all possible avenues of contract law. Mark wasn't an expert in litigation but he knew that a financed case with no risk to him or Jo was incredibly tempting.

'So where's the catch?' Mark said.

'No catch, however we are taking a huge risk here so it negates a considerable reward should we win.' Gordon said.

'Which is?'

'A million pounds.'

Mark was only one half of the claim to that money. Even though Gordon and his business partners were prepared to take the financial risk they couldn't do so without being given proxy papers to legally do so by both parties.

He had pondered on the offer for days. It was resurrecting a monster that had killed his marriage and almost his sanity, was it best to leave it? It seemed too good to be true, a million pounds each for him and Jo at zero risk. Then he realised that it could open another door if he did take them up on the offer. Mark would need Jo's signature, giving him a perfect excuse to go and find her, to perhaps give him a chance to spend an hour with her and while he explained it all she might see that he had changed. She had never replied to his letters and from what he knew through Lauren, Jo was back at her parent's in Rocklin. He could try writing to her first, but then they might not pass it onto her and most of all he wouldn't get the chance to make an entrance, to appear from thousands of miles away across the ocean with good news. Nobody could be upset at the chance to get a million pounds for free.

The final confirmation that made him determined to make the trip came from beyond the grave. Lauren had called him up one evening.

'Mark, do you have that Ramones LP that Stevie left you?'

'The yellow vinyl one, yeah, do you want it back?'

'No I want you to look inside it for me.'

Mark found the album and as he pulled the inner sleeve out a twenty pound note fell out followed by a fifty, then more. Thre was five hundred pounds in total.

'I don't understand.' He said, down the phone.

'Remember the letters that he left for me? He told me to give you that album and then call you and make sure you book a flight over to the states. I just felt now was the right time to call and check if you'd found it.'

'But I can't take your money Lauren.'

'It's not mine, he wanted you to have it.'

Mark said that he felt bad, it could go towards a holiday for the family but she was having none of it.

'It's his wish Mark, you can't argue with it and nor can I even though I don't think Jo will be pleased when you turn up.'

'Only one way to find out I guess.'

'There's one more thing,' she said, 'he mentions something about you having his old tartan punk trousers.'

Mark dropped the phone.

That night he played the bright yellow vinyl *Ramones* album *Road to Ruin* over and over and in the morning he made his way to the nearest travel agent.

CHAPTER TWENTY

Halfway to Sacramento the coach stopped at a diner, Mark stretched his legs and went to get something to eat. He ordered a huge omelette and a strong cup of black coffee. The diner was busy but he noticed a spare seat next to the window opposite a dark haired man reading a book.

'Mind if I sit here?' asked Mark.

The man held a finger in the page he was reading and looked up.

'Be my guest.' He moved his tray to make more space.

'Is it a good read?' Mark enquired.

The man looked at the book and inspected it. 'I think this is possibly the worst load of trash I ever read.' He laughed and offered his hand across the table. 'I'm Mikey, it's nice to meet you.'

Mikey was in his early forties. He had an angular, lived-in face with dark intense brown button eyes that reminded Mark of a shark. He looked very rough around the edges with black unkempt hair. Mark noticed a tattoo with musical notes on it.

'Are you a Musician?' Mark said.

He looked down at the tat. 'Kind of gives it away huh?'

'I play in bands myself.'

'Now we're talking, what sort of stuff?'

'Rock mostly.'

'You play guitar?'

'I stick to bass for live stuff as my mate Will's much better on lead, he likes Primal Scream, Black Crowes and then there's Stevie, he's into the Who, ... well he *was*.' Mark felt that empty feeling again.

'And you play all over Australia?' Mikey said,

'No, I'm from England.'

'I knew that, I was just yanking your chain. So are you guys gigging out here now or something?'

'No, we had to split up for a while, one of the guys had a family and priorities changed.'

'You can't replace him?'

Mark laughed. 'Oh boy, you couldn't replace Stevie. He was like Keith Moon on those drums, we were going to have a reunion last year but...'

Mikey waited for him to finish.

'Well he died so that was that.' Mark said, stabbing at his omelette with a fork.

'I'm real sorry to hear that.'

Mark drifted off for a second. 'Anyway, what do you play?'

'It's just me and an acoustic, guess it's sort of like John Cougar Mellencamp stuff, you heard of him?'

'*Jack and Diane.* My dad has that record.'

'Well your dad has good taste.'

'I don't know about that.' Mark laughed.

'So what does bring you this far from home?'

'My ex.'

Mikey lent forwards, 'You need a gun?'

Mark dropped the piece of omelette he was raising to his mouth from his fork. 'I can get you a gun.' Mikey whispered as a waitress arrived at the table with a coffee pot. Mikey let her fill up his mug whilst he studied Mark who in turn wanted to get up and leave or tell the waitress he needed help but she was already off to another table.

Mikey's face broke into a huge grin. 'Yanking yer chain again. I thought you guys had a sense of humour?' He clapped his hands together. 'I'm sorry, I like a joke as you can tell. So come on, why would you come all this way for your ex-wife?'

'She's not my ex-wife yet. I have some paperwork to deliver.'

'You not heard of DHL?'

'It's important that I explain this to her.'

'You still love her, you must do to come all this way out here?'

'I didn't exactly endear myself to her when we last saw each other.'

Mark took a mouthful of his coffee and looked out of the window at the trucks rolling past on the highway. It was becoming much more real now he had landed in her home state. There were a number of responses; he might be straight back on the plane with shredded papers and another slap around the face, her father might chase him down the road with his gun. On the other hand Jo might leap into his arms and tell him she still loved him.

Mikey leant forwards. 'You still love her don't you?'

'Well....'

'I mean you *really* love her I can see it in your eyes.'

'She was the one but I lost sight of what was important.'

'And what is that exactly?' Mikey asked.

'It's not money I know that much now.'

'Oh that's for sure. You chase that sucker and you're doomed.'

'Exactly, it's just a means to an end.'

'I always say to my wife if we won the state lottery I'd still be happy right where we are. I ain't ever happier than sitting on that back porch with that beautiful woman and a cold beer.'

'I forgot you have state lotteries over here.'

'Yup, the thing is I won't ever win it and you know why?' He leaned in close to Mark. 'Cos I don't buy any freaking tickets, that's why.'

Mark finished his coffee and put his mug down. They had been so busy talking that he'd forgotten all about the bus to Sacramento.

'Oh crap, what time does the bus go to Sacramento?'

Mikey looked outside. 'You mean that one pulling away there?'

Mark saw the back of the bus as it trundled onto the highway.

'Oh great.'

'There'll be more. Go check with the staff over there they know the whole timetable.'

Mark stood up.

'Unless you want a ride.' Mikey said.

Mark thought about it. He could hear his mother lecturing him as a boy about taking rides from strangers. 'I'll be fine. Thanks.'

'Well let me get your tab for you.' Mikey reached into the back of his jeans, got his wallet out and began flicking out ten-dollar bills.

'I can't let you pay.' Mark said.

'Call it a thank you for saving me from that awful book.'

Mikey wished him well and Mark made his way to the bus stop next door. It was going to be a long wait. He put his backpack down, made himself as comfortable as he could on a bench and began to doze off. It had been a long journey and now it was catching up with him.

The sound of a car horn startled Mark. He looked across the car lot, a grey pick-up truck sat ten feet away revving its engine and flashing its lights.

Mikey popped his head out of the window.

'You sure you don't want a ride? Come on. It'll be company for both of us.'

Mark could hear his mother again, *'Don't talk to strangers and for goodness sake don't get into their cars whatever you do.'*

CHAPTER TWENTY-ONE

Mark watched the suburbs of North California passing on both sides of highway 180. Outside the temperature was high; it was at least 35 degrees at that time of day. He lent on the car door, wind surfing with his hand. The band *Journey* came on the radio.

'Oh can we turn this up?' He asked.

Mikey smiled and jacked up the volume on *Don't stop believing* the old favourite of his. Despite his lack of sleep, Mark was excited to be there on an adventure again. Deep down he knew this wasn't about the money or the court case it was about life, about fighting for the right things, living in a moment and seeing where it could take you. It was a big world out there.

He was scared Jo might turn him away but it was worth the risk. He didn't want to be someone looking back over his life and wishing he'd travelled more or tried harder to follow his dreams. It was too easy to get carried along with the tide and that was one thing the lottery saga had ironically helped him face up to, to think about where his life was going. The music shop was a small step, some would have told him a step backwards after a cushy office job on twice the salary, but for Mark it was in the right direction and that was what mattered. He could do anything if he put his mind to it, that's what his dad used to tell him. *'Just make sure it's what you want to do in your heart and then give it your best.'* He would say.

'Do you want me to drop you off in any particular part of Sacramento?' Mikey said.

'Jo's parents are a bit further north, in Rocklin.'

'I know it well. I live about half hour away up in Colfax. I can drop you off.'

They stopped at a convenience store. Mikey got a six-pack of beer, blueberries and some flowers.

'If I forget these I'm a dead man.'

'The flowers?'

'No, the blueberries. I'll die without Carrie's cheesecake.'

'I love cheesecake.'

'Well maybe I'll save you a slice in case you want to drop by.' He smiled.

Mark helped to carry the bags to the truck. As they reached it Mikey handed him something.

'A souvenir.'

He looked down at the lotto scratchcard.

'Actually Mikey it's probably best if I leave this one for you.'

'You got a gambling issue or something?'

'Not exactly but trust me, you'd be more lucky than me with these.' He said, handing it back.

'Okay, suit yourself. We only got about a mile to go before your exit, whereabouts you staying in Rocklin Mark?'

'I'll find something, there are plenty of motels around I just don't feel ready to face Jo yet, not without some sleep and a clean up.'

'I can't just drop you in the middle of nowhere, it'd be wrong.'

'No honestly, it's fine. There's a motel right on the exit.'

'Mark, we've got a big house just a few miles up in Colfax. You're more than welcome to stay over and I'll drop you back in Rocklin in the morning.'

Mark heard his mothers voice again warning him about strangers but he was feeling so tired he could have slept in the back of the pick-up at that point.

'If you're sure?'

'Carrie will be mad if I pass up on bringing back a real Englishman for dinner. She's got all those stupid films like *Pride and Pickle Sandwiches* or whatever it is with Mr. Daffy.'

'You mean Darcy?'

'I just call him that to wind her up,' he winked, 'I can't compete with that actor, what's he called?'

'Colin Firth.'

'Yeah. See, you can talk about it to her, it just bores the shit out of me man you'd be giving me a night off!'

After leaving the highway they headed into the Sierra Foothills, Mark felt at home with so much greenery everywhere and remembered parts of the route from his trips to Lake Tahoe with Jo.

They reached Colfax, a quaint old railroad town, the buildings reminded Mark of a movie set and he felt a wave of excitement to be somewhere so different. The truck pulled down a track road and arrived at a large country house. Mikey lived on a hill with sprawling gardens, Mark had often thought about living in a similar place with Jo, not so far out but a suburb closer to one of the cities so they could dip in and out for the music scene and restaurants or head into the country for breaks.

On the porch was a petite lady in her thirties with brightly dyed ruffled hair. She beamed a huge smile at him.

'Oh my, we got another stray.'

'This is Mark and you'll never guess where he's from?'

'Jupiter?'

'Not exactly.' Mark said.

'You're English.' She put her arm around him.

'Crikey so he is guv.' Mikey said.

'Please excuse my husband's bad accent impressions. He ruins my DVDs all the time.'

'I hear that you like Colin Firth?'

'Tell me a woman who doesn't.' She laughed, leading him inside.

Mikey walked in behind them and closed the door, bolting it on the inside.

'Can we keep him Mikey, oh please let's keep him?' Carrie said.

'You'll scare him away. I told you Mark, you are going to get treated like royalty here man.'

'I've got *Pride and Prejudice* but I never met a real Englishman this is so exciting.'

'I'm more of a Simpsons fan myself.' Mark said, doing his Homer impression. They laughed and he decided that he liked them already, they were after all the first people to appreciate his impression.

Carrie made them a light snack while Mikey and Mark talked about music and jammed on an old Gretsch semi-acoustic guitar. Whenever Mark had a guitar in his hand he felt at home.

After eating they could tell that Mark was exhausted and showed him to an attic room where he collapsed on the bed falling quickly into a deep sleep. It had been a long journey.

Downstairs, Carrie took the blueberries and began to make her cheesecake while she quizzed Mikey about their guest.

'So you think he could be connected to Dean's prophecy?'

'Keep your voice down,' Mikey said, closing the door to the hallway, 'and don't go yappin off in front of him until we find out who he is.'

CHAPTER TWENTY-TWO

Mikey and Carrie had met in Seattle during the grunge music scene in the early nineties. At the time Mikey was a biker with problems longer than his ponytail. He'd had a really steady suburban upbringing but for some reason it bored him, he never liked his home town or felt like he fitted in and rebelled against everything his parents tried to teach him. After discovering music he got the travelling bug living at friend's houses and squats, he would roadie for bands, run errands and sometimes steal to make ends meet. He knew that he would have to stay tough to avoid people walking over him and whilst other friends back home were getting jobs with an upcoming company called *Microsoft*, he got his first full time job in a prison laundry room.

One night after being released from jail Mikey broke into a green Lincoln parked in a Church car lot. He hotwired it and was about to drive off when he saw the owner approaching, waving the keys at him. Mikey sat there in a half-drunk stupor looking at the man.

'You could have just come in and asked me for the keys. Have you broken the ignition?' The man looked inside and tutted. 'It's trashed, just look at it.'
The man was acting way too cool for Mikey who thought he must be stalling him before the cops arrived. He got out and began to walk away.

'Don't you want it now?' The man called after him.

'Freak.' Mikey shouted as he walked back up to the main road. No cop cars arrived or passed him and the incident bugged him all the way home and even that night he couldn't stop thinking about what had happened. People had always been so mad at him before, that's why he would strike first it was a defence mechanism he'd adapted. Normally they were afraid or crossed the road to avoid him, thinking that was going to thump or mug them or both.

It bugged him so much that this man had been so calm about the incident that he returned the next week and waited by the car. When he didn't show up Mikey walked over to the building and found him stood at the front of the Church. It was a huge place and easy to hide among the congregation so Mikey slipped in and watched as they sang a song. Within minutes Mikey was bored and thought he'd had enough. As he went to leave he heard someone calling out. The music stopped.

'I see we have a man in tonight who I had the pleasure to meet last week.'

Mikey looked at the faces turning towards him. Was this guy playing games to embarrass him? He marched down the front staring at people along the way recognising some of them, there were even some bikers he'd seen in the clubs. The man held out his hand. 'Pastor Louis. And you are?'

'Your worst nightmare.'

The Pastor laughed. 'I doubt that very much unless the end of the Bible has changed?'

'I want the keys.' Mikey held out his hands.

Pastor Louis looked at the congregation. 'He wants my car keys.' He turned towards the lectern. Mikey wondered if he had a gun, it wasn't unheard of for preachers to carry one in rougher neighbourhoods, instead he produced a set of keys. 'Well here you go you know which car is mine. Don't wreck the ignition this time, it cost me a hundred bucks to get it fixed.'

'This is a trick. You'll call the cops as soon as I reach the freeway.'

He glared at Louis.

'No. I won't.' People laughed. Why did they keep laughing, why weren't they afraid of things kicking off? He thought.

'You can be my witnesses then,' Mikey shouted at them, 'he just gave it to me and said I could drive it.'

'So what?' A tall skinny lady at the front said.

'We got a service to be getting on with if you don't mind so either park your butt or go for that ride.' Said a man behind her. Everyone roared with laughter.

Mikey ran out with the keys muttering about the lunatics inside. He approached the green Lincoln jumping in and firing it up. Now he had a sweet car to ride in and permission to take it. He looked back at the Church building. Nobody had followed him, in fact, as he wound the window down he could hear them singing. He put his foot down on the accelerator so it revved and thrashed. Still nothing.

He screeched out of the space towards the exit making one last check to see if he was being followed, there were no cops around. Turning the stereo on he whooped and hollered. There was some horrible music on the player so he threw the CD out of the window and tried the radio.

About five miles down the road Mikey pulled over. He should have been really buzzing but instead he sat there thinking about the people in the church and the pastor encouraging him to take his car and the tall skinny woman, unafraid waiting to get back to her singing. Something didn't feel right. *Mikey* didn't feel right.

He drove back to the church and waited. People began to file out and get into their cars and drive away. They all looked so happy, hugging each other which made him cringe, he couldn't remember hugging people that way it was alien to Mikey. They were all freaks and weirdo's who had been brainwashed and led like sheep by a system. Eventually Pastor Louis appeared. He shut the Church door and walked towards the car calmly. Mikey revved the engine and wheelspan it towards him stopping a foot away. The pastor looked unruffled.

Mikey got out of the car and threw the keys to him.

'It drives like an old man's car.' Mikey sneered.

'Well I guess at fifty I am almost an old man.'

'What are you anyway, some kind of head freak trying to psyche me out?'

'Head freak?'

'I know what you do in that building, it's mind control like that magician guy on TV and you get in their heads and you control people and take their money.'

'That's an interesting concept.' Pastor Louis looked him straight in the eyes. Mikey held the stare for as long as he could, he wanted to smash the man's face, to bust him up and stop him smiling, stop him offering his car to him, stop him hugging his friends, stop him being so ... nice. Instead Mikey did something he hadn't done for years, he turned and walked away.

'What are you doing?' Pastor Louis said.

'I'm leaving.'

'I mean with your life, aren't you sick of it?'

'I'm sick of you!' Mikey screamed, throwing his arms around.

'Stealing cars, living hand to mouth; was that the dream as a kid?'

'What do you know about me as a kid?' Mikey turned and started walking back towards him. 'You don't know shit about who I am, I could be anyone but all you see is another wallet, you want me to get a job, cut my hair and start putting into your collection plate. Isn't that it?'

Pastor Louis held his gaze again then put his hand on Mikey's tattooed shoulder. 'I'm not judging you and you're hair looks pretty cool actually, maybe could use a wash.'

Mikey couldn't believe what the man was saying. 'You'd better watch what you say to me old man because God ain't going to protect you if I choose to bust you up right now.'

'Okay, so it's just you and me here, free choice, you could take the car, beat me up run me down but you're still going to go home and feel the crappy way you do in the dark. That's when you can't lock it out isn't it, stuck inside that cage you're in with all the voices tormenting you?'

'I'm not in a freaking' cage, what are you talking about?'

Pastor Louis looked around the deserted car lot and started to walk back towards the doors of the Church building. 'You want a coffee there's half a pot to finish?'

'No I don't want a coffee I want to get as far away from you as possible you fruitloop.' He marched back up to the street. When he looked back he saw that the man sitting on the bonnet of the green Lincoln now had two coffee cups in his hand but Mikey just kept on walking.

The following week he detoured past the Church again. He saw Pastor Louis talking to a pretty woman in punky clothes, jet-black hair with pink highlights and a nose ring. Mikey recognised her from some of the gigs he'd been to. Pastor Louis saw him and waved but Mikey stuck his finger up then walked off, he wasn't in the mood for talking that evening. Later he went to meet his friends at a club and saw the woman again. He followed her to the bar and hovered, trying to think of something to say to her.

'Can I get you a drink too?' She asked, turning to him.

'Really?' He said, surprised. 'Just a lite beer thanks.'

'No problem.' She smiled.

'You were at that crazy church earlier weren't you?' Mikey said.

'And you were the one who drove off in Pastor Louis's car the other week, that was nice.'

'I brought it back. I didn't steal it.' Mikey snapped.

'I never said you did,' she handed him his beer, 'So you want to get something off your chest or do you have gas?'

He looked at her for a second. She smiled wider and Mikey broke into a chuckle then a big laugh. He hadn't laughed like that for a long time. The young woman introduced herself as Carrie.

'Do you hug people?' He said as they found a table to sit at.

'Why do you want one?'

When they said goodbye that night Mikey went to kiss her but she pushed him away. Carrie said that if he wanted to take her on a proper date then he would have to come to the Church at least three times first. Mikey really liked her and so he thought it was an easy trade to make. What Mikey didn't know was that those meetings would spark something deep inside him and change his life so profoundly that he would start his own controversial Church.

CHAPTER TWENTY-THREE

Mark opened the kitchen door onto the porch holding a mug of coffee and immediately discovered the see-through outer storm door the hard way, richocheing off it.

'Oh bloody great!' He cursed, wiping splashes of drink from his clothing.

Mikey had been outside on his hammock, concentrating on a baseball game on his handheld portable TV.

'Hey Mark, don't you have those back in England buddy?'

'Took me by surprise, it's okay.'

'You want to go change?'

'I'll be fine, I brought two pairs of jeans with me anyway.'

'Well take the weight off.'

Mikey kicked a wooden chair across towards him. 'So you got a plan for the day?' He enquired, still watching the TV set.

'I'll head to Jo's parents. See if I can track her down from there.'

'What side of Rocklin are they?'

Mark reached into his back pocket. He felt for the address slip and handed the piece of paper to Mikey. 'That's just a half hour drive from here. You wanna ride?'

'I can catch a bus.'

'Cute.'

Carrie stepped out onto the porch.

'Carrie, Mark is going to take the bus to Rocklin.'

She laughed and put her hands on her hips. 'Well that's fine if you got all day but you'll be waiting a long time.'

Mikey looked at his watch.

'I got some time this morning I'll run you over there.'

'It's just to hand some papers over.' Mark said.

'The mystery papers eh?'

Mark opened his mouth to speak but Mikey held his hand up.

'Just yanking yer chain. None of my business is it?'

'I'm not keeping you from things am I?' Mark said. 'What is it you guys do for work?'

'I'll show you later,' Mikey said, 'let's get some breakfast.'

~

Heading from Colfax to Rocklin Mark began to feel increasingly nervous. How would Jo's parents react to him turning up unannounced? All they might see was the man who took their daughter away and then returned her alone and in tears a year later, it wasn't a good resume and it was a long way to come to have a door slammed in your face. They pulled up outside and Mark got out of the truck.

'Go on, it's just a door.' Mikey laughed.

'You haven't met her mother.'

Mark walked slowly over to the house and up the pathway tentatively ringing the bell. He was about to turn and run when he saw a figure approaching through the rippled glass. It was too late now and he thought he was going to be sick with nerves. That might not have impressed Jo's mother but it couldn't have been much worse than the face she pulled when she saw him.

'You?' She put her hands to her cheeks. 'What are you doing here?'

'It's nice to see you too. I'm looking for Jo.'

'I don't think so.' She stammered.

'It's important.'

'I don't care, you aren't welcome here.'

'I wouldn't come all this way unless I had too. I tried to phone and I wrote e-mails.' He said.

'Well take the hint Einstein, she doesn't want to speak to you.' She began to close the door.

'It's about the lottery.'

Her eyes narrowed, 'It's about the lottery? That must be your catchphrase! You're just lucky her father isn't here.'

'Oh my God, I'm so sorry I never knew.' Mark said, holding his chest.

'He's not dead, he's out playing golf you moron.'

Mark frowned, she really didn't like him at all it was so obvious.

'I made mistakes and I'm not here for forgiveness, I just want to show her something.'

'If you expected a ticker-tape parade then I'm sorry buddy, you hurt our daughter so try coming back in, let me see, another lifetime?'

She shut the door firmly. Mark reached into his bag and took out a package placing it on the floor.

'Please ask her to take a look at this,' he shouted through the door, 'there's a number that she can reach me on the back.'

Jo's mum watched them as they drove away and walked back outside. She opened the package and looked at the contents. A newspaper with Mark on the cover and a letter addressed to Jo. She wondered whether to throw it in the bin and never mention it but it was a long way to come from England to drop off. It must be important like he said. As much as she hated it she picked up the phone and dialled her daughter.

'Jo? Darling you're never going to believe who just knocked on our front door.'

~

'You like Mexican food Mark? I'm meeting some good friends for lunch, why don't you tag along?'

Mikey was driving north towards Colfax, Mark had been quiet, deep in thought about whether Jo's mum would even pass on the package to her.

They pulled up outside a restaurant, three men sat at a table under a parasol drinking beer; *Dean*, a hard looking man in his thirties with spiky hair, *Jacob*, baby faced, late twenties with long hair and *Red*, named after his curly mop of ginger hair, mid forties with a weather beaten face.

'Gentlemen, this is Mark. He's come all the way from England.'

'Grab a beer.' Dean said.

'Thank you, it's pretty hot isn't it?' Mark said, reaching for a bottle from the ice bucket.

Red stared at him. 'The dude talks just like Austin Powers man.'

'He's Canadian you dummy.' Dean said.

'He just said England.'

'No, the actor who *plays* Austin Powers is Canadian. Mike Myers.'

Red looked at him curiously. 'Well you know what I mean.' He shrugged.

Mikey went to order some food. Dean offered to help him, 'You know this could be what that prophetic vision was all about?'

'Okay. Let's just take it one step at a time.' Mikey said, looking back out the window.

They ordered the special and joined the others.

'It's a long way to come just to turn around and go back again.' Jacob said.

'It depends on my ex really.'

'If you want my opinion, I think you need to stay here and enjoy the delights of North California. Try to work out what's happening with your life.' Mikey said.

'You believe in God Mark?' Dean said.

'Yes, I do. Although it's been tough this year.'

'You been baptised?'

'I was christened.'

'What's that?'

'It's like baptism as a baby.' Mikey said.

'You not had full immersion then?'

'Not as an adult,' Mark looked at them all and put his hands up, 'can I still eat with you if I haven't?'

'Best ask the Apostle.'

'*Apostle*?' Mark asked, confused.

'Let him drink his beer, he's on vacation.' Mikey said.

A waiter walked out and laid out some cutlery, a bowl of corn chips and salsa dip.

'What did he mean by Apostle?' Mark pressed.

'Well you wanted to know my job?' Mikey said leaning over and taking a handful of chips. Mark wondered if it was another prank, like the one in the diner. He was still trying to work Mikey out.

'You're telling me that you are an Apostle, seriously?'

'That's right.'

'But I thought they were the twelve disciples?'

'I look two thousand years old? We feed this guy and give him a room and that's the thanks we get.'

They all laughed. 'Sorry I didn't mean any disrespect it's just that's what I've read. I mean there aren't any modern ones that I've heard of.'

'It's from the Greek word *Apostolos,* it means messenger. I'm not claiming to be some divine being here. You only have to look in Ephesians to see how it was supposed to be but we've lost direction in the church along the years. All we got now is pastors, pastor for the choir, pastor for the youth team, pastor for stacking chairs.'

'You don't agree with them?' Mark dunked a chip into the salsa.

'They got their place but where are the leaders? The Apostles led the way, it's written that it would be upon the Apostles and Prophets that the church would be built. Now all we do is sit on the coat tails of society because it's out of whack and we've been left behind.'

'Interesting concept.' Mark said, putting a broken piece of corn chip back in the salsa.

'Hey no double dippin'.' Red yelled.

Mark sat up sharp in his chair. 'What did I do?'

'You stuck that corn chip in twice.'

Dean and Jacob were rolling up with laughter.

'Man, Red hates that so much.'

'Hey I'm sorry, I was so busy talking.'

'That's disgusting man, just don't do that please.' Red mumbled.

'You know what I hate Mark?' Mikey said.

Mark shook his head slowly.

'Being told that my Apostlistic calling is *an interesting concept.*

His eyes were drilling into Mark, the jovial guy had vanished and the others were quietly staring at their beers. They didn't need to see the look in Mikey's eyes to know when someone had hit one of his buttons. He may have changed since his wilder days but he was still fiercely guarded about his calling. Pastor Louis had been shocked when Mikey left Seattle to venture out on his own because he didn't understand his self-proclaimed title. That didn't stop Mikey taking half a dozen people with him to set up the new Church. These recruits trusted him completely.

'I'm sorry if I offended you.' Mark said.

Mikey stood up and threw the lotto scratch card down on the table, the one from the garage. He pointed at it and spoke in a firm but calm voice.

'It's either going to be strong leaders and a destiny or we're left with this bullshit Mark. Now you had better choose if you want to live with purpose and faith or wait for lady luck to run your life.'

Mark dipped another fresh corn chip carefully in the salsa and crunched it loudly. He chomped away and then decided to break the atmosphere with a change of subject.

'So, where is this Church?' He said.

Jacob pointed over into the distant mountains. 'Church is right over there.'

'In the mountains?'

'No it's more *inside* the mountains. At the Lake.'

CHAPTER TWENTY-FOUR

Dean ran towards the steep cliff edge at terrific speed and leapt off. He floated through the air before plunging down into the crystal clear water below. The others looked over the edge at the tiny circle rippling outwards. He resurfaced and waved up at them. Jacob followed feet first shouting as he plummeted. Audenlake Church was held at the side of Emerald bay, part of Lake Tahoe, surrounded by towering pine trees.

'Your turn.' Mikey pointed at the cliff edge.

'Bit high for me.' Mark backed away.

'Come on it's a rush. You want to feel alive?'

Mikey was dressed in cut down jeans and a Hawaiian shirt, he had a mad look about him at times. He could be really charming and engaging but there were moments Mark felt a little uneasy around him. It was what the others called Mikey's *passion for the cause* but to Mark it was something more elusive, perhaps that was why he decided to stick around despite the outburst at the restaurant, there was something exciting about the guy, unpredictable. Mark watched as he charged towards the edge and somersaulted down opening up in a perfect arc then piercing the water.

Just behind him at the edge of the woods Carrie and other women from the Church prepared food on a barbeque. They sang together and joked about the men. It seemed quaint to Mark, like an American TV show his parents used to watch called *The Waltons*. Mikey and Carrie also owned a pine-bound cottage by the lake. Every week they would head out there. Some people would be invited to stay, if Mikey felt God wanted to share something with them. It was considered a special honour if that happened to you. Most made their way back at the end of the weekend to their homes in neighbouring towns. Mikey seemed to dominate proceedings around the group when they were together, the men followed him and listened to his every word. When he spoke to them it was like a Captain addressing a platoon.

Mark had been warned about cults but nobody was being manipulated or told to stay against their will, they didn't all live in one location either, it was just a group of friendly people with one belief. He wished that John and Ben from England could have visited, he was sure they would have loved it however he wondered what John would have made of Mikey's *Apostle* title. He talked constantly about the revival of modern Apostles and the way God intended the family to be, the man at the head, the women making a home and taking care of the children, small communities sticking together. Some women Mark knew would have called him a sexist but Carrie and the wives there seemed to enjoy this order of things in fact they nodded in approval when the subject was raised.

Mark knew that the family unit as he remembered it in his youth had changed immensely. He would also be somewhere among the divorce statistics soon if he couldn't persuade Jo that he had changed.

Out in the bay there were boats circling a small island. 'What's that out there?' Mark asked Carrie.

'Dead Man's Island.' She said.

Mark thought it sounded like something from a pirate film.

'Can you get to it?'

'Sure. Mikey goes out there with the leaders for their big prayer sessions.'

Mark was reminded of that familiar question, *If you had to live on an island for a year what three items would you take?* Will used to say he'd take *The Dixie Chicks* and technically that was only one thing and that he could have two more choices.

Dead Man's Island, better known as *Fannette island*, was the only one on the whole lake. It had apparently survived over time as it sat on a rib of granite, something not lost on Mikey, as he'd set out to establish himself alone, apart from Pastor Louis and all the other Churches he'd left behind.

'If you stick around you might get invited over there I'm sure.' Carrie patted him on the shoulder. 'Can you do me a big favour, jump down there and tell the guys that it's time to eat?'

'It's a bit high for me.' He said.

'Come on, the kids jump it all the time.'

Mark felt like he had no choice. He took his shoes off rolling his jeans up, checked that there was a clearing below to dive into and took a few paces back. The sun warmed his face and suddenly he realised that he felt calm and open, ready to embrace anything that life showed him. He began to run towards the edge, his feet padded down on the smooth rocks as he got closer. Finally he saw the world open up in front of him and leapt out into the void, falling towards the water, embracing what adventure may come ... and screaming all the way down.

~

They had all eaten plenty from the barbeque and wine and beer flowed. It was so relaxed, more like a beach party than a Church service. Several times he noticed a pretty blonde woman looking over at him, he found out later that her name was Beth, a former dancer that Mikey and Carrie had met in Seattle.

After the music ended Mikey stood up to speak. He welcomed Mark to the Audenlake Church and they all clapped. He stood up and bowed.

'It's the people who make up the body of Christ,' Mikey said, 'whether they come from here or overseas *this* is real Church, it ain't a building. You can't contain something as big as God with bricks and mortar. When I left Seattle they said I was deluded but just like others who were told to move and they obeyed, here we are and we proved them wrong. Together we are living proof.'

Mikey held his cup in the air.

'And as I look at your wonderful faces with the exception of some damn scary ones too,' he laughed 'I can see that God has been faithful to his word. So here's to the *real* church.'

The others raised drinks and clapped their hands. They began to sing and Mark lay back on a rug looking up at the blue sky. Beth walked over and handed him a drink, she was the first woman that he'd looked at with any feeling of real attraction since Jo but he knew that no woman was going to replace the love of his life yet, he had to wait and see if he had one more chance somehow.

~

Several miles away in Rocklin Jo had arrived at her parent's house to collect the parcel. Nicholas wanted to see it too and they didn't have secrets, he had insisted on that.

'Did he look okay?' She asked her mum as they made coffee in the kitchen.

'I suppose so.'

'I mean did he look crazy or sad or what?' She probed.

'He looked like Mark.'

Nicholas walked into the room.

'Well, are you going to open it?'

'Let me get my coffee first. It's not going to disintegrate.'

Jo walked out to the back patio and sat down in the warm sunshine putting the coffee mug beside her. Nicholas was right behind, looking over her shoulder. He cuddled her and kissed her neck. She wished that he would leave her alone for a while to find out for herself what the mystery package from her estranged husband was. Could it be divorce papers? She wondered, maybe he had met someone too and wanted to get married again. That felt strangely hurtful but she brushed it aside and told herself that it would be fine because her and Nicholas would marry too someday. Wouldn't they?

She took out the newspaper article that Carly had written and the letter from Gordon's office. She sat quietly as she read the article first about Mark's journey since they had split, his regrets and how he had found faith and bigger meaning to his life. He spoke of how hard it was to see his friend die.

Jo stroked his picture on the page without thinking. He apologised in the article for his poor treatment of her as their relationship crumbled. She appreciated the gesture of kind words but she could never fully trust someone again who had taken her heart and broken it.

Nicholas read it over her shoulder and acted like the jealous boyfriend that she hoped had been left behind since their last stint together. He pointed to the wedding picture in the article.

'You deserved better than him, I mean look at that suit.'

'Nick will you quit it, I'm reading.'

'So what's the letter?' He said, grabbing it.

Jo grabbed it back. 'It's addressed to me, not you.' She opened it. It was from a solicitor in Cambridge, England.

'So, what does he want? A divorce hopefully, then we can...'

'Give me some space Nick for goodness sake.'

She read through the details. There was a second page with a stick on note in Mark's spidery handwriting.

> *I hope that I am explaining this to you face-to-face but if not then please consider it carefully and sign. I'll do the rest. I am planning to stay for two weeks. If I don't hear from you I won't bother you again. I hope you are well and happy. Mark.*

Her mother appeared and asked what the letter was about.

'These guys in England want to fund a new legal case.'

'Oh he hasn't changed a bit why didn't I just throw it in the bin?'

'I would have.' Nicholas agreed.

'They will take all risks and costs in return for a million pounds.' Jo said.

'It's a trick.' Nicholas took the letter from her.

'It's not a trick,' Jo said, snatching it back, 'that is a million pounds to the law firm and a million each if we win.'

'Can't you have it in dollars?' Nicholas said.

Jo shook her head. 'Go freshen my coffee will you I want to talk to mom.'

Nicholas picked up the coffee mug, kissed her on the cheek and walked to the house. Her mother sat down on the chair beside her.

'Listen to what Nicholas is saying, don't you think they would have won it last time if it was that easy?'

'It's no risk. Read it.' She handed the letter to her.

'I think you're forgetting *your* risk. He broke your heart last time, remember the state he left you in.'

'Exactly.' Nicholas said, through the open kitchen window where he had been listening.

'Just make the coffee.' Jo shouted.

'He wrote a number where he's staying on the back of the parcel,' her mother pointed out, 'there's no need for you to have to face him though, he can collect it from here.'

'No. I'd like to do this properly.'

'He'll upset you again.'

'No he won't Mom. He can't upset me anymore, Mark's history and this is business.'

CHAPTER TWENTY-FIVE

Nicholas was quiet on the drive back to his house. Jo knew when a sulk was taking place as he would chew his bottom lip until it was bright red.

'You're quiet.' She stroked his neck.

'I don't want you seeing him.' He snapped, leaning away from her hand.

'It's one meeting to check through the details and sign the papers.'

'You don't need to *actually* see him.'

'He's come across the Ocean Nick, the least I can do is see him.'

'The least you can do is tell him to go to hell.' He pressed the car accelerator.

'Nick, you are in serious danger of sounding like the person I left behind years ago.'

'Oh great, now it's about *me*. I'm suddenly the bad guy here?' The car swerved around a truck and cut back in.

'Watch your speed. There's always a patrol car up here.'

'Isn't that what you like Jo, a bit of danger? Unpredictable you called him.'

'Nick, you're scaring me slow down.'

'I'm serious Jo. You need to get your priorities in the right order, Mark belongs in the past and I'm your future.'

Nicholas saw the flashing lights pull out from a gap in the trees that lined the highway and slowed down. The police car pulled over behind them.

'See I told you.' Jo mumbled.

Nicholas went into the garden and sat on his own staring at the speeding ticket and fuming. Jo went into the hallway and took out the parcel from her bag. The number to call Mark was a fairly local code, probably his hotel she figured, to her surprise a female voice answered.

> *'Hey, the lovebirds aren't here right now. Please leave your message and we'll call you back. God bless you.'*

Jo hung up before the machine began recording. There was a pang of jealousy. She threw the parcel across the room; hit the re-dial and this time waited for the beep. 'Mark. This is Jo,' she said in a staccato beat, 'I'll be at my parent's tomorrow early evening from six. If you want to discuss this solicitor's letter then be there, it won't take long.'

~

'Hello again.' Mark said.

'Hm.'

'I got the message.'

'She's out back,' said Jo's mum pointing to the open garage, 'Oh and Mark, I don't want any scenes.'

He nodded at her and walked through the garage towards the rear garden, the lawnmower was sat in the same place next to the barbeque coal bags, the fishing poles and bicycles neatly hung on wall brackets. He felt a lump in his throat it was as if he was a ghost walking in his own footsteps. If only this could have been the last time he was here with Jo, she would be sat on a sun chair with a cold glass of lemonade, thrilled that he was there.

He could hear the sound of a basketball bouncing in the yard and stopped by the back door of the garage. There she was in the flesh, for the first time since she had walked out of his life. She had her hair tied back, shorts on and a T-shirt that read 'BITCH' in silver letters. His mouth was dry and he wanted to stroll over and embrace her like he'd done so many times but now he couldn't, she was off limits. This was worse than he had anticipated, being close to three million pounds and unable to touch it was a walk in the park compared to this.

Jo carried on throwing the ball unaware of Mark being in the doorway. One shot hit the side of the hoop and bounced to her left, she ran towards it and saw him. They stood there for a few seconds, unsure of what to say. She thought that his hair needed a good comb as usual and he had that stupid look on his face, the annoyingly sweet one that had tugged at her heart when they met. She was ready for him though, she had prepared for this. He wasn't going to worm his way back in. The T-shirt spelt out her manifesto for the meeting.

He slowly stepped out into the yard picking up the ball and throwing it to her. She caught it and spun it around in her hands.

'Well this is weird,' he said, 'are you okay?'

'I'm really good thanks. You?'

'Great. I'm living in Cornwall now.'

'Lauren said you'd found God, I didn't think you believed in all that I thought you made your own luck?'

'People change.' He said, trying out his best smile.

Jo's mother was peering out of the window. He waved. 'Your mum looks so pleased to see me.'

'Weird that isn't it?' Jo said.

'I did try to get in touch. I mean afterwards. After we...'

'And I told my folks to ignore any contact.'

Jo threw the ball. She missed the hoop and it bounced off towards Mark again. He kicked it with his toe and flipped it up into his hands looking pleased with himself.

'This solicitor guy seems too good to be true doesn't he?' Jo said.

'I thought so at first but I checked out his firm and it's there in black and white. A cool million each.'

'Was it an answer to prayer or just luck?' She said.

'I don't know, luck, fate, destiny or maybe it's part of the movie.' He bounced the ball to her. 'Jo, can I just say I'm sorry for everything I never meant for it to end the way it did.'

'How did you want it to end Mark?' She stared at him with that cold glare, the one that made his insides feel like they had just been scooped out. He hadn't seen it since the day she had driven away in that cab.

'You used to play a song when we met Mark, something about not taking the precious things in life apart to see how they work...'

'...because they never fit back together again?' He finished.

'You should have listened to that but you kept picking and pulling at what we had and eventually it all unravelled.'

Mark dropped his head down and wondered why he hadn't listened to Billy Bragg's *Valentine's Day is Over*, it could have saved him plenty of heartache.

'I can't change the past Jo.'

'Look can we skip the small talk about stuff that's long gone, you can't do this thing without my signature and that's why you're here isn't it?'

Mark wanted to say so many things and the lottery was low down on the list. He wanted to tell her that it was amazing just to see her again, that she still made him feel like the world had stopped and he wanted her back more than ever. Instead he just nodded.

'Good. Makes me feel so special.'

'I can't win here Jo. You said lets talk business and now you're fishing for stuff. I didn't want you to get upset.'

'Why would I be upset, you think I lay awake sobbing into my pillow, is that it, waiting for you to show up and tell me that none of that crap we went through mattered and we can go back to how we were, is that what you think?'

Mark looked at her, surprised by the outburst. He wasn't sure if she was about to cry or do a running jump kick on him.

'As long as we have each other?' Her voice began to quiver. 'How did I fall for that bullshit?'

She turned and marched into the house. Mark stood there unsure what to do. The door opened again, this time Jo's father appeared. He was a big man and Mark knew he liked to go hunting up in the mountains which didn't make him feel very relaxed at that moment with Jo almost in tears.

'I think you'd better leave Mark.'

'I was thinking the same thing.' he said, slowly walking to the garage doorway. 'I never meant to upset her, I just thought we deserved a free chance to get that money.'

'She's a bit confused by you turning up that's all. I don't like to see my daughter upset so you'll understand if I want you off our property, I'm sorry it has to be this way.'

Mark walked back through the garage into the street. Mikey had been waiting for him in the car. He started the engine but as Mark neared the vehicle he heard Jo call out. She was standing on the front porch with her arms folded, he walked back over to her wondering if now was the time to tell her how he felt; maybe there wouldn't be another.

She handed him the legal papers.

'This is what you came for isn't it? Unless I hear that I'm a millionairess then it really is goodbye this time.'

'Jo. I need to tell you something.'

'Me too.'

For a moment he felt like an invisible magnet was pulling them together, like their bodies were being drawn towards each other, their lips got closer and then Jo snapped him from the trance, stealing the breath between them.

'I want a divorce Mark.'

~

Mark sat in silence on the way back to Colfax, deep in thought. He had prepared to feel upset when he saw Jo but he was a complete wreck replaying the meeting in his mind, trying to remember everything she said, how she looked at him, how she smelt when he had got close at last. He felt sick to his stomach that he would never see her again. How had he been so stupid to let her slip away, what amount of money was worth that? Three million or three hundred million couldn't buy the way Jo made him feel when they were together. She had been his centre, the place where everything worked in balance.

They arrived back at Colfax and Mikey sat out on the porch, Mark went inside and looked at the signed documents. The next papers with her signature on it would be divorce papers. He reached into his pocket and took out his wallet, inside were three photos he'd kept of family and friends, him and his parents on holiday when he was a kid, him and the band on stage and one taken a week before the wedding with Will, Stevie, Lauren and Jo in a pub near Warwick Castle.

Carrie walked in with a plate of milk and cookies. 'Hey. I thought you might like a snack.'

'Thanks, I don't think I've had milk and cookies since I was a boy.'

He took one and bit it. Then he took a swig of the ice-cold milk.

'Blimey. I'd forgotten how good that is.'

Carrie smiled and sat down looking at the photographs now resting on the table beside his wallet. 'May I see?'

He handed them to her and pointed out the people but as he got to the one with Jo she could sense his mood dip again. 'She's very pretty. Reminds me of that actress.'

'Winona Ryder?'

'Yes. I can see you're upset at seeing her again. Did you get those papers signed though?'

'Yes.' He said, solemnly.

'You didn't want the papers, you wanted her back didn't you?'

Mark nodded. Carrie put her arm around him.

'I could tell it wasn't about the papers. You got that look in your eyes.'

'She wants a divorce so I better head back to England; I mean I got what I came for. I said to myself that I would either get another chance or closure and a divorce request is pretty much closure.'

'But you can stay longer I thought Mikey said you have two weeks.'

'I don't want to be in the way. I'm not sure I want to be this close to where Jo is either.'

'Rocklin's far enough for you not to bump into her Mark besides, I think there's someone in the church who would be sad if you disappeared.'

'Really?' Mark said.

'I can't say anymore than that but if you are looking for a lovely lady to take your mind off a broken heart then I'd stick around a bit longer.'

Mikey appeared at the door. 'Have you convinced him to stay?'

Carrie winked at him. 'I think I may be getting there.'

'I was hoping that you'd at least come to the mens prayer meeting this week Mark. It's over on the island and Carrie said you were keen to see it so why don't you sleep on it and let me know tomorrow?'

CHAPTER TWENTY-SIX

Emerald bay looked completely different in the late evening. Mikey's car headlights splintered into the dark road ahead. Along with Jacob, they were meeting the other leaders and then heading out to Dead Man's island. According to the congregation, Mark was very lucky to have been invited to the men's prayer meeting; it was only the chosen few that spent that sort of time with the leaders.

It was still warm and Mark had sprayed himself all over with bug repellent, they seemed to like English blood and he had come up in big bumps all over his legs and arms. They stopped by a cut out, the lights of the car illuminating the trees a ghostly grey. Jacob had brought his guitar, he slung it onto his shoulder like a rifle and they followed Mikey down a small trail, Mark carrying the cooler box and weaving in and out of tall pine trees. There was stillness around the lake at night, no noise from tourists, no boats or children playing, just the rhythm of the water against the edge of the land and small creatures in the woods.

They reached the jetty where a boat was moored. 'You wanna know why it's called dead man's island?' Mikey whispered turning the flashlight in his hand so that it was pointing at his face.

Mark laughed. 'Is it haunted?'

'Man don't say that, it's really bad to say that especially so close to the water here.' Jacob said.

'Can you hear that?'

Mark listened. There was a sound of a splash in the water.

'Mark you've woken it.'

'What?'

'Oh crap.' Jacob shouted.

Mark felt something on his neck, a cold wet slime. He dropped the cooler box and yelled out running down the jetty and stumbling onto the boat, which rocked so much it nearly flipped him out the other side. Mikey seemed more concerned about the beer rolling towards the water's edge. He was laughing and Mark turned to see Red holding a long branch that he'd dipped into the lake. Dean appeared out of the shadows laughing hard but it took a while before Mark saw the funny side, his adrenaline still pumping.

'Man you were scared of a wet stick.' Red said, still chuckling away.

They put the beer back in the cooler and boarded making their way out on the gentle tide towards Dead Man's Island. It looked like there was a small light up on the peak but he couldn't be certain. Looking back over at the mainland Mark could see tiny lights from some of the houses up the mountain. The sky, brilliant with stars, reflected down, cascading onto the water. Mark felt very small sat in their boat sailing along the huge bay with just the outboard motor blades humming beneath them.

They reached the island and jumped out of the boat heading up large steps carved out of the side of the earth to the peak. Mikey went ahead with a flashlight, then Dean and Red who had brought camping lamps. Mark and Jacob followed with the cooler box between them. They arrived at a flat area on the top of the island. A derelict stone building stood there, looking like it had seen better days.

'That's the tea house,' Jacob said, 'the place is better known as Fannette Island but it doesn't quite have the same ring to it.'

'We're a bit late for tea aren't we dear boy?' Red said in a bad attempt at the English accent. Mark was too busy looking out at the magnificent view. On the horizon where the bay opened up into the main Lake, the sky was a vibrant purple. He wished that he could have been there with Jo she would have loved it. He'd taken too many sunsets and views like that for granted and suddenly he remembered one at Sir David's Island. He hadn't even noticed he'd been so engrossed in telling the chef about the stupid lottery case instead of sharing it with her.

Mikey sat on a rock while Dean, Jacob and Red began to gather twigs and place them inside a stone circle on the ground. They lit them and soon had a fire going. They seemed to be experienced at outdoor living. Mark had started a fire once, rubbing sticks together. He'd got a badge for it in the scouts; it had been a wet day and he'd cheated a bit with matches. Mark picked out a beer from the cooler which exploded all over his arm.

'Well you shook them up buddy.' Dean said.

'It was you and the sodding sea beast.' He said, wiping a soaking arm on his jeans.

They sat watching the fire for a while, Jacob strummed chords on his guitar the atmosphere was relaxed and the night air across the water was cooling. Mikey told them that they were to just sit in contemplation for a while which everyone was happy to do. It went on for about half an hour. Mark's mind drifted. At first it was the sounds from the island, the wind blowing the crackle of twigs in the flames, the animals in the bushes then it was images, people, places, and Jo, he was struggling to forget that one. Eventually he managed to get into a state of calm, simply aware of his breathing and his heart beating. It felt nice, peaceful.

When he opened his eyes Jacob and Mikey had disappeared. Red was drinking a beer and Dean was pacing around.

'I never heard the others leave. Where did they go?'

'Apostle has some things to discuss with Jacob.'

He sat down opposite Mark. Red was wrapping a torch pole with rags and paraffin. He lit it, the smell was strong as the flames ignited.

'Do you believe God has a plan for your life Mark?' Dean asked.

'I think so.'

'I don't mean being in an organisation, like just going to Church on a Sunday, I mean God and you walking together, forget the rest.'

'I sense something now and then.' Mark picked up a twig and began scraping shapes on the ground.

'Sometimes you need a guide to help you. People are sent into your life at times to help you find your way,' Dean said, 'I was lost when Apostle Mikey found me. Same for Red here, Jacob, Beth, most of us owe him our lives because he led us all here to freedom.

'Yup.' Red said, draining his bottle of beer and opening another. 'Sometimes I hated him but I had to believe, y'know. Was hard when I'd been through life with so many people letting me down. But in the end the Apostle saw my calling.'

'Why did you hate him at times?' Mark said.

'He can be passionate about his calling and it comes over as anger.'

Dean agreed with him. 'Got us into trouble with the Church organisation we used to be in but he just sees stuff in people and wants to get it out, some of it's buried so far into you that he has to be brutal but it's the darkness inside of you that he's angry with that's what you have to remember.'

'You gotta get the roots out or that stuff grows back, you understand?' Red said.

They sat there watching the torch flame as it flickered in the night wind. Mark felt like he wanted to share some things, get them off his chest. 'I haven't told people much about my own faith but I've been really lost for a while now.'

'Then you've found a good place to be.' Dean said opening a Whisky flask and passing it to Mark. He wasn't much of a spirit lover and it stung his throat causing him to cough.

'I lost everything, my job, friends, then Jo. I had a meltdown,' Mark took another swig of whisky it seemed to go down easier this time, 'then when I found faith and hope I immediately lost someone close, I believed he'd be healed and he died just weeks after I prayed for him.'

The other two nodded slowly and listened. 'God's in control though,' Dean said, 'even when we can't see why something happens he sees the big picture.'

'We had a guy at Audenlake who got cured even when the Doctors wrote him off.' Red added.

'So why him and not bloody Stevie?' Mark stood up and felt a bit unsteady, the effects of the drink beginning to kick in.

Dean walked over and patted him on the shoulder. 'We don't know why friend. We just believe he's in control.'

Mark opened another beer and started gulping it down, a bad move with his low tolerance for drink. He waved the bottle around.

'But isn't that just random chaos theory bollocks? I mean that's like saying *shit happens,* some people are lucky and others aren't,' he threw his arms in the air, beer frothing up out the neck of the bottle and down his wrist, 'and I know about sodding bad luck when it comes to the odds.'

'You sound so angry man, relax.' Red said.

'Well I *am* angry. My friend isn't here for one thing, he died before he reached thirty and now his widow's raising his kids alone.' Mark had that sinking feeling, the one when suddenly life becomes too big to handle and comes tumbling on top of you like a huge wave.

'Don't let that steal your faith. Death is a part of life.' Dean said.

'But is life governed by luck or our belief system, I mean who really bloody knows?'

Mikey appeared from out of the darkness. 'This party's getting a little heated by the sounds of it.'

'I was just telling them about Stevie, why did he have to die?'

'I can't answer that.'

'Well I'm confused. You're supposed to have the answers aren't you, what with you being this modern Aristotle?' Mark said.

'I think you've maybe drank a little too much.'

Mark looked down. He had a beer in one hand and the whisky flask in the other. 'Can you pray things to help me with my headache in the morning?'

'Oh we have a special answer to prayer for these occasions.' Mikey said.

'Do you lay hands on?'

'No, we put these two magic tablets into a glass of water. They call them *aspirin.*'

Mark giggled, stumbling towards Mikey. 'You're alright for a God botherer.' He said, promptly falling onto the ground and passing out.

'Come on guys. I think it's time we headed back.' Mikey said.

'Where's Jacob?' Red asked.

'Oh he's fine, he's going to be doing some deep reflecting tonight.'
He exchanged a knowing glance with Dean and they packed up, Red carrying Mark back to the boat on his shoulder. He would occasionally mumble about stopping at *Take Bap* on the high street. When they reached Mikey's pine-bound cottage they laid Mark on a bed in one of the back rooms covering him with a huge blanket and then Mikey and Dean sat down in the main room.

'I want you to go back to the island in the morning just before sunrise and find Jacob. You know what to do if he still won't come round.' Mikey said.

Before Dean could answer they heard a crashing noise inside of the back room. Mark appeared at the doorway like a zombie, his hair pushed up on one side and dribble around his mouth.

'I think I just threw up in your wardrobe.'

CHAPTER TWENTY-SEVEN

'Do you take this woman to be your lawfully wedded wife?'

'I do.' Nicholas said.

'Then I pronounce you husband and wife.' Jo looked into Nicholas's eyes and kissed him. They embraced tightly and everyone in the Church cheered.

'I love you.' She smiled and waved across to the best man. Mark waved back and looked at Nicholas's suit, it was green. Why would anyone wear a green suit at a wedding? He wondered, and why had he agreed to be there at all. The organist was playing *I wanna be sedated* by the *Ramones* through the huge pipes. He looked closer at Nicholas's suit and could see patterns, they were grey tone and there were faces in there. He suddenly realised it was money; the suit was made from dollar bills. It would take loads to make a suit like that, hundreds, thousands, millions, about six million dollars he reckoned. 'That's my money he yelled out and that's my woman.'

The groom turned around. 'Shut up you loser.'

The Vicar lifted his robes up and turned into Stevie who punched Nicholas but his fist turned into a cheesecake that splattered everywhere. Nicholas morphed into a large piggy bank and floated up above the congregation. It was like the one Will used to have when he opened a bank account, he called it a *Pigurine*, 'It's like a figurine... but shaped like a pig,' he would say. Will appeared beside him dressed like Robin Hood. 'Don't worry mate, I'll handle this.' He drew back his bow and arrow and fired at the piggy bank, it exploded and coins showered down on them cracking on the floor. He looked for Jo to rescue her, she looked over but when she lifted her veil up it wasn't Jo, it was Philippa. 'Do you know what three million pounds looks like in notes Mark?' He recoiled but she grabbed him as he pushed her away, screaming. 'The size of a car, the size of a car, the size of a car...'

He turned around and could see Will with a miniature Nicholas in his hand explaining to Jo's parents, 'It's like a figurine, but shaped like a pig....'

Mark sat up in a sweat. He was no longer in the Church he was in a wood panelled room, there was a smell of bleach and he was still in his clothes. He noticed a lotto scratch card on the floor next to a mop and bucket, it looked like the one Mikey had tried to hand him at the garage the day they met. He put it into his back pocket, got up and walked to the window, outside he could hear voices on the porch and see water, a huge expanse of it. Mikey's face appeared making him jump. 'Feeling a bit rough today?' He laughed. 'Get yourself out here we're cooking up some breakfast.'

Mikey didn't have a regular job. As the Apostle of Audenlake Church he needed to spend time with God and hear His voice. He still had a routine though; he would get up at seven in the morning and get a coffee then sit out on the porch, maybe read a passage from the bible and meditate over it, listen to the spirit. Sometimes he would hear it clearly, sometimes there was nothing, he was just a vessel for it to work through; there was no obligation for God to be there just because Mikey was.

At half past eight Carrie would bring out his breakfast, French toast, eggs over easy, two sausages, two rashers of bacon and a glass of juice. She'd make sure there was another fresh pot of strong coffee for him and then head off to work in a hardware store. Mikey would then retire to his study at the rear of the house and count the tithes and offerings from the people of Audenlake Church. A tithe was ten percent of an income, gross, before tax. Then there was the *offering*. As Mikey pointed out, the *tithe* already belonged to God from what he had interpreted from the Bible, the offering was what you wanted to give over and above this from your heart. It was up to you although *God loved a happy giver,* as he would tell his followers. He wouldn't force them but sometimes they needed to be reminded of how much he had done for them. Mikey was leading them to eternal life at Audenlake and they should be thanking him and God in accordance to how much they felt grateful.

He would advise the group on their business affairs and careers so he also knew their income and that they could still give more if they were really serious about their faith. It would after all be returned tenfold he would tell them, *plant a seed and reap the harvest, if you plant nothing then expect nothing.*

Mikey and Carrie had bills to pay to keep two houses going. After a vision, God had told Mikey to buy the pine-bound cottage. One day on the way back from the Lake he had taken a track road to see where it led and stumbled across a large cottage for sale. It was beautiful and they fell in love with it. The porch balcony went around the corner of the frontage, you could see across the bay and as Mikey stood there he was overcome with emotion. Then he heard a voice.

'*Mikey, I led you to this cottage. It's yours because you obeyed me when I asked you to come here.*'

He caught up with Carrie who was staring across the Lake. 'Carrie. It's ours.'

'Mikey, we haven't got any money?'

'The Lord has spoken. He has given it to us.'

'We can't afford it though?'

'Trust God, He'll find a way.'

They returned to Colfax. The next day he received a call from one of the congregation. A couple from the church had decided to sell their fifteen foot camping trailer and donate the money to the Audenlake Church, their son had gone off to college and they felt they could make do with a tent for their breaks instead. They had felt God would want Audenlake to have the funds so Mikey put it down as a deposit on the Cottage by the lake. He used it at weekends staying there with Carrie and also it was ideal to crash over after midweek meetings with the leaders.

Mark had now been welcomed into this fold, deciding to stay on as long as he could and within weeks got used to a new routine of his own. He would help Carrie with the grocery trips and jobs around the house then in the afternoon Mikey would sit on the porch and study The Bible, teaching Mark. Midweek he would join the leaders at the Island, with the absence of Jacob who Mark hadn't seen since the first visit there. Mikey told him that he'd moved back to the city to tend to a sick relative.

Most evenings Carrie would make dinner. Mark tried to help out when he could and did his best to prepare an English roast for his American hosts. It wasn't quite like his mum's back home and the Yorkshire puddings were soggy but they enjoyed it. It was a relaxing time and he soon began to forget about the stresses he had left behind in England especially since sending signed papers back to Gordon who would have control by proxy of the lottery case. The music shop agreed to hire him again whenever he returned and Mark knew litigation could take years so what was the point of rushing back when there were so many fresh adventures in the USA? He wasn't with Jo but he had a new life so maybe it was all supposed to work out that way in *his movie*.

Two months passed and he grew to enjoy the outdoors more and more. He loved the fresh air, the tall pine trees and wildlife. The leaders took him fishing and white water rafting; they introduced him to a lifestyle he hadn't seen before, away from computers and mobile phones which Mikey discouraged except for his own use to run the church and emergencies, he said technology was stealing the art of real communication and community which Mark tended to agree with. For the first week he'd been there he had felt lost without these gadgets but in a similar pattern to his time in the retreat it was soon obvious that he could happily live without them. The only calls he made were on a landline once every few weeks to Will, Lauren and his parents to update them of his adventures. Will was open-minded and happy for his friend but he didn't want to get involved with debating belief, they always disagreed on that issue after Mark's *conversion*.

Mark on the other hand was embracing the ideas and ways of Audenlake Church. Where once he was mad at God, now he sat and listened to Mikey intently, he felt that being with him could lead him on to something deeply spiritual, beyond the physical concerns of the earthly body. The song *Meant to Live* by *Switchfoot* was often on the CD player in Mikey's house encouraging him to embrace the bigger picture in life and he challenged Mark in front of the other leaders in order to make him grow. He would say that he was *too immature to step up to the plate*, or *held back by spirits of doubt*. Mark sometimes got mad at first with Mikey for doing this but he realised there were going to be spiritual growing pains just like physical ones when maturing in faith. He thought that if he kept persevering and growing then God would find a way for him to remain there. Mark's epiphany wasn't exactly Peter Parker morphing into Spiderman but he knew that he could achieve so much more than he'd done so far.

Then there was Beth.

After a month she had told Mikey and Carrie about her feelings for the new Englishman and they arranged a day out. The weather was turning colder and so it was decided the four of them should go up into the mountains snowboarding followed by a *special* meal at the lakeside cottage.

Beth was very pretty and didn't wear much make up, a bit older than Mark and a good snowboarder. She helped show him the basics and he enjoyed getting close to her as she propped him up and demonstrated positions but he still spent most of the day on his backside or face down in the snow.

They returned to the pine-bound cottage on the lake and after a meal they were left alone on the porch. The different coloured Autumn leaves made the surroundings even more spectacular.

He watched Beth as she looked out over the bay with her thick long blonde hair moving gently in the breeze.

'Thanks for the help today.'

'Oh it was fun. I've never seen someone fall over so much.'

'You look very nice by the way.' He said.

'Even in dungarees and a bright red ski jacket?' she laughed. 'I always think I look like a giant tomato in this thing.'

'I love tomatoes I guess.' Mark laughed.

She reached into a woven bag, handing him a neatly wrapped parcel.

'Go on. You can open it, it's nothing much.'

He pulled at the neat ribbon and opened it. Inside was a small painting of him sitting by the lake.'

'Wow.'

'I did it from memory.'

He turned it over,

For our English friend, with blessings and love from Beth.

'I don't know what to say. It's amazing.'

Mark looked into her bright blue eyes and she smiled sweetly. The afternoon sun had made the porch warm and it was one of those moments he knew he'd always remember. They didn't come along many times in a lifetime.

'I can't believe we've never really talked to each other.' He said.

'All in God's timing. We have to be cautious, some men church hop looking for a woman and my calling is here at Audenlake so I like to keep my friendships close to home.'

He studied her face and felt that perhaps he could learn to love another woman eventually other than Jo or maybe it was his loins talking to his brain rather than any deep aching of the heart. All he knew was that she captivated him and the moment was perfect.

Inside the house Mikey sneaked a few looks from the kitchen.

'Leave them to it.' Carrie said.

'I'm just checking.'

'She's a grown woman Mikey.'

'Yeah, one who went astray once.'

'Why don't you just let go, she can handle herself.'

Mikey walked over to the coffee pot and put it onto a tray next to some mugs.

'The devil prowls around like a hungry lion, you know why I can't just let her go. I'm their spiritual guide, the father of the house Carrie.'

'I know that honey but you can't control everything that they do.'

Mikey slammed his fist on the table spilling the bag of coffee. 'I'm trying to help them so they don't make the mistakes I did out there.' Carrie grabbed his shoulders and looked into his eyes.

'Mikey, *God's in control*, that's what you are always telling me. Stop trying to do His job for him.'

'I want to know if it's him, the one Dean prophesied about. Why hasn't the spirit told me about the money yet?'

'Well why not bring the subject up with him?'

'He's gonna think I want something out of it then. I don't want him to think I'm after his money, that's not why I need to know but if God has plans for him to get it somehow and remain here then...,' Mikey took a deep breath and held Carrie tight, kissing her on the neck, 'I just want what's best for our people you know that.' He picked up the tray of coffee and iced tea and walked outside to the porch.

'Are you two getting along okay?'

'Oh we're fine.' Beth said, smiling at Mark. Carrie joined them with some cheesecake and they sat down.

'I think we should say a little prayer and give thanks for such an amazing day.' Beth said, taking Mark's hand in hers and Carrie's with the other.

Mark noticed that Beth had a small eagle tattooed on her wrist. He had also seen intricate fine patterns tattooed on her feet when they had first met. He wanted to know about them, how and where she had got them. As he listened to her pray in a soft sweet voice he thought that perhaps he could start a new life in America after all.

PART FOUR - WHERE THE HEART IS

'And with your love, I know with all my heart I can win. Cause I'm looking for something to believe in.'

- Ramones,
'Something to Believe In'.

CHAPTER TWENTY-EIGHT

Another month rolled by and Mark had only days before his visa expired which presented quite a few problems with immigration laws. Mikey suggested leaving the USA for a few weeks with Beth and go up into Canada. Re-entering was going to be difficult though as US Customs were some of the most stringent and thorough in the world. If they thought anything was slightly suspicious then they could ban Mark from entering for years. He didn't know how he would cope if that happened and breaking the law in a foreign country was not the most favourable road to be headed down in his opinion.

He had fallen for the new life he'd been introduced to over the past three months and couldn't just wave goodbye to Audenlake Church, to Mikey and Carrie and most of all Beth. Their relationship was growing daily and he thought that they might stand a good chance of becoming a permanent item. It was a very slow process compared to dating as he knew it, so many rules especially when it came to *no sex before marriage* but it forced them to talk more and pray together which formed a bond. If they messed up by jumping on each other too soon Mikey said it would be like opening a Christmas present in summer so they had people to account to within Audenlake Church. If they felt the *urge* to get physical then they had a number to call and people to counsel them through temptation.

There was one more idea up Mikey's sleeve and a possible way round his imminent departure date. It was significant that he delivered the news to him on Dead Man's Island. When the midweek meeting came round, Mikey drove him out to Emerald Bay. Dean and Red were already there as usual, waiting in the boat and they set off across the lake. It was getting colder now although Lake Tahoe hadn't been frozen over since the late eighties according to Dean.

Mark had made the journey many times since he arrived; it felt part of his routine however the moon over Emerald Bay looked especially beautiful that evening with some hazy smoke across the water. Maybe he was taking in more detail because he was conscious it was possibly his last trip for some time, he thought.

They sat around the crackling fire drinking hot apple cider from a flask, something Mark had been introduced to since living in Colfax. In the distance they could hear the occasional small boat cruising the bay. They reflected on the past three months together with Mark among them, the amount he had grown in his faith and trust, the humour he had brought into the group and their delight that he was treating Beth with such respect. It was noticeable how much they were fond of each other.

'I always knew you and I were supposed to meet that day.' Mikey told him.

Mark nodded. There were a lot of things that seemed to fit starting with the vision that John, the Pastor from the Church back in England had about him going overseas and the lake then there was Mikey buying the lotto card and most of all it seemed to be the ease with which he settled into life among these people who were like extended family to him now.

'There are some deep roots being put down here,' Mikey said, 'it's taken a while for God to speak clearly about this but he's told me something about why this happened. Dean and I had the same prophecy about you before you even came, a man from your country would find us and he would have a significant revelation while he was here.'

'You never told me before.' Mark said.

'We wanted to wait and see if it was you.'

'How did you know for sure?'

'There was something else, something only you would know.'

'Which is?'

'This person would have made a false idol and suffered as a consequence.'

It made sense to Mark, the false idol was obviously the lottery money and he had worshipped at its feet costing him everything, his wife, his job, his home and almost his sanity. There was a chance the court case would go through and they might still win but it didn't matter to him anymore. He hadn't heard from England in three months so maybe it had served its purpose, to lead him to Audenlake. Whatever happened with the case was inconsequential; he had a new path now. Like having small pieces of a jigsaw that didn't make much sense until you stood up and saw the full picture.

'What do I do Mikey I can't do anything about the visa and there's insurance for a start?'

'You don't need *in*surance when you have God's *as*surance.' Dean said.

'I know but that's not going to cut it at accident and emergency.'

Mark laughed.

Mikey leant forward. In the firelight his eyes seemed more intense.

'That's the least of your worries now. See, it's more dangerous to go back.'

'Dangerous?'

Mikey held his gaze. 'God led you here for a reason, are you going to just walk away from that?'

'I thought I was just coming out here to find Jo, I didn't expect all of this.'

'That was all part of God's plan, can't you see that now? It's time to choose Mark.'

Before he could answer two men approached carrying flashlights. At first Mark thought they were park rangers, there wasn't supposed to be overnight camping on the island but Mikey had insisted it was his right to be there. They all stood up and Dean pointed his flashlight back over at the men. The first man looked like he was in his early sixties, the second was thick set, younger with a beard. Pastor Louis and one of his elders called Wayne.

'What are you doing here Louis?' Mikey said.

'I was just passing.' He said in a very calm and deliberate voice.

'What do you want?'

'Who's this Mikey? A new recruit I see.' He pointed to Mark.

'He's our guest,' Mikey stepped between Mark and Louis, 'I'll ask you again, what do you want?'

'Mikey you need to stop this nonsense.' Louis said firmly.

'You came all the way here to preach at me?'

'We're here in peace. You know that Mikey.'

'You drew your sword the minute you set foot on my island Pastor.'

Mikey said the word *pastor* with disdain. The atmosphere was tense; Wayne looked like he wanted a piece of Mikey given half the chance, his fists balled up at his midriff. They had a history dating back to when Mikey had left the Church and caused friction and chaos.

'We've come so far to talk to you and reason things out. God himself has been asking me to come and intercede on His behalf it's been confirmed so come on, just a small piece of your valuable time?'

'I've told you a hundred times you need to stay back in Seattle with your sheep and keep to your own business.'

'Beware wolves in sheep's clothing.' Pastor Louis said. He seemed very sure of himself and unafraid of anything. Wayne was a more nervy character, shifting from foot to foot itching for trouble.

'How long have you been out here in the wilderness Mikey? Pastor Louis asked. 'And how many people are in this Church, a dozen, maybe twenty?'

Mikey stepped up to him slowly. Mark had never seen him so unsure of himself but somehow this older man had rocked him. 'I told you the last time you interfered it only needs one man to make a way. This isn't about how many people you can get into a nice new building Pastor.'

'Perhaps, but only those who saw Christ's resurrection can call themselves an Apostle Mikey, you know that deep down.'

'Is this a bible debate now?'

Wayne began speaking in a foreign tongue loudly. Mark had heard some of the men praying like that in both countries and it was still quite strange to him. Dean said that it was your spirit talking to The Holy Spirit, when you couldn't put something into words it spoke for you from deep in your soul.

Mikey yelled at him to shut up and pushed him away, Wayne responded by lashing out at him. Dean and Red were over him in seconds and threw him to the ground, he rolled over and pulled Dean's leg out from under him. Mark didn't know what to do, should he join in or watch, run perhaps, they could be armed. Wayne stood up and charged at Mikey knocking him to the ground. Mikey kicked his boot up into Wayne's groin and the big man slumped down to his knees. Mikey drew back his fist as he knelt up to strike again but Pastor Louis grabbed it. Mikey looked at him in the firelight and for a moment he saw the man who had saved him from a road to ruin. This image was swiftly replaced by the religious figure that had got in the way of his calling. He pulled his arm free and stood up.

Red was helping Dean back on his feet while Wayne rolled around cursing. Mark sat with his mouth open wondering if Pastor John and Ben ever had meetings like this in Cornwall. It was more like a wrestling bout.

'It's never too late.' Louis said to Mark, walking over to him.

'For what?'

He looked at him in the dim light and Mark caught a good glimpse of the man that had once tamed the younger and wilder Mikey.

'I pray that The Lord will answer in your heart somehow.'

'Leave him alone.' Mikey shouted.

Pastor Louis bent down and helped Wayne up who was still cursing and groaning. 'I'm sorry Wayne got over excited and we couldn't resolve anything tonight Mikey but we'll be praying for you.'

As they reached the top of the steps down to the water Pastor Louis turned. 'I love you Mikey.'

Mark was quite impressed, anyone who remained so calm when things were kicking off was pretty cool in his book. He wondered if he was with the right people. What about the answer Pastor Louis prayed for, what was it?

The leaders sat round the fire laughing about the bust up and drinking. To them it was just horseplay, they were used to a few punch ups now and then, not to initiate them but if someone *drew their sword* first then they had a right to defend themselves and their kin. Mikey had met with plenty of occasions when people challenged his authority as an Apostle.

'Why did he turn up tonight?' Mark said.

'It's a sign that you need to stay with us.' Dean said.

'How long for?'

Mikey looked straight at him with his dark penetrating eyes.

'Ten years.'

CHAPTER TWENTY-NINE

'An apprenticeship, that's good news.' Jan said.

'Well it's kind of *similar* to an apprenticeship Mum.' Mark explained on the other end of the phone. He had to phrase it carefully because if he repeated what Mikey had told him and how long he was going to be away for then they probably would have called the police.

'It's better than moping around.' She said, cupping the mouthpiece and looking at Roger, half asleep. They had been watching a Sunday afternoon movie.

'What about his bloody visa?' Roger said, yawning.

'Your dad says what about your bloody visa?'

'Mikey is sorting it out.'

'Well as long as you're happy. We do miss you.'

'I miss you too mum.' Mark said.

The phone line crackled.

'Hello, Mark? It's your dad, Roger.'

'I know who you are you don't have to keep saying that every time we speak on the phone.'

'I'm not paying for another bloody college course.'

'It's not like that one it's to do with Church leadership.'

'You just want to work Sundays I bet but it's not like that you should ask the Vicar round the corner from us.'

Before he could answer his mum's voice came back on.

'Don't listen to him he had too much red wine with his dinner he's been asleep through most of the film.'

Mark remembered his mum's roast dinners with crispy potatoes and loads of thick gravy.

'Is everything okay Mark?'

'Yes of course, it's fine Mum.' He said, feeling a bit homesick.

'I bumped into Will the other day at a petrol garage, he was with Lauren taking her and the kids to some fair bless him. He said he hadn't heard from you and the number there didn't work anymore?'

'Really? I'm out at the cottage at the moment, I'll check when I get back to the house. Tell him I'll give him a call soon. Everything is great here, honestly.'

~

'I never dated an Apostle before.'

Mark leant over and took Beth's hand. They had stopped the car near to the cottage where the others were preparing for the ceremony. *His* ceremony.

'It's bloody terrifying.'

'Does that mean this isn't goodbye?' She said.

'Well, that's the thing. Mikey has said that I can just stay on, working for the church under a study visa or something.'

'That's amazing, I knew this was meant to be.'

'Dean is going to get me some kind of part time job too.'

'Well I trust the Apostle I'm sure he's in control and whatever your concerns are he's the voice of God in our lives.'

'But what if Pastor Louis was right?'

'I'm going to pretend I never heard that.' She turned away and fiddled with the ignition keys.

'It's okay to challenge things Beth, we've still got our own minds. I thought you used to like Pastor Louis?'

'Everyone can be open to the enemy corrupting them besides, Pastor Louis isn't who I follow now. We can't serve two masters Mark.'

He desperately wanted to believe her, she seemed to come out with these things that were paraphrased from Mikey, almost robotic but when she looked into his eyes he knew that he wanted to be with her at Audenlake. What was he frightened of, didn't he want adventure and a new life away from the bad memories in England?

Mark was about to take some tough life changing decisions and Mikey had warned him that he would be tested in many ways and it could mean making sacrifices, even if that included leaving your past and all that it meant to you behind. How would he explain that to his best friend and family back in England? He wasn't sure how Will would take the news or understand about the call on his life, that Mark was according to Mikey, going to be an Apostle after ten years of preparation and start his own splinter church. Will was always flipping his views on spirituality but he fervently avoided any form of organised religion. A mixture of elation and panic ran through his body as he stroked Beth's hair and pulled her closer.

'So, are we going to your ceremony or am I dumping you here?' She said.

'You wouldn't do that.'

'Come on then, let's bury old Mark and raise the new one!'

~

As Mark prepared to leave the past behind, Will was anxiously trying to call him from England but the number was still out of order. He had been flicking channels on his TV when he noticed the Kabelson Industries logo flash up. The evening newsreader was discussing a court case.

> *'And Kabelson Industries are having a bad week. It looks like finally the couple from Warwick who lost a claim to their fortune are to get their day in court.'*

Will watched as Mark's legal representative appeared on the screen being interviewed. Gordon seemed excited and optimistic especially with the taped evidence available. The journalist turned to Nigel the inspector who had once offered the couple counselling.

> *'It was unfortunate that our representative said those things at the time. She is no longer with us. I am dealing with her old role and can confirm that was her own opinion at the time and not those of Kabelson Industries.'*

Will had not been in contact with Mark or heard from him for some time. It wasn't like him to leave it that long and something didn't feel right about the situation especially after hearing via his parents about a *Church Leader Apprenticeship.* He looked at a picture of them on top of his television taken on stage at a gig in St Albans.

'Come on Stevie, help us out, what would you do in a situation like this mate?' He said.

The phone rang. It was Lauren.

'I was just thinking of you, well Stevie actually.'

'Have you seen it on the telly?' She said, excitedly.

'I've just been watching it but I can't get hold of Mark. It's going to happen with or without them as they signed over by proxy to the legal team.'

'Shall I call Jo?'

'I think I might have a better idea.' Will said, looking at the picture of the band.

~

'You ready to die?' asked Mikey.

Mark nodded as he steadied himself in the water. Even though it was early Winter the giant outside spa pool at the pine-bound cottage could be used all year round. Steam blew up into the night sky. If it had been a few months previous then they could have baptised him in the lake but it had got too cold for that.

The leaders surrounded him holding his shoulders and arms. In a circle around the pool Beth and the other church members joined hands.

'Sometimes you're going to hate me. You're going to question how God could let you go through some of what is ahead of you,' Mikey said, 'but let me assure you in front of these people here we are all going to walk with you.'

As the crowd agreed in unison Mark felt the warm water swallow him and the sharp taste of chlorine in his mouth. The arms that had lowered him down pulled him back up through the water. As he broke through the surface everyone clapped and cheered. 'Welcome officially to Audenlake Church.' Dean said, patting his back hard.

Mikey hugged him.

'Welcome to your future!'

Watching them from a safe distance in the woods was someone who would do his best to prevent Mark being dragged any further into Mikey's world if he could. He knew that it was time to challenge this self- proclaimed leader before he got the new recruit more tangled in his complex web.

CHAPTER THIRTY

Jo circled the aisle once again, unsure from the first time if she really had seen the familiar figure. She walked towards him as he picked out a six-pack and looked at the price sticker. He began muttering about exchange rates in an English accent. It had to be him.

'Will?'

Will turned around, his eyes widened and a big grin spread across his face. He put the beer back into the fridge and scooped her into his arms.

'It's really you? I can't believe it.' She said, holding him around the neck.

'Yeah it's me.' He said, squeezing her tightly and planting a big kiss on her cheek. To onlookers it might seem like they were lovers. It didn't help that they included Jo's boyfriend.

'Hey buddy, what do you think you're doing?'

They looked up the aisle to see Nicholas standing there with a basket in one hand and a melon in the other.

'Nick, this is Will.'

He shrugged.

'Mark's best man?' She added as Will hugged her again.

'Hey will you stop touching her.' Nicholas said, angrily.

'Nick, he's my friend, cool it.'

'He was all over you, what's the deal here?'

'I love her.' Will said, proudly, flicking back his mop of wavy hair.

'Oh you love her?' Nicholas spluttered.

'Yes I do and if you let me into your life I could learn to love you too.' Will held out his long arms and walked towards him. Nicholas backed away.

'Get away from me you jerk.'

Will started to laugh and so did Jo. Nicholas remained long faced which made them laugh harder.

'What the hell is he doing here anyway?'

'That's actually a good question, what *are* you doing here Will?'

'I was going to call but there seems to be something a bit odd going on with Mark.'

'Oh great.' Nicholas said.

'Why don't I get this pack of beer and we can go talk about it?' Will grinned. 'Bloody cheap booze over here isn't it?'

~

'He's not staying at my house!'

'Nick. He's my friend.'

Nicholas poked the barbeque grill and flipped a burger.

'He's your ex husband's friend. Why can't he stay at your parents?'

'Because my mother hates Will almost as much as Mark,' Jo said, remembering the wedding speeches, 'and Mom has no sense of humour.'

'Jo. I won't allow this.'

'Quiet. He'll hear you.'

Will poked his head out from the upstairs window and waved. He had a giant towel wrapped round his head that made him look like a big Smurf.

'Great shower! I feel ten times better. Are you sure this is okay me staying here?'

'Sure, make yourself at home then come get some food it's nearly ready.'

He disappeared.

'Mark could be in trouble. You don't know what he's like.' Jo said to Nicholas.

'Who cares? He hurt you so forget him and his friends.' Nicholas said slapping his metal spatula onto the burger, this time squishing it in half.

'Stop it Nick.'

'We've loads more in the freezer.'

'You know what I mean, stop running Mark down.'

'Why, because I'm right? You just have to sit back and if they win the case over there then you get a cheque.'

'But what if Mark's in danger, why can't anyone reach him? He was obsessed with this case when it started.'

'Whether or not he's lost in the mountains or dead in a ditch it doesn't involve us.' Nicholas said. Jo sat there and wondered why she cared. Maybe Nicholas was right, it didn't really involve her anymore.

Will walked out into the garden with a doorknob in his hand.

'Hey I'm sorry but is this supposed to come off like that?'

Nicholas looked at him as he handed it over and then reached into his pocket producing a little spring.

'Erm, and this bit sort of fell out too.'

~

It took them a few days to work out where Mark was staying in Colfax. Even though the number was out of order the exchange still listed a residential address and they made their way up there, through the smaller roads at the mountain foothills. Nicholas had surprisingly offered to drive them but it wasn't out of kindness, deep down he didn't trust Jo with this stranger from England. His plan was to dump Will wherever Mark was and so he had persuaded him to take his case and put it in the back of the car.

They pulled up to Mikey's track road; a grey pick-up truck was in the driveway. Jo recognised it from the day Mark had come to collect the papers. 'Maybe it's best we don't go in mob handed eh?' Will said.

'Do you want me to come?' Jo asked.

'I'll knock first and see.' Will got out and walked up the driveway, banging on the door. There was no answer. He could hear the sound of a radio coming from the back yard and went to open the gate. Jo called out of the window. 'What if there's a dog?'

'Hopefully he'll eat him.' Nicholas muttered.

'I'm good with animals,' Will said, 'I used to have a guinea pig.'

Will walked along the pathway that ran alongside the house, the sound of the radio got louder. As he turned the corner he could see it, it was actually a small hand-held TV set left on a hammock that was still swinging. He peered into the house but couldn't see anyone.

'Hello?' He said.

'Hello.' Replied the voice in his ear.

He spun around to see Mikey just feet away. Will physically jumped in the air. 'Bloody hell, where did you come from?'

'Well I should ask you the same thing but judging by the accent you're probably from Australia.'

'England.' Will wheezed, still catching his breath.

'Yanking yer chain, I knew that. Let me see, Warwick perhaps but originally somewhere further south?'

'How did you know that?'

'Mark told me all about this guy called Will and you pretty much fit the description.'

'So I'm in the right place then. Is the fellah around?' Will said, creating a bit of space between them and looking inside the house for signs of Mark.

'He's out. You want to wait?'

'That would be wonderful.' Nicholas shouted, standing with Will's case by the gate. Jo walked past him and over to Will.

'You okay with that or you can come back with us if you want?'

Will looked over at Nicholas who was shaking his head subtly at him.

'I...I better stay here for when Mark gets back. Thanks.'

Mikey watched them studiously, it made her uncomfortable and she wasn't sure she wanted Will just dumped there.

'It's not far for us to come and get you, we'll be back tonight, you're our guest at the moment.'

'You must be Jo,' Mikey introduced himself and took her hand kissing the back of it, 'I can definitely see why Mark was so heartbroken when I found him.'

She took her hand back and wiped it on her jeans. Nicholas stared at Mikey, he didn't like people touching Jo very much.

'What's Mark still doing here, I thought he was supposed to be back in the UK?' She said.

'He's hanging out with us having fun. Lots to keep him here now too, the people love him, one in particular. Very nice girl, pretty, blonde!'

He wanted to test to see if she still had feelings for Mark. Mikey had become very astute at gauging people, even the slightest twitch could say so much, the actual words people spoke apparently made up just seven percent of what they meant during communicating, tonality was around thirty eight percent but the body however indicated a huge fifty five percent. You just had to know what to look for.

'Come on Jo, we need to be heading back.' Nicholas said.

'Drop by anytime.' Mikey said.

Jo picked up the case again and they walked back to the car.

'We intend to. Be back around ten to get you okay?'

Mikey put his arm around his shoulder as they watched the car pull away.

'Tell me Will, do you like beer?'

CHAPTER THIRTY-ONE

Mark returned from the grocery store with Carrie and walked into the house. He put the food bags on the table then looked out onto the porch. Although it was late in the year when the sun shone it was still beautiful to be outside in the fresh air.

'Hey Mikey,' Mark shouted, then noticing the other guest, 'Hey Will.'

'Grab yourself a beer.' Mikey said.

Mark stopped dead in his tracks.

'You okay?' Carrie asked, 'you look like you just saw a ghost.'

He burst out onto the porch.

'Will? I don't believe it.'

'I've been trying to contact you for ages'

'What are you doing here?'

'I was worried about you mate you went right off the radar.

'Blimey.'

'Plus I bring tidings of great news Caesar.' Will said dramatically.

Mark laughed, he'd missed his best friend, they knew each other so well.

'What news? Come on spill it you idiot.'

'Your lottery case, it's on apparently?' Mikey said, watching Mark for his reaction.

~

Nicholas and Jo had been arguing since they dropped Will off. He hadn't liked the closeness they shared or her new interest in Mark. They were due to have her parents over for dinner but she had called and cancelled. Nicholas had spent a while putting wood into the log burner while Jo tried to calm him down. Eventually he had gone upstairs, returning with a handful of letters that Jo recognised at once. They were the ones from her shoebox.

'I was hoping it wouldn't come to this.'

'Where did you get them?' Jo said.

'It doesn't matter. What the hell have you got them for?'

'You don't have anything from your ex-girlfriends?' Jo walked over to him snatching the letters. 'What about the photo collage from *Cindy* under the bed?'

'From years ago, so what? I read those letters Jo. They're from after your break up and that's different to memorabilia.'

'I can't believe this. You don't have the right to go through my personal things.'

'Burn them.'

'What?'

Nick pointed to the log burner. 'Burn them now. Say good riddance to Mark and his crackpot friend and we'll forget about it.'

Jo looked at the letters, angry that he had been through her things. She did love him, she thought, but what about Mark, did she still love him too and who was the mystery blonde Mikey mentioned, had he moved on after all? Jo looked down at the letters as Nicholas prodded the logs, prompting the flames to lick around the burner. Jo squeezed the letters tight.

'If you want to spend your future with me then you need to let them go,' he said, 'I have your things packed in a case and I'm not fooling around anymore. You need to choose what you want.'

Jo hesitated. She lowered them forwards towards the heat and took one off the top handing it into the flames. One of the corners began to take and Nicholas grew impatient flicking the whole lot out of her hand before she had let go and she watched as the white envelopes turned to brown then black and finally to ash in the flames.

'Now the rest.'

'The rest?' She said.

'The shoebox, it's in the kitchen. It's all got to go.'

'But those are my CD's. Surely ...'

'It's all got to end now Jo. Come on, be a good girl and fetch the box.'

'But Nick, it is just music.'

'It's *Mark* music.'

Jo walked into the kitchen and saw the shoebox, he had rummaged through everything, the CD's, notes from Mark, cards, a Valentine he'd made with a picture of them stuck onto cartoon bodies. She picked up a concert ticket, *Wembley Arena* when Mark had got them front row for *The Cure*.

She was being asked to burn it all, but she could still keep some in her mind. Would Nicholas want her to forget *memories* too eventually? In the other room he was joyfully playing with the ashes of the letters, waiting for the other bits. He kept calling, calling her to come, to *be a good girl* and burn the bridges with her past forever.

~

Mikey went back inside the house to fetch some more beers leaving Mark and Will alone for the first time. The wind was blowing around the back yard and Will shivered. 'Bit parky here isn't it?'

'You get used to the weather, I love being outdoors now.' Mark said.

'It is nice around here,' Will said, you've been up on the mountains then?'

'We go snowboarding every week it's brilliant.'

'Nice. I didn't know you could use a board.'

'They taught me. I feel bad actually, I should have told Mikey about the court case, he seemed a bit annoyed I didn't mention it before.'

'It's your business, why should he have to know everything?'

'Oh mate, Mikey has changed my life since I came here.'

'Yeah, you seem happy but you should have let us know you were okay, what happened to the landline and your mobile phone?'

'Doesn't work out here, it's not tri-band.'

'My e-mails, you never replied?'

'Mikey teaches us to avoid technology, he thinks that it's killed off our ability to communicate.'

'Well it backfired this time, I just spent hundreds on a flight when an e-mail would have cost me nothing.'

'You know what I mean.'

'Hang on,' Will said, 'I saw a laptop in the lounge and a mobile phone on his belt?'

'They're for running church affairs and emergencies.'

Will wasn't convinced but at least he had traced his friend and could now set about getting him to return to England.

'So come on, how's Jo?' Mark said, changing the subject.

'Good. It was really great to see her again.'

'Has she got really out of shape and become ugly in the last three months?'

'Absolutely.' Will said, looking the other way.

'You're lying aren't you?'

'Yup she's still gorgeous. She's coming to pick me up later with her new bloke. Total nob.'

'She wanted a divorce, I knew there would be someone else.'

Mikey walked back onto the porch handing them beers.

'So what exactly does your day job involve as an Epistle?' Will said.

'*Apostle.*' Mikey corrected him.

'I say *Epistle*, you say *Apostle*.' Will sang . He could see Mikey wasn't impressed and stopped quickly and took a swig of beer.

'It varies,' Mikey said, 'I have to look after people's welfare and keep the church running and...'

'... which I hear is a lakeside cottage and a barbeque? Sounds cushy.' Will said.

'Cushy?'

'It means easy.' Will beamed, clinking his beer bottle on Mikey's.

'You couldn't begin to grasp the magnitude of what I do I'm afraid.' Mikey said sternly.

'Yeah but someone pays for this house, where does the money come from? It doesn't fall from the sky so it probably comes via the congregation I expect, like most organised religion.'

'This isn't religion pal, this is a *relationship*.' Mikey snapped.

'That may be but what's stopping you having a day job too like the others who pay into this system and keep a roof over your head.'

'Will!' Mark interrupted.

'I'm only asking.'

'It's okay, the man asked me a fair question.' Mikey said, staring at Will. 'It's not about what it pays me, it's what it takes out of me that's significant. It'll cost you everything you have to be an Apostle. You risk being ridiculed, hated, despised and misunderstood.'

'Sounds like my life mate, maybe I should be one.' Will nudged Mark.

Mikey was getting annoyed with his flippancy.

'For one *you* don't choose this, you are chosen and second, it will cost you your heart and soul. You willing to do that?'

Will picked at the beer bottle label.

'I couldn't really because I don't believe in the soul. I believe in eternal forces.'

'Oh no, here we go.' Said Mark.

'I've been working on my theory see that it's a continuous sort of energy.'

'And what do you call this energy?'

'*The Giant Mingmop*.'

Mark spat his beer out and nearly choked.

'The what?' Mikey said.

'Just my own name for an eternal infinite force that can't be contained, labelled or worshipped.'

'And how do you know this?' Mikey said.

'The Giant Mingmop told me.'

Mikey looked more confused.

'I'm just making a point mate,' Will said, 'you call it one thing, I call it another but lets look at the facts as reasonable men here, we are finite creatures with finite minds, the universe is infinite and therefore cannot be contained in our brains.'

'What are you talking about?' Mikey said.

'Look at it this way, trying to understand the universe is like trying to put the sea into a plastic cup where the cup represents you or me and the sea represents the universe. No matter how much water you scoop up you can't ever hold that cup up and say *look, here is the entire sea*. It can't be done.'

Mark sat open mouthed, his friend may have been nuts but he actually put his point over well. Mikey looked into the yard for ages in silence then stood up.

'I'm going to check on dinner.'

As soon as he disappeared Will turned to Mark. 'You don't believe all that Apostle stuff do you?' He whispered.

Mark looked disappointed. He had hoped that Will might be a bit more open-minded. 'This is why I never called you about it, you don't get it at all, you and *The Giant Mingmop* I mean what the f...?'

'It's no more outrageous than all this mumbo jumbo about you staying here for your destiny.'

'He's a good guy Will.'

'He's a work shy freeloader living off vulnerable people, even I can work that out and I've only been here for a day.'

'Mikey works hard spiritually, it takes time to commune with the spirit that's all. You can't do that when you're working.'

'He's really got to you hasn't he?' Will shook his head. 'There aren't modern Apostles even I know that.'

'Who told you that, The Giant Mingmop?'

Mark was getting frustrated with him. 'He's not saying I'm the second coming or anything, it simply means *a messenger* that's all, from the Greek word *Apostolos*.'

'It's also the name of a kid I went to school with. He used to put salad in my parker hood at break times.'

'See, it's just a name.'

'It's making me uncomfortable. What would Stevie say if he was here?'

'I don't know.' Mark put his head in his hands.

'He'd tell you that you were a bollock head and throw you head first into that bin over there. Then we'd go and watch some cheerleaders in a bar or something and have a laugh.'

'Mate, it's not all about having a laugh it's about life and death. Once you meet the others you'll see they are just normal people.'

'I came out here to find you, not start dancing in the moonlight around a lake. What about the case, are you going to come back?'

'No point.' Mark shrugged.

Will shook his head. 'But your visa waiver must be due to expire, I thought you have to leave anyway?'

'I've been hired by the Church on a study visa.'

'Show me.'

'It's not on paper, it's Mikey's word.'

'Oh my God, this is bad mate, you'll get banged up. The Sheriff round here won't swallow all this you know.' He shook his head.

'Will, just back off, I'm happy here so don't ruin it.'

'I'm going to use the bog,' Will said, standing up, 'don't turn into a spirit walker or Bigfoot while I'm gone.'

Will went to walk into the kitchen but hadn't seen the clear storm door, promptly bouncing his head off it.

'And mind the storm door.' Mark said.

Will said hello to Carrie as he passed her in the kitchen, still rubbing his head.

'Don't tell me, the storm door?' She laughed.

'We don't have those where I live.'

'Mark did it when he first came here too. I'm fixing to make some cheesecake if you're staying a while longer?' She said.

'That sounds nice.'

'I love your accent. It's sort of different from Marks.'

'I'm from further south.' He said.

Carrie asked him to say a few different phrases. Will soon had her laughing hysterically. Mikey walked into the doorway holding some records that he wanted to show them, hopefully changing the subject from the nonsense Will was coming out with. It was either that or he would end up assaulting the annoying idiot.

'Not interrupting?' He said.

Will turned and felt the full blast of Mikey's cold stare. 'I was just giving your wife a few phrases from back home.'

'Did you need the bathroom son? It's through there.'

Will smiled at Carrie and ambled past Mikey towards the hallway.

'He's cute.' Said Carrie in a hushed tone as Mikey put the records down and went to the fridge. He took out three beers and began taking the tops off with his hands.

'He's trouble Carrie, that's what he is so mind what you say to him you hear me?'

'Sure, I think it's nice that Mark has people who care about him enough to come looking.'

'Mark's very vulnerable and if we lose him now he might never come back.'

'It's weird that you were right about this money thing not being over.' She said, stroking his hair.

Mikey looked out onto the porch at Mark and spoke quietly.

'I'm trying to find out as much as I can. If he goes to England and they win the money then who knows what that could do to him.'

Will, who had been standing in the hallway listening, was now more worried than ever that Mark was in over his head.

CHAPTER THIRTY-TWO

Will sat in Jo's parents lounge. He looked around and saw a picture of Jo on her wedding day. Mark's image had been obscured with a new photo inserted into the frame of Nicholas on the beach in bright yellow shorts next to Jo in her glamorous dress.

Her parents looked at him and shook their heads, they weren't expecting anymore people from England to appear on the doorstep like this, even if he had been invited by their daughter.

'Would it help if I said sorry again for that speech at the wedding?' Will said.

Jo's father stood up. 'I'm going to clean my gun,' he looked at Will, 'Rifle Club this afternoon if you'll excuse me.'

'Is it a big gun?' Will stammered as Jo walked in with coffee.

'There you go. You look like you need it almost as much as I do.'

'I just want to get this clear in my head Joanna,' said her mother, she didn't call her *Joanna* unless she was very stressed, 'You've left Nicholas and want to move back home, you also want this *person* to stay for a while as you try to convince Mark, your ex-husband to leave a strange religious group?'

Jo looked up at the ceiling and bit her lip. 'That's about the measure of it except that Mark is my estranged husband, not my ex.'

Her mum looked at the suitcase by the door, the last time it had been there Jo had been leaving to start a new life with Nicholas, good old dependable, clean living boy that he was. On top of the case was a shoebox, safe and unharmed by any flames.

Jo had never truly felt like it was home at Nicholas's house and after his increasingly controlling behaviour and demands she had left him, collecting Will from outside Mikey's house in Colfax before showing up at her parents.

Will had explained the situation regarding Mark and *The Apostle*. With Nicholas out of the picture she was free to help Will if she wanted to without all the guilt. That was if she *really* wanted to help. Mark was buried in her past but maybe he still had the power to dig it up again and that scared her.

'I'm going to have a lay down.' Jo's mother said, shaking her head and walking out.

Jo put her head in her hands.

'I wondered why Mark hadn't responded to the divorce papers, he was half an hour away all this time.'

'You definitely don't have feelings for him anymore?'

'The jury is out on that for now. After Stevie died I kept dreaming that Mark came out here and we were back together. I guess I'll only know if I see him face to face.'

Will reached into his coat and pulled out a folded piece of paper.

'I didn't know if I should give this to you or not but now you've left that bloke I suppose it's okay.'

Jo opened it up. It was in Mark's scrawly writing.

'What is it?'

'The song he started working on when you split.'

> *I heard our song the other day,*
> *the one we got on our second date and I*
> *thought it would be forever.*
> *For just a moment we were on the sand again,*
> *dreams held tight between our hands but then,*
> *first love always comes at a price... and oh love*
> *it passes in a second, love, don't let it slip away.*
> *And I want to be, long to be, I want to be with you.*

Jo read the rest of the song quietly, hearing Mark's voice speaking the words in her head.

'Okay, I want to help. Just tell me what you need me to do.'

'They invited me to one of their gatherings on Sunday which I passed on and then he was going on about some special meeting mid-week but Mikey said that one was *chosen people only* and I didn't like the way he said it.'

Jo sipped at her drink and toyed with the old wedding ring that she'd found buried in the shoebox. 'We're not really talking crazy cult here are we?'

'It's too subtle for that but then again that's how people get drawn in, they're seduced with mind games,' Will said, 'people don't go following some bloke with a shopping trolley who talks to bushes.'

'He's only been here three months though.'

'They can do it in an hour like that neuro-linguine.'

'You mean linguistics?' Jo said.

'Yeah, they get people into an emotional state and then set up a catch phrase or something and then they can use that catch phrase to put them in that state.'

'He's been hypnotised?' Jo said.

'Not quite but that's just the start, see this Mikey bloke would have got

Mark feeling lost and depressed after he found out you wanted the divorce and then offered Mark a positive lifeline, a way through the pain that's how co-dependency works.'

'How do you know all this stuff Will?'

'I read a lot of magazines in the bath.'

She laughed. It was good to have him around again he always put a light touch on any situation, so had Mark when she first met him.

'So what shall we do? He's an adult and you can't just kidnap him plus, if he's started to believe this guy then he's going to resent interference.'

'Have we got time to find *The A-team*?'

'Damn fool Will. I suggest we get a good nights sleep and then tomorrow we can start researching who these people are.'

Jo got up and pulled the window curtains shut, unaware of the stranger sat in the car opposite that had been watching them for the last hour.

~

The Audenlake Church leaders had been on Dead Man's Island since sunset. It was cold and they huddled around the fire in their overcoats handing around hot apple cider. Mark was there for the final part of his induction, in order to show his commitment to the church. He felt so different out at the lake, removed from all that lottery nonsense and heartache with Jo. Pastor John from Cornwall had seen this place in his future and Mikey and the leaders had confirmed it. It was too much of a coincidence not to be real. The Mark that had suffered the frustrations, divorce and breakdown was going to be history and the new Mark was at the beginning of a *breakthrough*.

It had been great to see Will again but in some ways, like Mikey said, God had arranged for that as a sort of closure, he couldn't help it if his friend didn't understand; they both had their own lives to lead.

Red had made a torch from a branch and some rags soaked in paraffin. They walked down towards the back end of the island, a flat patch of land with trees surrounding a tiny copse with a small dome tent in the middle. Red put the torch into the ground and lit a prepared fire for him.

'This is where we come to die.' Mikey said.

'What?'

'Metaphorically, die from the old life.'

'Oh. Right.'

'Although there was an English Captain who built a tomb on here once.

He wanted to be laid to rest here.'

'What happened to him?'

'His body was never found, it's somewhere at sea I heard'.

'Don't tell me, it wanders the island?'

'No, you sicko, I'm just telling you the island's history. We want you to stay here, meditate, think, seek.'

Dean threw him some blankets, a mountaineering sleeping bag and a food parcel.

'How long am I being left for?'

'We'll be back tomorrow to get you. It will be a new dawn. Don't just sleep, listen because God is in the detail Mark.'

'Why does it have to be out here?'

Mikey walked up to him and put a hand on his shoulder. 'We're here to bury you, to remove those things that aren't of God.'

Mark remembered his cousin burying him in sand as a boy, it was really frightening and he got cramp. 'I'll get claustrophobic. Can't I just sit in the tent?'

They laughed. 'He means metaphorically,' Dean said, 'we're not literally burying you. Look there's even a small propane heater if you want to use it.'

'Blimey, you had me worried.'

'All the fear and insecurities, the new Mark won't need them cos he's going to walk tall from this night onwards.'

'And don't be afraid of the wild creatures.'

'Metaphorically you mean?'

'No he means real ones,' Red said, 'we got bears, big cats and coyote so stay by the fire and just don't show em you're afraid, if they smell it on you then it's feedin time at the zoo my friend.'

They climbed back up toward the top of the island leaving Mark to lay the blanket across the tent entrance and make himself comfortable. The water lapped against the island, the moon shone brightly and the night wind that crept around his neck felt like soft hands. He pulled his collar up. 'Walk tall.' He said to himself, watching the torch burn.

He heard the outboard motor start up around the other side of the island. The leaders sailed away, leaving him there completely alone. He felt anxious at first, it wasn't the most normal thing he'd ever done but as Apostle Mikey said, life was about adventure, about boyhood dreams of the wild frontiers and exploring. Why stop there? Just because the masses got sucked into tedium and routine, it was up to you to break out and find the life God wanted you to lead if you had enough guts to seek it out. Don't be crushed by mediocrity, Stevie used to tell him. He remembered something they had agreed when forming the band, '*We have to be really good or really bad but never ever mediocre.*'

The leaders had left him with a guitar, Mark still loved to play as often as possible. He sat strumming chords for a while, remembering songs, one of them was a song for Jo from the time she left. He looked around for the food box, eating a cheese roll washing it down with the last of the hot apple cider.

The sound of scuffling in the dark was unnerving. It was probably a mountain squirrel after his food if they even had squirrels in the mountains, he wondered. He now knew they had bears and big cats and coyotes but it wasn't that was it; surely they wouldn't really leave him on an island with savage creatures? He felt something on his leg. He slapped at it. Mosquitoes. It wasn't good for him to be near water late at night. He found the bug spray that he always kept close to hand and drenched himself in it.

Coughing and spluttering he decided to escape the cloud of smelly clinical repellent he had created and go for a pee. He turned his flashlight on and walked to some bushes near the water about twenty feet away. On the way back he began to shine the flashlight beam around like a laser, a light sabre. He made noises and pretended to strike an opponent, he was Luke Skywalker waiting for Darth Vader. Cut, thrust, advance, pounce and then trip over a tree root. 'Shit.' He rolled on the floor half laughing and half in pain. It was the same leg he'd bashed on the lottery sign the year before and the ligament still ached now and then, especially in the cold. It was going to be a long night.

CHAPTER THIRTY-THREE

Jo and Will knocked at the door of Mikey's large house. There was no pick-up truck in the drive this time and no noise from the back yard either. It was getting dark and they didn't know where the pine-bound cottage was. The weather forecasted possible snow and Jo didn't fancy getting the wheel chains out if she could help it.

They hadn't managed to find out much about *Audenlake Church* apart from some comments on an online forum. Nothing too sinister just some aggrieved person who had crossed paths and disagreed with Mikey's views. Their login ID was *Wayne68*.

As they drove back up the track road they passed another car which pulled over to let them through. Will had a picture of Mark and he waved it out of the passenger window as they drew parallel.

'Excuse me, can I ask you if you've seen this man?'

The old man in the other car looked at him curiously and nodded, driving into the top of his driveway and getting out. Will walked over to him and held the picture up again. The man squinted in the dusk, raised his glasses onto his head and then smiled.

'Oh I know this guy. Speaks just like you and hangs around with Captain Kooky.'

'Captain Kooky?'

'Our neighbour, he thinks he's a prophet or sumthin.'

'An Epistle?'

'Apostle.'

Will broke into song. 'Epistle, Apostle, ta-da-da, let's call the whole thing off.'

'Are you on drugs?' The old man said.

'Sorry, it's a code, I was just checking you out.'

'Is this guy in trouble, are you with the police?'

Will took the picture back from the man.

'I'm from Interpol and over there, that's agent Juliet Foxpants.'

Jo couldn't hear what Will was saying so she waved and smiled sweetly.

The old man waved back slowly.

'We're worried about this man because he is in danger. Do you know where Captain Kooky and the group he's with might be now?'

The old man went into the glove box of his car and pulled out a map of the area. 'They were at the store earlier, here, heading off towards the Lake, Marv and Mary at the store reckon they go to this area,' he pointed towards Emerald Bay, 'you know they forecast snow earlier so you don't really want to be headed over there tonight.'

Jo had joined them and looked down where the man pointed. 'I know that area but it's going to be tough finding him and it's getting late, maybe we should wait until they get back.'

'Nah, we'll spot him.'

'Will, Lake Tahoe is around twenty two miles long and twelve miles wide.'

'Oh. Can you narrow it down to roughly where they were going in that case?'

The old man scratched his beard. 'I was chatting with his wife last year, she brought us over a cheesecake and seemed pretty normal but you never can tell. She mentioned an island and there's only one on the entire lake.

'They said something about *Dead Man's Island.*' Will said.

'Nobody calls it that anymore, it's called Fannette Island.'

'Well the first one does have a more mysterious ring to it.'

'We need to make a move. Thanks for your help.' Jo said.

'No problem, good luck with your search Officers.'

She looked at him quizzically as they walked back to the car.

'That was a funny thing to say.'

'I know, old people eh?' Will waved back at him.

As they drove out of the track road onto the highway a car and trailer followed them from a safe distance.

~

At first Mark had found it hard to meditate with all the distractions but he finally managed to block them out, the itch on his leg eased up and the noise in the shrubbery quietened. He was moving into a deep trance state, strumming a chord on the guitar over and over again. He found a sense of calm, losing himself in it and discovering that there was just the moment he was in and wonderful peace.

Mark felt the cold night air in his lungs, the blood rushing around his body, the sound of his heart slowed, his breathing became rhythmic and relaxed. It took a lot to find those places in the modern world but the rewards were well worthwhile. When he eventually opened his eyes again an hour later the flame was out on the big torch. Through the night a distant sound echoed around the bay, too harsh to be an animal, it was a man made sound.

~

The car behind sounded its horn again and Jo cursed. She couldn't believe how impatient the driver was. The headlights dazzled in the mirrors so she decided to let him pass at the first opportunity, pulling into a cut out. The vehicle that had been following them for miles pulled in behind her.

'What is he doing?' She said, annoyed. 'He's been dying to get past for ages.'

'Shall I go speak to him?' Will said. 'I used to do martial arts.'

'No you didn't.'

'I did, I joined in a demonstration in the town centre.'

'Yeah and that little boy threw you over his shoulder.'

'He caught me off guard.'

Jo looked back at the car and saw the door opening.

'He's getting out.'

'Maybe he's just lost, he hasn't got a gun has he?' Will said, pushing his door lock down.

Jo wondered if she should drive off, the car looked like it was towing a boat on a small trailer so she might be able to lose him easy enough. It was too late though as the man sidled alongside the car and knocked on her window. Jo wound the window down a little.

'Can I help you?' She said.

~

It had been four hours since Mark had been left on the island and now he was wide-awake. The meditation session had been good but now he was jumpy. There was a boat on the water and it seemed to be getting closer. The leaders weren't supposed to be returning until the morning so who else could it be, Park Rangers, teenagers with beer out to get loaded? His mind began racing with all sorts of things. Maybe it was Mikey and the others, they wanted him to deal with his fear so it could just be a test to say they were leaving him there on a cold night and then come back. He began to creep round the side of the island. If the boat didn't go past then whoever it was would find him there by the fire and the heater, they were like beacons.

The boat's motor spluttered to a halt. Mark's breathing was deep and heavy he could feel his heart pounding in his chest; so much for calming meditation, he thought. There were two people moving closer, hushed voices, one was a woman's. He could see them in silhouette as they walked up the steps towards the stone teahouse their footsteps passing across the peak towards where the leaders had left him. Then another thought rushed him, what if it was Pastor Louis, back to try and confront Mikey?

As he reached the main steps that led to the small jetty he could see a boat and it wasn't the same boat the leaders used. He panicked. There was no time to think, he had to get off the island. He ran down the remaining steps and began to untie the boat, there was just time if he was quiet to push it away from the shore before starting the motor. He wondered what would he do at the mainland though, it was miles from the nearest house and freezing cold and he didn't have a car?

There were heavy footsteps to the right of him, twigs snapping as a figure approached from the bushes switching on a flashlight. He span around ready to defend himself.

'I appear to be lost,' came a familiar voice, 'I think I should have turned right at Dover.'

Mark squinted in the bright beam.

'Will?'

CHAPTER THIRTY-FOUR

They huddled around the fire and propane heater and shared a flask of soup that Jo had brought along. Mark was surprised she had accompanied Will to find him and even more surprised to see the man who had led them there. Jacob told Mark about the real reason for his sudden departure from Audenlake. Mikey had challenged him over his commitment to the Church because he had issues with some of the methods the Apostle employed with people. Jacob was fine with it for years but then as he matured he felt restricted and undermined by Mikey, his own thoughts and opinions seemed to be robotic versions of the Apostle.

Mikey's view was that Audenlake came first and as long as your other interests didn't interfere with that then you were cool. Jacob had met a woman from another church in a nearby town one day and asked her along to Audenlake. She found Mikey overbearing and preferred her own Church so Jacob wanted to go to try it out and get to know her more as he really liked her but Mikey acted strangely towards him when he went back a second time. He gave him an ultimatum and that was why he had left him on the island that night, to choose. Jacob lived with Dean and his wife and when Jacob still felt the same in the morning Dean had been instructed to give him a ride home and then pack his things, requesting that he did not contact the others.

Jacob knew what Mark would be going through especially the fear of leaving. Mikey said that if you left Audenlake then you were out of God's protection and would be in danger, you could even *die*. Usually this meant spiritually, he loved dramatic metaphors to drive home a point. Mikey would tell stories of people who had left and who had eventually come back to the fold or there were some who had left and had accidents. The truth was, as Jacob discovered, people had accidents' anyway as it was part of everyday life. When you were looking for significance in something you'd see it so this occurrence would be seen wrongly as punishment for not being obedient.

During his own deprogramming Jacob had read an article about the way the brain processed information using the example of a car. If you decided to buy a bright blue Chevrolet compact then you'd start to see them everywhere but most of the time your brain filtered out this information as unimportant although it was always there. The mind could only store and process a certain amount of information so you wouldn't have paid much attention to every blue Chevrolet compact car you saw before, it wasn't important. Suddenly, when you thought about buying one, it took on a more significant relevance and you noticed them.

Jacob used logical things like this when he became depressed as triggers set up by Mikey had previously led him to believe everything was a divine sign to keep him where he wanted him to be, not by force but by clever manipulation in the mind. It took a lot of counselling and understanding for Jacob to be able to break free completely. He didn't lose his faith in God but he became wary of groups with a framework like Audenlake.

'I'd never fall for all that trigger stuff though.' Mark said.

'I was in your position once. There's more ways to control people than physically. I'm not saying Mikey is trying to hurt you, he genuinely thinks that he is doing us some kind of divine favour but it's feeding a need for him too.'

'Co-dependency.' Will said.

'That's right, Mark you need to hear me out and meet some of the people who have also left groups like this, you can't do it alone.'

'Are you going home with Will for the court case then?' Jo said.

'I don't know. This is so much to take on board, why is it that when I work something out in my head another load of crap comes in to mix it all up again?'

'Nothing's stopping you coming back, we're not here to kidnap you.' Will said.

'Don't be afraid, I can help you with all the stuff going through your head.' Jacob said.

'But it made sense because I had prophecies, some in England relating to the Lake and then the chance meeting with Mikey and the lotto scratch card he bought suddenly, he never knew about my past the day we met.'

'It's the car thing again.' Will said.

'Mikey said that I was going to be someone eventually and I like it here.'

'You already *are* someone Mark.' Jo said.

'Doesn't matter where you are, over here or in Warwick, it's what's inside you that counts.' Will added.

'You can never make it big in your home town, Mikey had to leave Seattle and I remember from the band days we were always more welcome further afield.'

His mind was spinning, why had they come to the island and disrupted his meditation when he was just about to find peace?

'It's another way to control people, he calls it *Love Bucketing*.' Jacob said.

'Blimey, what sort of weird stuff has been going on?' Will joked.

'Don't laugh at me.' Mark snapped.

'We're not laughing at you oh great Love Bucket.'

'Shut up Will! Everything is a joke to you but my faith is something that can't be taken away; whatever happens at the Lake or in England, it's still there not like that money, not like a relationship going wrong. If I go back I might lose the plot again.'

'Mark, we're here to help you.' Jo said.

He stood up and paced around the fire.

'No, *you* are the test. This is to trick me from my calling, all this rubbish about bloody blue cars.'

Jo was getting frustrated, she'd had a long couple of days too. 'We're a test? Lauren has been phoning up wondering if you are ever going back, Will has just flown thousands of miles because he was worried about you, Jacob has driven up from Seattle and I'm here on a freezing island with my ex-husband when I could be relaxing in a hot tub. And you have the nerve to say that we are trying to test you or somehow drag you away from this place?'

'I'm not your ex-husband yet.' He muttered.

'If you'd gone home when you were supposed to then you would have found the papers.'

'Don't worry I'll sign them.' He shouted.

From the darkness they heard the sound of clapping. It got louder as Mikey walked out of the trees into the copse, flanked by Dean and Red.

'Who do we have here?'

'I don't want trouble Mikey.' Jacob said.

'You shouldn't have drawn your sword then.'

'They've got sodding swords?' Will whispered to Jacob, picking up a branch of wood.

'He means metaphorically.'

Will put the branch down by his side. Mikey walked over to Mark putting his arm around his shoulders.

'You okay buddy, how you liking the night so far?'

Mark felt like he was on a fairground ride, being alone on the island was one thing but seeing your worlds collide like this was too much to compute in his brain.

'So, what has Jacob been telling you Mark?'

'He just helped the guys find me.'

'Did he now? In some ways this has turned out better than expected. It was your night to be tested and choose so maybe I should thank him.'

Mark looked at Jacob, maybe it was a set up to test Mark's loyalty to Audenlake perhaps Jacob was like a double agent? He thought.

'A divided army is a weak one,' Mikey walked over to Will, 'mind if I take that?' He grabbed the stick from his hand and laid it on the fire. 'You know, when I left Seattle I had nothing, just me, Carrie, a few of these guys you see here,' he looked up at Jacob, 'when God calls you it's a deep knowing inside. You hear that voice and you *know*. It's stronger than loyalty to any place or any person.'

'Is this about me or Mark?' Jacob said, defensively.

'Both of you I guess. You can always come back Jacob you know that, unless you are enjoying life with the happy deluded masses out there?'

'No thanks.'

'Pity. So that leaves you Mark, are you with us?'

'Mikey you know I'm with you.'

'One hundred and ten percent?'

'That's actually impossible.' Will said.

'I'm sorry, did I ask you to talk?' Mikey spat.

'No but I need to point out the flaw in that statement because there's no such thing as one hundred and ten percent.'

'Do you ever stop running that mouth of yours man?'

'I enjoy freedom of speech.'

'Are you mocking me?'

'I don't know, am a mocking you Mr Epistle?' Will smiled.

'Apostle!' Mikey shouted, getting up in his face, Will still towered above him and couldn't resist doing it once more.

'*Let's call the whole thing off!*' He sang and then clapped Mikey's cheeks.

Mikey was livid and pushed him hard in the chest. As Will rocked back Mark went to intervene but Dean and Red were on him, holding his arms. Jo stepped in between them all.

'Hey, he's just joking with you, back off.'

Mikey looked her up and down. 'And what about you Miss, what brings you to my humble island?' He had an intense look in his eyes that gave her the creeps but she wasn't afraid of him.

'I think you'll find it's Emerald State Park's island.' She said.

'Really, you hearing this guys?' Dean and Red laughed.

'Maybe you can ask one of the rangers, I'm sure they'll be here soon.' Will said.

'Is that so?' Mikey took a deep breath. ' Let's see shall we, Mr Ranger?' he bellowed, 'come on guys, help out.'

Dean and Red joined in, calling out loudly. Mikey turned to Jo, 'Nah, I don't think anyone's coming but don't worry we're not here to hurt you.'

'Oh I'm sorry, did I look scared?' Jo said, in a squeaky voice.

'I can see why you married her now Mark. She's got spirit, I take it you've told her about Beth?'

'No.'

'Our Mark here is quite taken with his new lady and she loves his accent as you can imagine.'

'Congratulations.' She said.

'It's not like that...'

Mikey interrupted, 'If you go back and get that money then would Beth be enough to make you return Mark, would your calling play on your mind or would you just go back to worshipping money because I hear it didn't work out very well last time, right Jo?'

She knew it was a cheap dig but countered with one of her own.

'And correct me if I'm wrong but don't you have some sort of tithing system here?'

'We do. What's your point?'

'If Mark won the money then that's not a bad Christmas bonus, ten percent of a million pounds.'

'Nobody forces members to pay a tithe.'

'But it's preached so he'd feel compelled with a bit of encouragement to hand it over?' Will interjected, 'Thousands of dollars, it's subtle control all of this can't you see Mark?'

'Mikey thought that you would bring money for the future of the Church,' Jacob said, 'they looked you up on the internet.'

Mark looked at Mikey who was shifting around the fire poking at it.

'Is that true?'

'God can use anything at his disposal, we had to make sure it was the person in Dean's vision but that's not why I wanted you with us.'

Will laughed, 'If you believe that then you really do need help. Come on Mark, let's get out of here and go home.'

'But where is Mark's home?' Dean said.

'England.'

'You can't say that for sure because then you're trying to control him just like you're accusing us, smartass.'

'I think you'll find it's on his passport.' Will said, dryly.

'Okay, we're going round in circles here,' Mikey said, 'if Mark wants to leave the island and Audenlake then it's with my blessing. I don't want your money Mark, I don't want to control you I was just offering you a chance to be what

God intended you to be. If you are going to be used to help others and fulfil your destiny then it means sacrifice, it's not like getting a swanky job with loads of benefits, it's hard and it costs.'

'And what if I don't?'

'He'll raise up others for the job, he doesn't *need* you, He's offering you something, do you really want to walk away from all of that?' Mikey threw a stick on the fire and walked over to him. 'It took a lot of orchestration for God to lead you here so it's time to choose carefully. There are two boats tied up on the island and whoever is in the other boat when we hit that jetty on the mainland, they're out of your life forever. You make a stand here tonight and bury that part of your life but it's your choice entirely.'

Mark looked between the leaders and his friends. 'Don't make me choose, why can't I just have everyone in my life?'

'You can't have divided loyalties,' Mikey said, 'stand with us and we promise we will walk you through what God has prepared for you, it was waiting for you even before you were born. Alternately go back to slavery and bondage.'

'Don't call us that,' Will said, turning to Jo 'why the weird nicknames?'

'Come on, it's getting late and I am freezing cold,' she said, 'Mark, you have to do what you have to but this sounds like a bunch of crap if you want my two cents worth.'

Mark was exhausted, there was much at Audenlake that he wanted to believe in but to make it so permanent? Hours before when he stepped onto the island he wanted to spend his life there and within an hour of Jo and Will showing up his faith and direction were under fire. He weighed up the other path, Jo was with someone new and wanted a divorce, Will was a grown man and as much as he would miss him, surely he'd be okay? He knew that coming to the States had been cathartic, Mark felt like a new person and Beth was helping him to learn to love again.

All eyes were now on him as he decided his next move. Mikey pulled the torch out of the ground, re-lit it and handed it to Mark.

'It's up to you now. You lead the way to the boats and make your choice.'

They walked up to the top of the island and down the steps on the other side where he could see the two boats. He turned around and looked at the people who were getting into each one, contemplating each journey that the vessel would take him on over and over in his mind.

'Okay, I've chosen.'

CHAPTER THIRTY-FIVE

The boat cut quietly through the water. Mark sat watching the other boat adjacent to them. They were perhaps only thirty feet apart yet significantly separated as they were headed towards the same shore but on two very different voyages.

It had been a difficult decision but he thought it was the right one. Weighing up what mattered in life compared to comfort zones and familiarity meant sometimes choosing the less trodden path. Mikey was right, he would have to learn to trust him even when sometimes he didn't understand what was going on. If Mark was destined to be an Apostle and help others in the future like Mikey and Dean predicted then that would also mean personal sacrifices like leaving the past behind and staying for ten years. Jacob and the others had tried their best to reason with Mark but he was an adult and had his own decisions to make. You could listen to as much advice as you wanted but eventually you had a choice, and that was your own.

Will had been distraught by the decision but he wanted to support his friend, they had said an emotional goodbye and it had been one of the most difficult things he had ever done. Jo was quiet as she embraced him and kissed him on the side of the cheek. For a moment Mark remembered everything they had ever been, just from the smell of her skin. As he let go of her she seemed to hang on for a bit longer, almost tugging at him not to go but it was too late. They had made their way to the boats and set off. Mikey seemed quietly triumphant but he didn't gloat out loud or go on about it as he'd waited for Mark to board and sail off.

Halfway across to the land on the other side, Will shone a flashlight over towards Mark.

'Don't forget there's no real beer here mate.'

'Or a decent cup of tea.' Jo added.

'What about Sunday Roast?' Will added.

Dean could see Mark was wrestling with his decision as he listened and watched his friends across the water. 'You did the right thing man. I left lots of friends in Seattle when we came here, it gets easier.'

'I've known Will since I was a teenager.' Mark said.

'We'll be closer than friends, we're you're family now, joined by the spirit. You have a good woman in Beth too and that lady over there, she's your past.'

'I'll sign the divorce papers Jo,' Mark shouted over, 'just post a copy to the house.'

There was a few seconds silence then her voice came back across the water.

'No rush, I'm single again for now.'

Mikey watched Mark's face change. Even in the low light he could see mechanisms in his brain clicking into life. The new recruit wasn't landed just yet. Mark stood up, he felt like someone had just woken him from a deep sleep. Mikey and the others told him to stop rocking the boat and sit down but he ignored them.

'I thought you had someone else now?' He called over to Jo.

'I did until he asked me to burn my CD's.'

Mark grabbed a flashlight from Dean and shone it across to the other boat. It found her in the darkness and lit up her face. Jo put her hand up.

'That's right, shine it in my eyes you tit.' She yelled.

'What CD's?'

'Stuff from our time together like the one you got me in Stratford.'

'Why didn't you burn them?'

'Same reason I didn't burn the valentine card you made me, the ones with the silly faces and the notes you used to leave around the place.'

'You kept all that?'

'Of course I kept them.'

'Remember the sirens on the rocks?' Mikey warned him. 'Don't be fooled man, she'll run you aground.'

'That wasn't in the bible, that was in Jason and the Argonauts or something.' Mark said, looking down at him.

It had started to snow and Mikey blinked up at him, his face anxious and twitching. He hadn't seen him like that since Pastor Louis had showed up on the island. They told him to sit down again but he wasn't hearing them, his mind raced. Jo wasn't involved with anyone and she'd kept all those things that must mean she still had feelings for him and that changed everything, wasn't that the reason he had gone out there in the first place, maybe he was being fooled by Mikey?

He looked at Jo's silhouette on the other boat. Why did he have to choose like this? Surely life wasn't just about clear hard lines in black and white, it was grey, blurred and patchy, it overlapped. You couldn't put it into boxes and keep them separate because life was messy.

'I still have the silver pick holder you got me.' He hollered.

'Your favourite picks were shark fin shaped right?'

'And your favourite colour is blue,' Will joined in using a high pitched voice that used to make Mark laugh, 'and you have a birthmark that looks like a bird dopping on your leg.'

'Do you reckon there are sharks in the water here then?' Mark cried out.

'I don't think so, it's too cold.' Jo laughed, her voice wavering with tears that had begun spilling onto her cheeks. He shone his flashlight over again through the falling snow which dissolved on impact with the dark water. The boats were close as they approached the mainland and there wasn't much time left.

'You said when we hit the jetty the other boat would be my past?'

'Yes, so say your good-byes and sit the hell down!' ordered Mikey.

'You also said the choice was mine?' Mark patted him on the head.

'What the hell are you doing?'

'God speed my friends. God speed!'

'It's too late to change your damn mind.'

'It's never too late.'

Mark leapt overboard into the water, the splash soaking the leaders.

'It's bloody freezing.' He screamed, swimming towards the other boat.

'Get back here, you Jonah.' Red shouted after him but Mark didn't hear, he just kept pulling at the water with his hands and kicking his legs, swimming as hard as he could. It was so cold he wondered if he would make it.

'You'll die out there.' Dean called.

Jacob had turned the boat towards him.

'Come on Mark, you can make it.'

'Shall we go after him?' Red asked Mikey.

'Why would you do that you idiot? I don't chase anyone, they come to me.'

'I was trying to help.'

'Well it would help if you shut the hell up.'

'Hey Mikey, calm down and stop cussing.' Dean said.

'You want to make me?' He stood up, nearly tipping the boat over.

Mark reached the other boat and they pulled him on board, flopping around like a seal gasping for air, they covered him with blankets. Jo held him in her arms as they watched Mikey and the leaders shouting at each other, drifting in the water.

'You chose us then.' Jo said.

He nodded, shivering as his teeth chattered away.

'Why didn't you burn that stuff?'

She smiled, kissing him on the forehead.

'That's a good question.'

CHAPTER THIRTY-SIX

Will looked around the diner overrun with women in various soccer tops.

'Am I hallucinating?'

'There's a ladies soccer tournament, I saw it on the welcome board in the foyer.' Jacob said, as a woman in an Arsenal top walked past and smiled.

'Right, I think this is my territory. Tell you what, you get the beers in, a few bowls of chips and salsa and I'll find us a table.'

They had stopped at a motel and restaurant complex, the snow had got heavier and it seemed a far better idea to stay for the night somewhere warm rather than putting the wheel chains on and attempting the mountain roads. Will and Jacob had gone looking for food leaving Mark and Jo to talk.

Next door in the motel room she wrapped a huge towel around her and walked into the main suite. On the TV music channel was a video, *Just For Tonight* by an English band *One Night Only*.

Mark lay on the bed with his eyes half-closed. 'Remember this on the mix CD I did for you?'

'I do. You like alot of songs with the word *just* in it. Any reason?' Jo said.

'I *just* do that's all.'

She sat on the end of the bed and shook her head. His jokes were still awful.

'Does it make you homesick for England?

'Makes me homesick for what I had and lost.' He said.

'Come on, the showers free.' Jo said. 'Don't get all soppy on me now.'

'I'm too tired to move let alone shower.'

She walked over to him.

'I'll count to three.'

'Huh?'

'One, two...'

'I just need to sleep.'

'Three.' She grabbed him by the arm and pulled him off the bed.

He lay there moaning.

'You stink of lake water. You aren't sleeping with me like that.'

'Are we sleeping together?' He said.

'You know what I mean, unless you want to share with Will? I said I'd sleep on the same bed not inside it and you're stinking the room out.'

He stood up and stretched. 'Thanks for coming to get me.'

'It was Will who wanted to, I'm just the taxi ride.' Jo said.

Mark began to unbutton his shirt.

'I can't believe that bloke asked you to burn the CD's.'

'Well, obviously I couldn't believe it either or I wouldn't be stood here with my dirty ex in a motel.'

'Dirty, what sort of dirty?' Mark pulled the last of his buttons open and grinned. He did his Mr Bean dance.

'Oh my God you are still as corny as ever. Just shower will you?'

'I will I'm just a bit freaked out by tonight, it's surreal you turning up and all that Audenlake stuff in my head, I don't know what to think.'

'Give it time, you've been through a lot.'

'I think I may owe you for showing up. Having you there tonight made me think differently when it mattered.'

'Come on, even if you had stayed on that boat you wouldn't have seriously spent ten years with those people, would you?'

'I really thought I was going to.' He said.

'Well, go wash and get some sleep, plenty of time in the morning to think about all of this.'

Mark padded over to the bathroom door then turned around, looking at the music video, remembering when he had danced around to it with Jo in a pub back in Warwick.

'Thanks for keeping all that stuff Jo.'

'Not all of it, I'm afraid the letters ended up in the fire.'

'Letters?'

'The ones you sent from Cornwall.'

'I didn't think you got them, you never wrote back.'

'You hurt me Mark. What did you want me to do?'

He looked sheepish, removing his shirt and throwing it at the linen basket in the corner.

'What if they were right, what if I'm running from my destiny Jo?'

'I can't answer that but I know Jacob's been through every situation that you're going to go through so you're not alone.'

'I never came here for the Church Jo, I came to find you and I'm so sorry for what happened between us. I was hoping that maybe now we could spend some time together?'

Jo looked at him and was about to say yes but then she thought about the break up. 'Mark it's been a weird couple of days for me too, it's too late to do this tonight.'

'It's never too late,' Mark said, 'that's what you used to say.'

'Shower!' She walked over and pushed him into the bathroom, closing the door between them.

By the time Mark had got out of the shower Jo was fast asleep on the bed with a blanket over her. He borrowed a big T-shirt and jeans from Will's case and climbed in beside her. In the dim moonlit room it felt just like they were back in their house in Warwick. He got as close as he could without disturbing her, the smell of her skin and gentle breathing on his face was still so familiar. Jo's hand moved and touched his. She mumbled something about waking the baby. Whatever she was dreaming about she looked peaceful and so he squeezed her hand gently and drifted into a deep sleep.

~

Mark woke up mid-morning. Jacob was asleep in the other bed and Will was on the Sofa groaning and waving his hand around.

'I don't like you or your manky chips.' He mumbled.

'Will.'

'No, I want the chilli sauce on them still you twot.'

Mark sat up and walked over, shaking his friend.

'Where's my kebab?' Will said.

'Never mind your kebab, where's Jo?'

Will stretched. 'I was having a dream about Take Bap. Did you know it's changed managers now?'

'Great stuff, but have you seen Jo?'

'I came back about four this morning and she was there beside you.'

Mark walked to the door; he looked across the car lot as a group of women in soccer gear walked past the space where Jo's car had been. The snow had turned to slush in the morning sun and she had gone without saying goodbye.

Mark kept pulling the long jeans up, he'd already rolled the legs over and over, Will was much taller than he was and his own clothes were still damp.

'I would have brought some shorts if I'd known, they'd fit you like normal trousers I reckon.' Will said.

'These will have to do for now.'

'We need to get your stuff back, where is it?'

'Mikey's place, I'm not going there.'

'What about your passport?'

'Shit.'

'I'll get them,' Jacob said, sitting up, 'I ain't afraid of him anymore. What's he going to do?'

'Okay, we'll all go together after I've seen Beth,' Mark said, 'I'm invisible to him now anyway, I chose the other boat.' He scratched his head and laughed.

'So, did you and Jo, you know, *play horses?*' Will said.

'No, it wasn't like that we just slept beside each other, I can't believe she just left without waking me up.'

'Looked more than just sleepy time to me. You were wrapped in each other's arms when I came in.'

'Were we?'

'Yeah, mind you I was a bit drunk. I thought you were a giant badger at first, scared the life out of me and I think I fell over a chair.'

'Where did you get to anyway?'

Will pulled the curtain back and saw the women in soccer gear. One of them looked up and waved.

'You wouldn't believe me if I told you mate.'

Mark walked over to the kettle. 'I'm looking forward to a decent cup of tea when I get back,' he said, unplugging it and taking it to the bathroom sink to fill up. Propped against the mirror was a note written on motel headed paper.

> *Mark, by the time you read this I'll be back in Rocklin and getting changed for my shift. (Some of us have to work for a living!) Good luck in court. If I don't receive a cheque in a few months I'll assume you have run off with the winnings or we lost the case.*
>
> *It was strange and wonderful to see you again but maybe it's best to remember things as they were (before you went weird!) rather than attempt to patch it back together. Love Jo.*
>
> *PS. I will send copies of the divorce papers to Lauren, just sign then whenever you're ready.*
>
> *PPS. You still make that little gurgling noise when you sleep.*

~

Jacob stopped at Beth's house on the outskirts of Colfax. He got out of the car and walked up the driveway. Just inside the porch was his red backpack with his belongings, Mikey had been there first, it didn't surprise him. He checked and found his passport, waving it to the others in the car.

He remembered all those dates when Beth had appeared at the doorway looking so beautiful. He knocked on the door. There was no response but he could hear *Taylor Swift* singing *Cold As You* from the stereo inside.

'Beth, please open up I need to talk to you. I know Mikey's been here.'

There was the sound of feet approaching, a clicking of the lock then there she was, long blonde hair back in a pony tail, her face red from crying. He moved to hold her.

'Don't touch me.' She backed away.

'Beth I need to explain.'

'You lied to me.'

'I didn't lie.'

'Mikey told me everything.'

'That's not a surprise, he's a control freak.'

'You're running away, you chose your ex over me Mark.'

'Is that what he said?'

'Are you denying she came to get you and you left with her?'

'No, I mean yes, I mean no, she came with my friend Will because they were worried about me. Look he's right over there in the car.'

She stepped out slowly onto the porch. Looking down the road she could see Will and Jacob sat on the car bonnet. Will waved furiously and gave a big beaming smile.

'Is he, you know, *special* or something?' She said.

'Yeah he's very special, come and say hello to the guys.'

She shook her head.

'But you have to say hello to Jacob, you were friends for years?'

'He chose to leave us too.'

'Mikey must have told three different stories but it was because Jacob fell in love with someone and wanted to be with her, did you hear that version?'

Beth played with the door handle nervously.

'It's a free country Beth, he can choose what he likes, just like I have, just like you can there doesn't have to be a divide, it's nonsense.'

'You're scaring me Mark I thought you'd chosen the Apostle's vision, I mean he baptised you and they accepted you into the leadership circle, why are you doing this?'

'Something snapped when my friends showed up, like I'd been sleepwalking. I was in a bad place Beth, I was rebuilding my life when I came out here to find Jo and then I got sidetracked. I don't think being at Audenlake is where I should be anymore.'

'Sidetracked? You were led to us, you told me you were.'

'Or maybe it was a series of small coincidences that I wanted to find more significance in. Have you ever wanted a blue compact car?'

'What?'

'Maybe that's the wrong analogy, can I come in and talk properly please it's cold out here?' He pleaded.

'We can't be together now. I shouldn't even be talking to you.'

'After all we've been through I thought we had something, we can still give it a go can't we?'

Beth shook her head. 'It changed the moment you bailed out of Mikey's boat.'

'I can show you England. I'll be your very own tour guide, you can always come back here, it's not forever.'

'I've seen what it's like out there in the world and it nearly killed me. This is my home now, with Mikey, Carrie and my family at Audenlake.'

'But I thought you loved me?'

'I loved the Mark who was going to be an Apostle,' she said, 'not the Mark who bailed on us, I don't know that person.' Her blue eyes pierced him. The sparkle that he had grown accustomed to had gone. In its place was a cold stare, just like the look Jo had when she left him.

She turned, went inside and shut the door.

Mark went to knock again but there was no point he knew she was so deeply involved with Audenlake that he'd lost her.

He picked up his backpack and went back to the car.

'She wouldn't even come and say hello to you Jacob. You knew each other for years though?'

'She's in for the duration I'm afraid.'

'Women are weird mate.' Will patted Mark's shoulder.

'So what now?' Jacob said. 'I can drop you anywhere you want to go guys.'

Mark looked at Beth's house one last time then down at his passport.

'The Airport please, my good man.'

CHAPTER THIRTY-SEVEN

It had been nearly a month since Mark had returned to England. Regular contact over the phone with Jacob helped his recovery. Mark began to understand what had happened like finding a trail of thread in deep woods, he slowly found his way back home mentally. It wasn't easy and sometimes in the night he would have flashbacks, quotes Mikey had drilled into him about a *Jonah complex*, running from your calling.

Jacob however, had been through a much more intense attachment to Mikey and Audenlake than Mark, having been there for many years. He pointed Mark to information about mind control and spiritual abuse and the more he researched the more boxes he ticked of what essentially equated to being in a *cult* when it came to the way Audenlake operated. It wasn't the stereotype one that he had often seen depicted but there were key signs to look for, the programmed cloning of the leader, a dependency on decision making via the leaders, individuals' lives coming second to the leader's direction and plans, former members like himself were ostracised as *losing the way* or *unable to hear the truth*.

Were there *Modern Apostles*? It wasn't for Mark to judge or decide, all he knew was that whatever Mikey and people like him called themselves or believed they would behave in the same way when it came to their behaviour and interacting with other people. He still wanted to believe in God but he had so many questions, maybe even more than before. Was his life governed by luck and random chance or by beliefs and a higher power? For now he decided that he'd work things out in his own head and heart day by day leaving an open door. There were times he really missed the certainty he once had, maybe one day he'd regain it but for now it would be a private matter. He was simply happy to be back in England with his friends and family.

The long litigation case with Kabelson Industries was about to come to a conclusion at The High Court. Litigation wasn't won or lost by a jury, it was a judge's decision based on contract details. Mark and Will decided to journey down to London and watch as both sides presented their cases. Most of the lengthy summing up went over Mark's head and he couldn't work out quite which way the result was going.

'We've been awarded our costs.' Gordon said, leaning over to him.

'So Mark and Jo won?' Will asked, excitedly.

'I'm afraid not.' Gordon motioned towards the exit. As they filed out of the courtroom he explained that the judge said it was unfortunate and he sympa-thised with them but he had no way to enforce payment of the lottery jackpot winnings from Kabelson.'

Outside, on the steps of the High Court, the press were swarming around Nigel who had been promoted to head of public relations at Kabelson Indus-tries in a reshuffle.

'This confirms that we were always right in our decision.' Nigel said smugly.

'Or just too mean?' Said another.

'No we had to protect the integrity of the lottery.'

'Is that why you paid out to all the other people?'

'Will you people get your facts straight?' Nigel snapped.

'More precedents than the USA wasn't it?' Will shouted over the top of the pack.

Nigel pushed past the cameras and got into a waiting limousine. Mark was next out of the court onto the steps.

'Are you disappointed?' A journalist asked.

'Yes and no I mean you would be over three million wouldn't you? But we got to hear a Judge make a decision here today and that was what I always wanted.'

'So what now for the future?' A voice asked from the crowd.

'It's over, I have to move on it's all anyone can do.' He began to walk away.

'We heard that you're going to write a book, is this true Mark?'

'I need to get myself together, it's been a crazy couple of years and there's plenty of time for that.'

'A final word for the people watching?' A journalist said.

Mark thought about it for a moment. 'I have three actually.'

He stared into the closest TV camera imagining who might see that broadcast, not just in the UK but also around the world. It was his last comment on the saga and everyone hushed down and waited.

'I miss you.'

~

They returned to Warwick and Mark moved in with Will temporarily. It was fun again like when they shared a house at college. Despite losing the court case, Mark was returning to his old positive self with each passing day. He even used to smile when he saw the bright orange ball logo in shops and on the television. It was nearly Christmas and they started to rehearse some old band songs using a drum machine. They gaffer taped it on top of a mike stand and called it *Spirit of Stevie*. Then they decided it would be a good idea to call up some old faces and have a festive pub-crawl of old haunts and of course the take away shop on the avenue, under new management and now called *Take Bap! VII*.

The next morning Will woke up to his phone ringing. He looked around at the kebab wrappers and beer cans and realised he was still on his sofa and the option screen to a console game was playing repeatedly on the TV. His mouth was so dry he could barely muster a croaky answer down the phone.

'Yergh?'

'Will, it's Lauren. Are you okay?'

'Yergh.' He crowed again.

'Is Mark there?'

'Hang on.' Will cleared his throat and called out but there was no response. He winced as he sat up and stumbled around looking in the rooms unable to locate his friend. 'He's not here and he hasn't even got a mobile at the moment.'

'Where could he be? It's important.' She said.

~

Mark stood outside the church and watched the happy couple coming out with their friends and family behind them. The photographer asked them to pose and then wait while people filed out and got the confetti ready. Even on a cold winter day it was a wonderful atmosphere. On cue they showered them with the multi coloured bits of paper, each flake full of hope and optimism as it landed. He wished that he could close his eyes and open them to see Jo under all that confetti, to have her back again and a new start. All he had was memories and they still hurt him.

He watched the newlyweds get into a car and drive away, some of the kids began throwing more confetti about before they were told off by their parents and whisked away to the reception lunch. He noticed that some of the coloured pieces of paper had landed near to him, in fact some were still falling down around his head but that was impossible unless someone was throwing it. He turned around to see Will in a green jesters hat with mistletoe on the end.

'Been looking for you mate,' he said, I was worried you'd fallen down a drain or joined another cult or something.'

'You were wasted last night.'

'I can't even remember getting home.'

'We played that new TV game but you kept falling asleep, I think I won by seventeen goals.'

'What are you doing here anyway?'

'Remembering.'

'I thought you were over Jo since all that stuff in America?'

His friend was right, he'd have to stop visiting places like this to remember Jo or he'd never move on. Maybe her stupid boyfriend over there had been right, get rid of the past and everything to do with it if you wanted to be free of it.

'You've been through a lot what with the lottery, Jo then Stevie and the cult business but you'll get there mate. I think we've learnt loads.'

'Have we? I still don't know if this is about luck or belief.'

'Or The Giant Mingmop.'

'Or The Giant bloody Mingmop.' Mark laughed, shaking his head.

'Hang on,' Will said, checking his pockets.

'What?'

'The rings.'

'Rings?' Mark said.

'Oh here they are.'

Will took his hand out of his pocket and opened his palm. Inside was Mark's wedding ring.

'What are you doing with that?'

He opened his other hand to reveal Jo's wedding ring.

'And what the hell are you doing with that?'

Will grinned at him and nodded over towards the Church. Mark turned around and at the doors, in jeans, a black three quarter length army jacket and flashing Santa hat, was Jo. He walked over towards her, not quite knowing if he was dreaming, perhaps he would wake up in a moment in Will's spare room covered in stale beer and take-away wrappers.

'What are you doing here?'

'I got your message.' She said.

'What message?'

'Lauren put the TV clip from the court up on the web and sent me a link.'

'And you came over?'

'Recognise this?' She placed her engagement ring in his hand. 'The question is, do I put this on and maybe even the other one or do I file those divorce papers`, have you signed yours yet?'

Mark shook his head slowly. He looked deep into her brown eyes and felt the dryness in his mouth and the buzz through his body, only Jo could make him feel that way.

'I can't lose you again, marry me.' He blurted.

'We are married!' She laughed.

'Stay for Christmas, give me a chance to show you I'm different.'

'I don't want you to be different I want you to be you,' she said, taking his hand. Mark lent forward and kissed her but she moved away.

'Hang on. Is there anything I should know first? Now is the time to spill if we're going to make anything of this relationship again.'

Mark flipped through his brain for any confessions, then he noticed a *Hey Ho, Let's Go!* badge on Jo's lapel.

'I do need to get something off your chest.' He said.

'You mean *your* chest?' She said, raising her eyebrow.

'No, I meant your badge, I never played with the Ramones.'

'Are you serious?'

'We just met the drummer in London once.'

'You expect me to trust you after everything you told me about that gig, the times you bored me and anyone else who would listen?'

'Yeah.'

'Lauren told me ages ago, I always knew.' She laughed.

'So do I get my chance?' He said.

Jo put her hands to his face and pursed her lips.

'What about your destiny in the States?'

'I was hoping that I'm looking at it now.'

'That was a good answer.'

'So what about you?'

Her eyes seemed to glow again and the light that had gone out for so long was back. 'If you ever hurt me again then you're a dead man, you understand?'

He nodded. 'As long as we have each other...'

'... the rest will fall into place.' She finished.

Will opened his long coat to reveal a small belt-clip guitar speaker and the opening bars of *Just Like Heaven* by *The Cure* played.

He handed over the rings and the couple returned them to each other's fingers.

'By the power vested in me I would like to pronounce myself truly hung over and in need of a bacon sandwich so hurry up and kiss her.'

Mark leant forwards, pulled Jo's santa hat off. Her hair fell down and he pushed it gently away from her face, kissing her full on the mouth. They knew once and for all that wherever they were in the world, home would be in each others arms. Jo thrust her hands deep inside his jean pockets and squeezed him close, as she did a piece of card fell onto the path. Will picked it up.

'What's this?'

'That's the lotto card Mikey got on the day we met.' Mark said.

'You haven't scratched it, you might have won.'

Mark looked at it and reached into his pocket for a coin.

'Will, you have it. Win or lose... it's yours mate.' He said, flipping the coin over to him.

As Mark and Jo danced around to their song Will began to scratch off the foil sections of the lotto card. Small pieces of paper are sometimes worthless and sometimes they are worth a fortune. Mark had journeyed so far since they had first stood at that church. One thing he had learnt was that whether life was governed by *luck* or *belief* or even *The Giant Mingmop*, it was the person in your arms and the people around you who love you and stand by you that matter the most. For that is where you can find *real* treasure, fulfilment and happiness along the way.

The End.

Six Magic Numbers

The Real Story

Six Magic Numbers

This book was inspired by real events that happened to me. Originally I was going to write a factual account but it became laborious and bogged down in places with things that really didn't seem relevant anymore. The idea was shelved for years but people always seemed entertained by the essence of the story whenever it came up in conversation. Many people still dream of winning the lottery and equally dread losing the winning ticket.

The moment I moved towards fiction everything fell into place, I was no longer worried about every fact being correct or detailing long legal cases, I was simply using my experiences as reference and I could create a whole set of fictional characters in new locations. It was only then that the book and screenplay came alive and so did the love story between Mark and Jo. This surprised me as their relationship developed in directions I hadn't planned and not only added another layer to the story, it *became* the main story.

I hope that you enjoy Six Magic Numbers and it makes you think, even if it's just *'Hey did I check my lottery ticket this week?'*

Watch the trailer and find out more about my other books at the websites:

www.martyntott.com

and

www.sixmagicnumbers.info

Lightning Source UK Ltd.
Milton Keynes UK

173504UK00001B/32/P